F*CK THIS
MURDER

F*CK THIS MURDER
2025 The Unpopular Publishing Co.
Copyright © 2025 Elizabeth Land Quant & Signe E. Land

Editing: Jordan Rosenfeld
Illustrations: Bread & Clutter
Cover & Interior Layout: Fresh Design

ISBN Paperback: 979-8-9994392-0-8
ISBN Hardback: 979-8-9994392-1-5
ISBN ebook: 979-8-9994392-2-2

F THIS MURDER SERIES · BOOK I

F*CK THIS MURDER

Elizabeth Land Quant
& Signe E. Land

For

Ashley, Camie, Cecilio, Dad, Henry, Jack,

Kane, Karen Elise, Kim, Roger, Sam, Scott, Shawn,

Solveig, Big Solveig (Mom), & Cosmo

Praise For
F*CK THIS MURDER

★ ★ ★

"Our Verdict: Get it!"
—KIRKUS REVIEWS

★ ★ ★

"Impeccably written, fabulously illustrated, witty, charming, surprising, and wry, *F*ck This Murder* is the wacky page-turner I didn't know I needed to read. The Autistic Aunties strike gold with their unforgettable cast of quirky, lovable characters and a plot that will keep you up all night reading. Book two can't come soon enough!"

—JENA SCHWARTZ, author of *Fierce Encouragement*.

★ ★ ★

"Takeaway: Hilarious B&B murder mystery
with unexpected heart."
—BOOKLIFE REVIEWS, EDITOR'S PICK!

"Signe E. Land and Elizabeth Land Quant have created a sparkling cozy mystery that is snarky, inclusive, and gloriously unhinged, all with humor, plot twists, and convincing portrayals of unconventional characters. I love sarcastic sleuths, chaotic queer energy, and cozy mysteries with bite, and this book has all that and then some."

—NINA MCCONIGLEY, author of *Cowboys and East Indians*, winner of the PEN Open Book Award.

★★★

"*F*ck This Murder* delivers exactly the right blend of humor and pathos to make you laugh, scream and demand your bestie read this book next. In a time when things are tilting toward tyranny, this joyfully neurodivergent book, which celebrates our differences and our intersections, lets you sink into a world you'll be reluctant to leave."

—JORDAN ROSENFELD, author of *Fallout* and *The Sound of Story*.

★★★

"Need an escape? Treat yourself to *F*ck This Murder*: a heartfelt, fast-paced screwball cozy mystery that's wonderfully neurodivergent and joyously queer. Can't wait to see what's in store next for Maggie and the gang in book two!"

—JENNIFER PASTILOFF, bestselling author of *On Being & Proof of Life*.

"This rollicking murder mystery presents intrigue and fun in equal measure, with a gift of disability and queer representation. I deeply enjoyed the twists and turns, and I'll be thinking for a long time about the engaging protagonist with her real and embodied challenges amid her humor, humanity, and loving community."

—SONYA HUBER, author of *Pain Woman Takes Your Keys and Other Essays from a Nervous System.*

"*F*ck This Murder* is a fresh, fun, quirky take on the mystery genre, and I loved the twist at the end that I did not see coming! The characters represent a diverse bunch in all forms of the word, but I never felt like the story was trying to prove a point by including these perspectives. They felt genuine and only served to increase the depth of characters, making them all more believable humans. Ultimately, this mystery is cozy like a cup of hot cocoa with a splash of bourbon, and one I'd highly recommend you pick up now!"

—KAYLEIGH SUGGETT, author of *Alibi by Accident.*

"Elizabeth Land Quant and Signe E. Land have written a hilarious, buoyant, and smart mystery that will have readers turning the pages with both anticipation and pleasure. The real gift of *F*ck This Murder* is the characters, many of whom will stick with readers long after they've finished the book. Don't miss this entertaining read!"

—CHRISTIE TATE, author of *Group: How One Therapist and a Circle of Strangers Saved My Life*, a Reese's Book Club Pick.

Table of Contents

Cast of Characters

MAGGIE LIVINGSTON: She/her. Autistic, divorced, intrepid B&B owner-in-debt, overalls & clogs, deals with chronic illness, might still be in love with ex-girlfriend Alice, a local game and fish warden, who is dating someone else. Cousin to Detective Mark.

MIA HERNANDEZ WEBBER: She/her. Cat and cat show enthusiast, accountant-but-questioning, ADHD, best friend to Maggie and Sutton, wife to James, mother to Shaun and Brianna.

SUTTON ANTONOFF: He/him. Mia and Maggie's bestie, attorney, swing choir alum, intestinal issues, into pocket squares, bad boys, and seersucker.

HEIDI KRISTENSEN: She/her. Owner of Heidi's Cafe, girlfriend to handsome ER doc Nic, wickedly fun sense of humor, adolescent saboteur of bullies, the friend who would help you hide a body.

ABIGAIL (ABBY) MARSH: She/her. Maid of honor, wedding planner, pageant winner and ballet dancer, experiences weird joint pain, loves lists, order and deadlines. Her one trait she struggles with: She "cares too much."

JAMES WEBBER: He/him. General contractor, loves animal themed clothes, dedicated and sweet husband to Mia, dad to Shaun and Brianna, unintentional nudist.

ALICE GIANNOPOULOS: She/her. Game and Fish warden, Maggie's ex, fierce animal & possum advocate, Jenny's girlfriend, sexy in hiking boots and a sports bra, can park a trailer in reverse without a camera. Younger sister to Nic; cousin to Adrian.

JENNY CLARK: She/her. Wedding attendant, Herschel's twin, dock builder, chops wood, Alice's girlfriend.

HERSCHEL CLARK: He/him. Wedding attendant, Jenny's twin, big guy-sports a blond mullet, personal trainer, has a family and chickens.

TRIG SANDERS: He/him. "Best dude" to Noah, wears hats with questionable joke slogans, works wonders with bongs both beer and jane, trumpet first chair in high school, successful attorney.

ADRIAN GIANNOPOULOS: They/them. Wedding attendant, peacemaker, cousin to game warden Alice and her brother handsome ER doc Nic, rocks flowy scarves, loves live jazz.

NOAH ALLERTON: They/them. Spouse-to-be, marrying Tamsin, nice to everyone, owns successful charity consulting business, played trombone in Jazz band, amateur ghost hunter.

TAMSIN CARLYON: She/her. Bride-to-be, marathon runner, supports Hugs-4-Dogs, high school popular girl and second chair flute.

LENA-ELISE TURNER: She/her. Wedding attendant, girlfriend to William, quiet, played the French horn.

WILLIAM GELT: He/him. Preppy, psychologist, boyfriend to Lena-Elise, loves renaissance festivals.

VIRGINIA TORRES: She/her. Wedding attendant, mom to two boys, head of physical therapy at a Kansas City hospital, led the school team to state soccer championship.

NIC GIANNOPOULOS: He/him. Hot ER doctor, boyfriend to Heidi, older brother to Alice, dad to two girls.

SHAUN WEBBER: Son of James and Mia, 5 years old, carries a stuffed elephant, prefers grape jelly.

BRIANNA (BRI) WEBBER: Daughter of James and Mia, 8 years old, loves drawing, animals and bracelets, is autistic, invents games.

MARK DONNELLY: He/him. Detective, cousin to Maggie, wears plaid, high school state wrestling champ, has secret crush on Regina the goth coroner.

REGINA BERAN: She/her. Hot goth county coroner, best sense of humor, nobody eff's with her, wears a lot of black, high school mathlete.

MISS VERA: She/her. Neighbor to Maggie, hates Maggies's B&B and any changes to the neighborhood, claims the noise bothers her African gray parrot Richard.

MR. TREMBOLT: He/him. Maggie's first unofficial guest at her B & B.

MR. GUSTAFFSON: He/him. An old retired high school janitor. (Probably nothing to see here.)

TREVOR: He/him. Head of Parks and Rec, James' friend, loose tongued.

CARL GLEET: He/him. Friend from high school.

HARLAN PETERSON: He/him. Policeman with an apparent grudge.

LYNN NGUYEN: She/her. Young, smart, and fair policewoman, family owns town hardware store.

MR. JABLONSKI: He/him. Neighbor across the cove, owns B & B where Tamsin and Noah stayed with their families.

YOGA PAT: She/they. Owner of Patty's Bait and Tackle, in-demand yoga and fishing instructor. "Ya Gotta Earn It!"

GARY: He/him. Owns Gary's Gators n' More, tour guide at The Old Treasure Caves.

COSMO: Maggie's Boxer dog - loves hose water, frisbees, attention.

NOODLE: Maggie's Tuxedo cat, "cathole," likes to collect dead bugs, toe biter, feckless.

ATHENA: Wayward baby possum.

REBECCA: Miss Vera's shrill elderly corgi.

RICHARD: Miss Vera's nervous and molting African gray parrot.

Welcome to Henry's Point
Bed & Breakfast where you'll
find all the comforts of home
and so much more.

CHAPTER ONE
The Inspector & the Corpse

Three more corpses and it wasn't even noon. My cranky tuxedo cat Noodle had left *another* pile of dead crickets in the living room, and I kicked their mutilated bodies under the couch as I rushed to answer the door. Wishing for the umpteenth time that I could wear my "uniform" of soft overalls and a t-shirt, I smoothed down my itchy, crisp, white blouse with the stiff collar and tucked in a few bouncy auburn curls that had escaped my braid in the humidity. I was determined to look like a well-organized, relaxed, and successful innkeeper welcoming her first guests, and *not* a chronically ill and desperate for money, almost divorced, thirty-something autistic woman who had just moved back down south to rent out her beloved ancestral home to strangers.

"Welcome." I initiated awkward eye contact as I opened my front door to a gust of hot wind. *Please lord do not send us another bad storm today.* I glanced up at the darkening sky and swaying pine tops. I hoped the health inspector did not notice the paint chips sailing down onto the scraped and faded hundred-year-old oak floors.

"Miss Maggie Livingston, how nice to see you again." Mr. Raffin, a smallish, sharp faced man with a thready combover, did indeed watch the moss green flecks of paint float down before snapping his eyes back to me. "I hope you didn't mind the schedule change?"

"Not at all," I lied. "I have everything under control."

I motioned Mr. Raffin inside, thankful to finally break eye contact as I followed the inspector in. The lie was fair. I *would have* had everything under control for my B&B's grand opening, except that an unexpected heat wave just murdered our ancient air conditioner and was currently holding our tiny mountain tourist town captive. As if that wasn't enough, my first group of guests, who just happened to include my old high-school nemeses, was supposed to arrive today. If Mr. Raffin found out I'd booked guests before he signed off on the inspection, he would shut me down.

"Don't you have people coming today?" Raffin asked. "Friends of yours, you said, to try out the new place?" Mr. Raffin swept past me into the kitchen and ran his hands along a well-hidden, floor-to-ceiling wood-paneled door that was painted the same moss green color as the rest of the kitchen paneling.

My eyebrow twitched. I had to go along with this, since Mr. Raffin hadn't signed off on our inspection yet, but I could barely stand the subterfuge of calling my childhood bullies "friends." Taking a deep breath, I nodded to both questions, trying to smile serenely at the same time and stuck my hand in my pocket.

Rubbing my thumb against a smooth rock I'd found earlier, with its cool glossy finish, soothed my nerves.

"Can I look inside this secret passage?" Mr. Raffin asked, his fingers tracing the well-worn grooves in the paneled door. "I've read about your home at the Majestic Springs Historical Society. Such grand history right here from your ancestors' moonshining days!" The inspector popped the door open and peered into the dark passage that connected all three floors of my home. I hoped that he would glance past the dusty staircase and shelving stuffed with extra blankets, a dirty dog bed, and some other junk that had been cluttering up the living room. The cobwebs and the mildew smell were not helping my situation.

I did think it was cool that my moonshining ancestors and our home were considered "grand history." My grandma used to tell me stories about my infamous great-great-grandparent's bootlegging days during prohibition. I loved how the entire family got involved: uncles whooping and hollering, playing and swinging squealing children up in the air to the sounds of old Bluegrass music, all while they ran the moonshine still day and night. Under cover of darkness, the lake was a perfect means to distribute illegal hooch undetected. As a child I had pretended to be my law-breaking ancestors, playing inside the secret passages, fleeing law enforcement, running up and down the rickety stairs between the floors and shining my Raggedy Ann flashlight down the spider-filled tunnel that led from our basement out into the forest. I hoped Mr. Raffin's enthusiasm for my house would be reflected in this last inspection, so I could finally, officially open my B&B. I was really pushing my luck scheduling guests to check in today, the day of my last inspection, but I couldn't help it. This was the day they had to check in or they would have to book somewhere else.

I glanced over at Mr. Raffin, who still had his head stuck into the secret passageway. "Just to let you know," I called out, "we should get started because my guests, er, I mean my friends, are arriving this afternoon." I shuffled some overdue utility and mortgage bills under a *House Beautiful* magazine and then grabbed a framed embroidery off the wall that read, *Drink Water & Take Your Medicine, Bitch!* stitched in rainbow letters. As I slipped the embroidery into a drawer, I added under my breath, "Right in time for a lovely sunset cocktail hour." Another event thrown at me last minute, thanks to the pale-cheeked, raven-haired Bridezilla Tamsin Carlyon, and her impossible-to-please former ballerina and maid-of-honor, the tall, blonde, primped and determined Abby.

Mr. Raffin emerged from the secret passageway's panel door and started to say something when a loud THUMP followed by a muffled shriek came from somewhere upstairs where my two best friends Mia and Sutton were serving breakfast in bed to my very first *unofficial* guest, Mr. Trembolt. Mr. Raffin and I both stared up at the ceiling in unison.

"What was that?" Mr. Raffin asked.

"Nobody," I said, a bit too fast and loud before I recovered and blinked twice. Sutton, Mia, and Mr. Trembolt wouldn't make that much noise. "I don't hear anything," I added, despite an evident scuttling and scraping above our heads. My mind raced wondering what the hell was going on above us. *Thunder? A tree falling on the house?* Nothing could go wrong today.

Another THUMP. "That!" Mr. Raffin exclaimed, pointing upwards. "What was THAT?" His beady eyes penetrated mine.

"It's probably my uncle," I lied. "He's staying here." Sweat slid down between my breasts. *Squirrels in the attic? More thunder? Maybe that tree fell that the tree guy said I should cut down but I couldn't afford to?* I hoped I was not visibly squirming as I rearranged my too-tight bra and stalled for time. There had to be something going on with Mr. Trembolt's room. The air conditioning probably wasn't cool enough in there, and Mia and Sutton were likely up there solving the problem. I didn't even want Mr. Trembolt to stay here, but he was apparently an old acquaintance of my dad's and had begged me to stay for a few nights "for old time's sake." Something about missing the old days and all the people from town who were now deceased like my dad. *Get in line, Mr. Trembolt, get in line.*

"Are you going to answer your phone?" Mr. Raffin stared at the ceiling, squinting hard like he could see through the layers of plaster and wood to the cause of the thumping noises above.

I was so focused on what was going on upstairs that I had tuned out my phone blasting the Buffy the Vampire Slayer theme song.

"I'm so sorry!" I squeaked, making *more* meaningful eye contact to convey my apology, but apparently *too* meaningfully, because Raffin backed up a few feet. I was going to turn the ringer off, but then I saw Mia had been FaceTiming me over and over. "Oh my, I need to take this," I said, using my calmest voice ever, because nothing good could be at the other end of this FaceTime. I steered Mr. Raffin toward the kitchen island and told him to look around while I dashed into the pantry and shut the heavy oak door.

"What?" I whispered, looking at a close-up of Mia's face. "I'm with the . . ."

"I KNOW," Mia hissed. "You CAN'T bring him up here! A few of Mia's black braids had fallen from her flowered headscarf, partially obscuring her deep brown eyes. I was going to ask *why* we couldn't go upstairs when my other best friend, Sutton, grabbed the phone, his normally tan complexion a sickly white.

"HE'S DEAD. MR. TREMBOLT IS DEAD. VERY, VERY DEAD."

Then the phone screen went black.

I stood in the dark pantry, clutching the phone and staring at the canned peas for a good thirty seconds as I let this sink in. *Dead?* A dead body, here in my ancestral home, *with the health inspector?* My left eye twitched and I rubbed my comfort rock vigorously. Before I could call Sutton and Mia back, the inspector knocked on the pantry door and I jumped, knocking a stack of metal trays to the floor with a crash.

"Goodness!" Mr. Raffin yelped through the door. "Are you alright in there? I'm ready to go upstairs and check on what we went over during my last inspection, including the bathrooms." *And the freshly dead corpse!* When I couldn't even get a sound out, he asked, again. "I said, everything okay in there?"

Think, Maggie. I mashed my damp auburn curls up from my face. "Almost done!" I practically barfed out. THINK. The secret passageways were out for moving the body because the snooping Mr. Raffin had left the paneled kitchen door wide open. Another knock at the pantry door. "Hold oooonnnn," I sang. *Wait. The back staircase to the upstairs bedrooms!* I quickly FaceTimed Mia.

"Listen, I need you to do something," I whispered, pushing the horror of what I was about to ask out of my mind. Mia's wide eyes stared back at me in desperation, her normally perfectly applied eyeliner starting to run just a bit. "The inspector and I have to come upstairs, *right now.* He will *know* something is wrong if we don't come upstairs, and if we *do* come up and he sees a . . ." I stopped, realizing I could not say "dead body" out loud. I swallowed the coffee-and creamer-laced gag that was rising up my esophagus and kept going, trying to find a neutral way to describe the unfolding horror in case Mr. Raffin was listening. "If the inspector sees Mr. Trembolt," I mouthed "dead," before I continued breathlessly, "then we will have no business. Raffin will shut me down and that means I will have to accept the offers to sell Dad's beloved lake property because I couldn't keep my shit together to pay the bills!" I practically shrieked before lowering my voice again. "Please, you've got to help."

I had a vision of hauling boxes of my dad's fossil collection and my grandma's books into the street. My remaining family heirlooms thrown out in a dumpster because I lost our home.

"Okay," Mia quickly wiped her flushed brown cheeks, her face glistening with sweat.

"Okay," I said, my voice shaking. "No passageways because the kitchen door is still wide open down here. So, when you hear us go up the front stairs, you guys and Mr. Trembolt go down the back stairs."

"Look, you absolute ghoul . . ." Sutton spat out, his pale freckled face pushing past Mia's into my phone screen before Mia pushed him away again.

"Okay. Okay," Mia shushed Sutton. Then, to me: "How?"

I straightened a few cans of beans to stop the shaking. "Just, um, put his stuff in his bag and . . . and oh!" I just thought of an *Unsolved Mystery* episode I'd watched where the murderer got the body out of his house without leaving evidence. "Wrap him in the shower curtain and carry him down."

"Oh, good," Sutton interjected. "You mean your new cat-print shower curtain with rainbows coming out of the cats' butts?" He giggled hysterically before I heard Mia whack him.

Shit! I forgot to change that funky curtain to a more demure, flowered one. What had Mr. Trembolt thought . . .

"Are you coming out of the pantry, Maggie?" Mr. Raffin's muffled voice was strained with irritation through the wooden door. "I have another appointment, and I hate to be late." I could see his tiny foot tapping out the rhythm to "Hips Don't Lie" through the crack at the bottom.

"Ah, yes!" I called out, hoping that he would keep grooving to the music in the kitchen. "So sorry," I blabbed. "It's my aunt on the phone . . . her parakeet Napoleon just died. Her, uh, her cat learned how to open the cage, and it's a real blood bath over there, feathers in every room."

"Stop talking, *oh my god*," Sutton hissed over the phone. "First of all," his eyes narrowed. "My future godchild who currently grows within Mia's belly will *not* be carrying a dead body. It's unseemly."

The phone went dark a moment to the sound of shuffling, then Mia appeared. "Unseemly my fine ass," she snorted, her face dewy but determined. "Pregnant or not, I can carry any dead body you can, Sutton."

"Sutton! Mia! Focus!" I yelped, interrupting them both, and trying hard not to think about my own two missed periods after my last very unwise trip up north to see my soon-to-be ex-husband, Lance. An anxiety-laden fog was descending so I shook my head. *Focus!* "Raffin is outside the pantry door. We have to do *something*."

Mia broke in: "We can get Trembolt down the stairs, Maggie, that's the first step."

"And where the hell are we supposed to place our recently deceased guest once we get him downstairs?" Sutton's face reappeared as he flipped his sandy brown hair out of his eyes and glared.

"We could put him in his car until the inspector goes?" Mia threw out. "It's right outside the mudroom by the back door."

I nodded along to Mia's plan. Our countless hours spent watching murder movies on *Lifetime* had finally paid off. "And then I can call Mark and Regina to discreetly come get him."

Mark, my male doppelgänger cousin with his pale ruddy cheeks, curly auburn hair and sturdy build, was our plaid-wearing town detective. Mark's secret crush, Regina, was the county undertaker and coroner. I wished they would get together because they would have amazing kids. Curvy and hot as hell in her black stretchy scrubs and tattoos, Regina sported big round black glasses that gave her a distinct owl-like appearance, which dove-tailed nicely with her profession.

Mr. Trembolt was just an old man who had most likely died of a stroke or heart attack in his sleep. It wasn't like we had to preserve a crime scene. I was *almost* not breaking any laws at all, I thought, as my eye twitched again and my shaking hand almost dropped the phone. "I definitely think we will have enough time before the guests come so no one knows he died here, especially if we park the car away from the house."

"On it," Mia said. Before I hung up, I heard Sutton seething about how people were supposed to *bury* a body, not *carry* one secretly through the halls. When I came out of the pantry, Mr. Raffin was frowning and patting his perspiring forehead with a soggy glob of paper towel. I apologized profusely before pointing out the restored wainscoting and the vintage light fixtures.

"AND HERE WE ARE AT THE STAIRS." I grandly gestured about like we had just teleported to the Taj Mahal.

"Yes, I see that." When Mr. Raffin tried going around me, I humiliated us both by grabbing his hand and swinging it like we were in a Hallmark movie. Our hands were wet with perspiration, and they made a squelching sound when I squeezed them together. A part of me died, but I hung on tight until I heard movement in the upstairs hallway.

Mr. Raffin jerked his hand away as though disturbed by the obvious boundary violation. "What are . . ."

"I got a little dizzy," I blurted out, which wasn't a total lie. In all the heat and hubbub of this morning, I'd forgotten to take my morning meds for my very annoying autoimmune disease and now the staircase seemed precariously tall.

"Oh . . . well," Mr. Raffin stammered. "Are you okay?"

I was trying to listen for the thumps of moving a body, so Mr. Raffin had to ask again.

"Totally fine," I answered. "But we just need to stay right here, not moving, until I get un-dizzy." We stood on the first step for a few seconds until I heard the tell-tale "ka-thud" of my guest being quietly dragged down the stairs. "We can go now!"

I clambered as fast as my aching knee joints would allow up the stairs hoping that Mr. Raffin would be right behind me. If he stayed down there too long, he would see two people carrying a body-shaped cats-pooping-rainbows-print shower curtain and there would be no way to un-ring that bell.

"All the bathrooms are in order, and I see that you took care of everything on the list I gave you," Mr. Raffin said as he came out of my dad's old bedroom suite, taking notes and pictures on his phone. "The railing is slightly loose going up the second part of the stairs, but that won't take much to fix. So now I just need to see the last bedroom on this floor."

My Aunt Mary died in that room at the end of the hall, where now, coincidentally, Mr. Trembolt had also entered his eternal slumber. And now Mia and Sutton had just bounced him down the stairs like a sack of potatoes. Aunt Mary's door was shut, and as I opened it, I prayed that there was no blood or floating apparitions or anything that hinted of recently dead people. My eyes darted from Mary's delicate rosebud wallpaper to the white desk and dresser, looking for any sign of trouble that I would need to hide from Mr. Raffin. As I walked around the four-poster bed, I carefully pushed Mr. Trembolt's breakfast tray and suitcase farther underneath the bed with my foot while pretending to straighten the bedspread.

I started to breathe a sigh of relief, but then it got caught in my throat. My boxer dog Cosmo loudly alerted the neighborhood that someone new was on the property. Through the lace curtained window, I saw several cars pull up and park at the back of my house. Oh god. Some guests, otherwise known as "friends" to Mr. Raffin, had arrived early looking way too much like dressed up *paying* "guests," which were a no-no. I jumped up and stood in front of the window, blocking Raffin's view. I needed to focus. We were so close, as long as I could stop Raffin from seeing what was going on *outside* the house while Mia and Sutton moved a DEAD man down to the back door *inside* the house.

I texted Sutton: **Stash Mr T under blankies downstairs. Mudroom. Now!**

I only had time to read the first part of Sutton's response: **WHAT THE F—?** before Mr. Raffin burst into the room, startling me to death.

"I still need to check that back staircase railing and the last bathroom before I move down to the kitchen," Raffin announced. "That's in the mudroom, isn't it?"

"YES, MR. RAFFIN," I all but yelled toward the back staircase, hoping Mia and Sutton would hear. "THE BATHROOM YOU STILL HAVE TO CHECK IS IN THE MUDROOM, YOU ARE RIGHT."

I heard Sutton groan on the stairs, then a loud thud.

"What was that?" Mr. Raffin asked, eyes narrowing suspiciously.

"My cat Noodle. He has the . . . er, asthma. From the crickets. And also, he falls a lot." Before I could say more, Mr. Raffin expertly dodged my outstretched hand and weaved around me so fast he was in the hallway, striding towards the back stairway before I could blink.

"OKAY LEAD THE WAY MR. RAFFIN SIR. I AM COMING RIGHT AFTER YOU DOWN THE STAIRS INTO THE MUDROOM." *Please please please let them hear us*, I prayed as we marched down the stairs.

"Oh, hello," a smooth, deep female voice announced. "I'm Mia, Maggie's friend. I didn't realize you were here already."

I practically sprinted to follow Mr. Raffin all the way through the mudroom into the kitchen, where Mia had greeted him and was bending over the stove, pulling out sweet-smelling muffins from the oven. She smiled her most dazzling smile at the inspector, making sure that she stood up very slowly so that Mr. Raffin was completely absorbed in her damp and ample pregnant bosom while Sutton quietly stepped out of the pantry and closed the door.

"My goodness," Mr. Raffin stammered, patting his stringy comb-over down flat over his pasty scalp, creating a greasy bar code effect on the top of his head. To be fair, he was trying, as most people did around Mia. "Do you need help with that heavy pan?" As Mr. Raffin stared hopefully at Mia and her glorious muffins, Sutton sidestepped behind Raffin and drew his finger across his own neck in a cutthroat gesture before pointing frantically to the closed pantry door. Oh god. Dead Mr. Trembolt was right there in the pantry.

"Ehhhgggg," I accidentally blurted aloud, still trying to catch my breath.

"What was that, Ms. Livingston?" Mr. Raffin turned around and backed his rear right into Sutton's rear, who squealed and jumped back. "Who . . .?"

"Hot muffins?" Mia asked, holding up a steaming platter. I leapt over beside Mia and handed Raffin a flowered plate, then dished him up a warm blueberry muffin topped with a pat of melting butter. Then, while Raffin was absorbed in Mia and muffins, Sutton snuck out the back door to deal with the early, *curse them*, guests.

I glanced out the window and saw the pine branches starting to move more in the wind, and was the dock bobbing up and down too? Great. More steamy, hot gusts and a sea-sickness-inducing dock for the party, plus special lakeside toasts the bride had planned for tonight. Flowers, vines and lights on the dock now twisted and entangled with each other in the wind—decorations that the bride Tamsin and her wedding planner and maid-of-honor Abby had strung up on the dock.

The doorbell rang and everyone's heads swiveled from the kitchen toward the hall. *What now?* As I was heading to the front door, Mr. Raffin requested sugar for the coffee that Mia was pouring him. With a gasp, I realized that the sugar was, of course, in the pantry, aka our new domestic pop-up morgue. I stopped and made a frantic motion at Mia, but Mia pointed me towards the front door so confidently, I went ahead.

"Heidi!" I smiled, surprised when I opened the door since I wasn't expecting her for a bit longer. Leave it to Heidi to come early to help. Heidi smiled back, her sea blue eyes twinkling under her expertly applied makeup, while lilac and lavender scents wafted off her flowing, honey-blond hair.

We all had major crushes on Heidi in high school, shamelessly hanging around the lifeguard station and admiring her in her swim trunks. Heidi transitioned after college and took over the local coffee shop, and now we all hung out there respectfully admiring her in her cute skirts and ruffled aprons while stuffing ourselves with her delightful pastries.

"Hey, y'all," Heidi called back toward Mia and Sutton. "I tried the back door, but no one answered. Here, Maggie." Heidi handed me two large bags as she gracefully rebalanced a large serving tray of meats and cheeses. My chest muscles relaxed now that the cavalry had come.

She placed various delicacies on the counter and turned to me. "I saw Herschel and Trig playing fetch with Cosmo outside by the dock. They were throwing a frisbee, but a wind gust blew up and the frisbee flew into the lake." She started sorting cheeses. "Cosmo ran onto the dock to watch the frisbee float away, but when he did, I noticed the dock was really rocking and all those decorations were—hey, have you checked the dock lately, to make sure all the bolts are tightened up, hon?"

"Yes, they all should be in good shape," I said. I looked past Heidi toward my dog playing with that mullet-headed blonde jock, Herschel, and his ridiculous friend Trig, who always had to wear a baseball cap with something offensive on it. The wind couldn't make up its mind to blow or die down as usual here in the mountains. Our boats were bobbing up and down with my dad's old floating dock, but the bolts were holding. I hoped Trig and Herschel would stay busy with Cosmo because we had to move Mr. Trembolt and now would likely have to involve Heidi. Trig's hat blew off and after Cosmo grabbed it, they started playing tug-of-war, nearly trampling my new flower garden.

"Typical of that crowd to be early," Heidi said. "No regard for others. I'm going to put this in the fridge and then I'll get the rest of the serving dishes. I understand they want the foods and drinks set out by the dock for the toasts." Heidi sashayed past me, her white eyelet dress skimming the tops of her Ariat cowboy boots.

At least Sutton had found Herschel and Trig something to do, though that wasn't hard; give them a ball and some beer and they were good to go. *What jerks.* I would have rather ripped my own fingernails off than fill my home with the perfect, raven-haired Tamsin Carlyon's wedding party. However, when her dad promised me a huge bonus, I couldn't refuse. That bonus for a job well done was the only way for me to pay off months of overdue bills and make sure the bank couldn't take my home if I didn't sell to the highest bidder.

"They're very early," I said to Heidi as she walked toward the kitchen. Before I closed the front door, I scanned the yard for places to hide Mr. Trembolt. I spied Sutton sneaking around the back of the house like a murderer, and I got an idea. If Cosmo could keep Trig and Herschel occupied, we might be able to sneak Mr. Trembolt into his car and get the inspector out without anyone seeing anyone else.

"Hey Sutton," I called out as I followed Heidi into the kitchen. The inspector was currently munching on another muffin and thoroughly enamored now with both Mia *and* Heidi. I knew that he had to check the pantry next, the current resting place for my first and only *ever* guest if we didn't act now. "Could you help me put these bags away in the pantry?"

"I . . . what?" Sutton's eyes grew round, his mouth squinched up. He was patting his perspiring forehead with the bottom of his shirt. "I don't think . . ."

"I also have something we need to take to the car," I said, which got Mia's attention, so now both Mia and Sutton were very slowly shaking their heads at me in horror while I took a deep breath and stepped with intention toward the pantry. "Mia," I announced, "could you and Heidi show Mr. Raffin the screen porch before he has to inspect *the rest of the kitchen and also the pantry?*"

Knowledge dawned on Mia's and Sutton's faces, while Heidi and the inspector just looked perplexed. Mia set her shoulders and nodded to me, then steered Mr. Raffin to the door leading to the screen porch, beckoning Heidi to come along.

Meanwhile, I opened the pantry door and peered in only to come face to face with my deceased guest, whose cat shower curtain wrapping was scrunched down below his bushy-bearded neck. I tilted my head to the side.

"Doesn't he look familiar to you?" I whispered to Sutton as I tried to pull the makeshift wrap back up over Trembolt's face and prepared to lift him. Sutton had recoiled briefly but was recovering himself as I nodded approvingly at him. Trembolt had similar coloring to me, pale with freckles, but with black hair. How could I appraise Mr. Trembolt so calmly? I had a gift. One gift. And that was to compartmentalize the hell out of any given situation and shine like a trooper in emergencies. Most people would be horrified coming face to face with a dead body, but I was solely focused on the mission to save my home and not the repulsiveness of manhandling a fresh corpse.

"Well now that you mention it," Sutton whispered, peering at Mr. Trembolt before we covered his bearded and mustached face all the way up. "Lift his feet, Maggie, I'll take his shoulders."

"He's familiar like someone famous, maybe. He said he knew my dad, but I swear I'd never met him before this week." I hoisted up my guest by his lower legs while Sutton manned his upper body. "Oh wow, this is harder than it looks on TV." I stumbled back through the opening of the pantry, furtively looking around for the inspector.

"Go!" Sutton hissed.

"I'm *trying*," I hissed back, lurching backwards over the short distance toward the mudroom. My swollen ankles buckled, and I went down hard on my ass just over the mudroom threshold near the aged, 70's-green washing machine. Trembolt's cold rubbery feet landed, *ewwww*, right between my legs before I hoisted myself and Mr. Trembolt up to make it out the mudroom door to the outside and down the stairs to the driveway.

Mr. Trembolt's butt bounced on the last stair, which was bad enough, but things got way worse when Heidi spotted us and yelped, dropping a food tray and scattering crackers and breadsticks all over the gravel driveway.

"All okay up there?" Trig, *that jock bastard*, yelled from the dock. Herschel, the bastard with the mullet stood beside Trig peering up and trying to spot us.

"Get down!" I hissed to Sutton, who was already down and spread out over the body, a little black paw on the shower curtain cat design peeking out under Sutton's armpit. I put my hands up to Heidi, motioning her to stay calm, as she was standing very still and not making a sound in a way that told me I was going to need a rational, totally not criminal explanation for all of this.

"We didn't kill him, and he died in his sleep and if the inspector sees this, I am going to lose my home!" I said in a rush.

Heidi paused, still clutching the tray. She looked from me to Sutton, then back to me. "The cats," she began, before blinking several times and straightening her shoulders and starting again:

"The cats on your corpse bag are pooping rainbows. Now, what do you need me to do?"

You learn who your real friends are when there's a body to be dealt with. I took the car keys from Sutton and unlocked the front passenger door, then the three of us extracted Mr. Trembolt from the cat curtain and placed him in the seat, arranging him to look like he was taking a nice catnap.

"Will people wonder why he would be sitting in the passenger side of his own car?" Heidi asked, her arms crossed tightly around her as she peered at the body-shaped curtain. "And why isn't he wearing pajamas?"

The woman had a point. Sutton and I stared at each other, the exhaustion apparent on our pale, sweaty faces. We had to resolve this, and we were out of time.

"Listen," I said, a thought occurring to me. "Sutton, you need to drive Mr. Trembolt's car away from here, so the new guests do not see a 'sleeping'"—I drew air quotes and rolled my eyes—"man in my driveway. Heidi, can you go up and get his suitcase?"

Heidi nodded and ran back into the house while Sutton and I discussed the best place to have my detective cousin Mark and Regina the coroner "find" the car. I trusted them to discreetly take care of poor Mr. Trembolt who "happened" to "die" after pulling over to the side of the road, even though Regina would know in seconds that he didn't. She was the kind of person to watch first and ask questions later, which was turning out to be a great quality in my friends.

All the bad stuff that could have gone wrong already did go wrong, right? Ensconced in my little log cabin by the lake shore where I stayed when guests slept in my home, I wiped yet another layer of sweat from my face and then piled my unruly hair on top of my head, securing it with bobby pins that Sutton had bejeweled for me. I shooed Noodle the tuxedo cat away from my make-up brushes that he liked to munch and applied a second coat of mascara. I just needed to survive this week by being exactly the opposite of myself. After that, I simply had to ignore the fact that I manhandled a dead body and would be fighting all week long to save my family home.

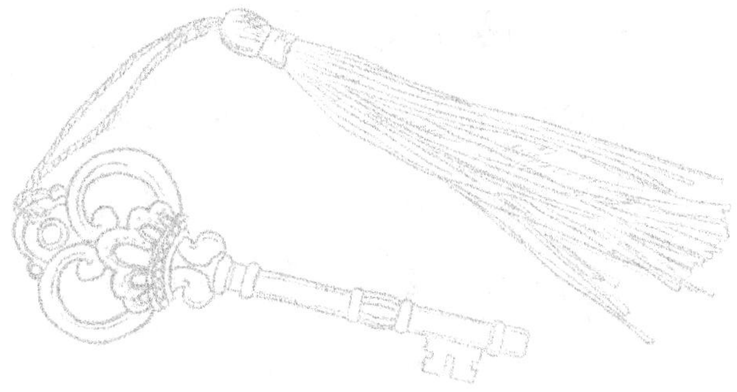

Open your mind to new
relaxation possibilities here at
Henry's Point B & B, where extra
feather pillows, fluffy towels,
blankets & amenities are always
available on request.

CHAPTER TWO
The More, the Merrier

Don't think about the dead body don't think about the dead body don't think . . . shit. What was Abby saying? I turned my favorite yellow melamine bowl over to dry at the kitchen sink and grabbed another dish.

"Did you hear what I said, *Maggie*? We need to get the rooms sorted and prepare for tonight's sunset cocktail hour!" Abigail Marsh, the tall, blonde ballerina of our high school class flipped her beauty pageant hair off her shoulder, her fuchsia nails glinting in the light. She was sporting a tan that made her normally light skin look slightly Oompa Loompa-ish.

"Uh, yes," I answered, trying not to look at my pantry, aka dead Mr. Trembolt's final pit stop after my friends dragged him through here in a shower curtain. At least he had gotten a full tour. I tried to ignore the laundry room screen door banging loudly in the wind so I could get through this planning session with Abby. "So, Abby, which keys . . ."

If rolling eyes could make a sound, hers scoffed. "I want *all* the keys so I can distribute them when the wedding party comes." Abby sniffed, discreetly wiping away a bead of perspiration trailing down her forehead. With effort, she lifted the large, sparkling wedding binder she'd bedazzled in rhinestones, and I swear to god, real feathers. Noodle pawed at wayward feathers that had made a mess of pink glitter on the floor. Great. Another thing I'd have to clean up.

Abby continued barking orders like I wasn't standing directly in front of her: "Everyone gets keys except Herschel's twin Jenny because she lives here in town, obviously. Also the spouses-to-be, Tamsin and Noah, of course are staying with their families across the cove right over . . . Maggie, where is it again?"

I pointed.

"Where? I don't see it?"

I had a momentary flashback to being paired with demanding Abby in high school for an assignment before I pointed silently again, resisting covering my ears against Abby's loud questions as she peered across the choppy water. She had skipped right over the fact that I'd gone mute with stress—I guessed it was comforting that some things never changed.

Abby finally spotted the other house through the thick band of pine, maple and spruce trees lining our shoreline. "Oh wow. Impressive." She squinted at the three-story log home, then looked back at my big, but less impressively landscaped yard. "There's enough room there on the patio by the dock for the cocktail party tonight, right? And you've checked the weather? It's been blowing like crazy sometimes today, and I'm responsible for *everything*, you understand." She thumped her chest with the palm of her hand. "I had to go secure the decorations on the dock in the wind when I also have to do everything else."

Abby threw me an urgently beleaguered look like she was under the most pressure here. I wanted to flick her forehead, hard; I was the one who could lose my family home. What did *she* have on the line? Nothing. Absolutely nothing. Come to think of it, more than just my home was on the line. I'd just gotten my ass handed to me by my cousin Mark for breaking more than a few laws, including abusing a corpse.

"We lovingly, not abusingly, carried Mr. Trembolt to his car," I'd insisted. There had been no need to mention dropping Mr. Trembolt on the stairs or bending his creaking appendages to cram his stiff corpse into the seat. Nor did we discuss how Sutton barfed on my shoe after he'd accidentally poked Trembolt's eye and some yellow goo oozed out. Unlike Sutton, *I* had held it together, and Mark should be happy I called him right away. Well, almost right away. And *then*, I had barely gotten Mark out the door before Abby's Mercedes came flying around the corner, kicking up half my gravel. If anyone was the hero here, it was me.

Abby was still glaring at me.

"Of course, Abby. Yes, I understand that you've got all the stress and we need to make tonight magical," I said, trying to make my voice sound light. I had said yes to this evening's soirée without thinking about whether the lawn and patio in the middle of my wooded lake property *would* comfortably hold all the guests because it *had* to hold all the guests. And I had no control over the weather. I folded a blue and white dishrag over my gleaming white double farm sink and then pulled out a bunch of keys. "Room number and name written on each tag . . ."

"Thank you." Abby snatched the keys from my hands, briefly checking whether I had labelled them correctly, before asking, "Did you put people in the rooms exactly like I specified on the floor plans here in the binderr-rr . . . oh no! Noodle, No!"

I had to look away so I wouldn't laugh. Abby had been, no lie, stroking the wedding binder like it was a rhinestoned, puffy-feathered therapy chicken, and Noodle had just run off with a huge chunk of white feathers in his mouth, glitter trailing in his wake.

Just then, Sutton's voice boomed from the back entry that led to the mudroom and parking area: "This way, everybody!"

A sharp pang gripped my chest as I stared at my ex-girlfriend Alice's hippy-dippy cousin Adrian flapping their woven sandals into my kitchen for the first time in years. Alice and Adrian were dead ringers for each other, each of them blessed with luscious dark hair (albeit a windblown blunt cut under her Game and Fish hat in Alice's case), a strong Greek nose, and expressive brown eyes you could drown in. Adrian's hair flowed long and wavy down their back when it wasn't swirled up in a man bun.

"Adrian, so good to see you," I managed to squeak out as I tried not to think about how badly I had hurt Alice all those years ago. My husband—almost ex-husband—Lance had been a badly misjudged hookup at a national high school student government conference back when Alice and I had been dating on and off for over a year in high school. Now, my hand flew to my belly as I once again regretted a one-nighter with Lance three months ago. I couldn't even think about it. There was no way *a pregnancy* could happen in a single last stupid fling with Lance after all those expensive years of trying without results. Right? I was supposed to be divorcing him, not planning for a baby with him now. I'd bought a pregnancy test the other day, but I couldn't bring myself to open it. I shook myself and noticed Sutton was lurking behind Adrian. He gave me a quizzical look before I turned back to Adrian.

Adrian bowed toward me slightly, their full pink lips—another shared trait that deliciously conjured Alice—stretched across their straight white teeth into a huge smile. "Thank you for having us all to stay with you," Adrian said, looking around, their linen tunic and pants hanging perfectly despite the humidity. "Hey, does anyone know why the coroner's van was in the area? Kinda spooky, right?"

My mind drew a terror-fueled blank. Had Adrian seen us moving Mr. Trembolt?

Abby whipped around to glare at me, a poof of glitter from the wedding binder flying up around her face. "Why was the coroner here?"

"Oh yeah, I saw Regina the sexy goth coroner too." Sutton waved his hand around dismissively. "She and some other law enforcement officers were out, um, testing their vehicles. Totally routine. I got a memo about it and everything." Luckily Sutton was on the ball because I was completely out of lies.

"Huh, okay." Adrian pursed their gorgeous lips together and nodded solemnly, their body lanky and relaxed in the doorframe, a stark contrast to tense Sutton and his nervous babbling.

Abby jumped in the conversation. "Why would *you* get a memo about law enforcement procedures, Sutton? You're a defense lawyer, last time I checked."

Sutton straightened up so he could look down at her, which was about an inch at most. "I'm on the town council, *Abby*. I happen to be particularly important in town."

Good lord it was high school all over again. Adrian gallantly changed the subject before this hostile mess could escalate. "Hey Abby, so good to see you." Adrian kissed Abby's cheek and while doing so gently pulled her away from Sutton into a graceful ballroom-style spin, the stray feathers of the binder in Abby's hand floating around the pair. Abby blushed and giggled then went back to studying her binder at the kitchen island.

Adrian turned to address me. "Wow, Maggie, the house hasn't changed a bit." We both took a moment to look around. Things had been spruced up, but much was still the same here from when we were kids. The same comfy couch and recliner surrounded the fireplace in a corner of the kitchen where we all used to cuddle up and watch horror movies before high-school cliques split us apart. I glanced up at the stained glass, wrought ironed framed pendants that Mia and I had just cleaned and re-hung over the island. We used to turn all the other lights off at night to see the muted reds, blues and yellows make a kaleidoscope pattern on the white cupboards and moss-colored walls.

"Hellooo," Abby said, rattling the binder and interrupting my reverie. She opened it and pointed at the floor plans page showing where the guests were staying. "We have work to do, Maggie. Sorry, Adrian, but we don't have time to reminisce. Like I keep saying, we need to get people situated and then get ready for the sunset toasts on the dock. Did you get everyone arranged in the rooms like I put in here?" Silver glitter rose up in a *poof* when she tapped a page with her long fingernail.

I caught Adrian's eyes flicking mischievously between Abby and me. It was clear Adrian could see Abby was stressing, but they held up a placating hand toward her, which had always worked when we were younger. "Hold on just one more moment, Abby, and then you'll get Maggie back." Adrian, always the peacemaker with their little prayer hands and calm demeanor. At least they were trying. I caught my own thought. When had I gotten so cynical? I was basically finding something to hate about every single one of these people.

Adrian continued, "Didn't we used to pretend that we were in a circus tent and those were our spotlights? You always insisted that you were an elephant . . . I can't remember what I was . . ." Adrian's voice petered off, deep in thought. "Wow, that was a long time ago."

Before we got to be teenagers and my weirdnesses made most of my friends drop me like a hot potato. I tried not to allow my feelings to show on my face. With the exceptions of Alice, Mia, Heidi, and Sutton, most of my small graduating class stopped hanging around with me as my social idiosyncrasies became more apparent. My thoughts returned to Adrian. In high school, they had always had impeccable taste in clothes, both feminine and masculine styles, and today they hung a gorgeous summer-silk shawl on a peg before calling back into the darkened back hallway, "Hey, Herschel, quit playing with Cosmo, and tell Jenny to get in here to say hey."

My head swiveled so hard toward Adrian it nearly snapped off. "I'm sorry . . . Jenny is here?" I squeaked. *Lumberjack Jenny? The town dock-builder, Jenny? My ex-girlfriend Alice's current girlfriend Jenny?* "Erm, I mean, how nice that Jenny is here." I could have slapped my own forehead. Of course, it made sense Jenny was here; Jenny was the mullet-y jock Herschel's twin, and they were both part of the wedding party. I just never connected that Jenny would show up here today because she wasn't staying here. But that was ridiculous because we were having the toasts on the dock tonight for the happy couple. I was not ready for this.

Abby and Sutton had both clocked my alarm and were now looking on with interest, which meant gossiping would be a rekindled joint hobby between those two. They made meaningful eye contact as if to say they'd *talk about all this later.*

"Oh yes," Adrian said. "Everyone's looking forward to seeing you, Maggie, Jenny too." It felt as though Adrian was going to say something more when their cell dinged. "Excuse me, sorry," Adrian said, frowning, before scurrying to another part of the kitchen.

Sutton eyed me and my belly suspiciously before pulling two oversized suitcases in from the hallway. "I guess *I'll* get everyone's luggage into the kitchen then," he said, as he glared at me and clowned, pretending to struggle under the weight of the suitcases. But Sutton was of sturdy stock, and now he looked positively fetching as his biceps flexed. He was being an amazing sport about all of this. Earlier, he had changed into khaki shorts and a forest green polo shirt, after discarding five other outfits. "I want to look like I'm a successful lawyer about town, but also into quiet luxury," Sutton had said as he filled in his brows with my Sephora brow kit. "You know, like I don't care what these peasants think."

Abby leaned over the kitchen island and snapped her fingers three times in front of my face. I suppressed an urgent and immediate need to smack her. This was going to be a long week. *Breathe, one, two. Breathe, three, four.* Sutton gave me an encouraging look and my anger calmed. I could do this. I gave Sutton a thank you wink.

"Yes, Abby," I sighed, "You, Trig, and another bridesmaid are up on the third floor. Where is Trig, by the way?" I hadn't seen him or his omnipresent, offensively themed baseball caps since we'd seen him and Herschel playing with Cosmo down by the dock while we were securing dear Mr. Trembolt into his car. *No, brain, don't think about Mr. Trembolt's waxy dead skin or Sutton barfing on a fire ant hill.*

"Trig went to visit his aunt at her store downtown," Abby said. "Of course, I *myself* will be sharing a bathroom with everyone on the third floor." Abby said this like she was donating a kidney to someone. "Trig texted me that he'd check in sometime before the cocktail hour, which you said will go *very well.* I noticed the wind blowing, but I'm sure you've got it handled."

"That's right, Abby," I muttered under my breath. "Among my many talents is 'handling the wind.'" I shuddered and opened my own Abby-created miniature white, rhinestoned feather wedding binder (Abby's big white feather binder was having glitter-pooping babies, apparently) to check who was on the second floor. A few white feathers floated to the floor as I quickly flipped through the plastic inserts. "Along with two other guests, Adrian and Herschel are on the second floor. Herschel is in the room where . . ." *Oh no, where poor Mr. Trembolt died.* I floundered.

Sutton saw my distress and jumped in. "Herschel will love it! It's a super cute bedroom with comfy furniture. Such a comfortable bed too. He'll sleep like the *dead.*" The second Sutton uttered the word "dead," his eyes flew wide in horror and he dropped the suitcase. "No. Not dead . . . what I mean is," he sputtered, "what I'm meaning is that he will not ever want to wake up." Sutton's face twitched like he was glitching.

"Thank you, Sutton," I said pointedly as I gave him a clear shut-the-fuck-up look. I had to finish looking at floor plans with Abby. *Did lightning ever strike someone if they prayed for it hard enough? I silently wondered.* "Okay," I said. "The room that Herschel is in will be lovely and . . ."

"Oh look, Maggie," Sutton chirped, pulling his polo shirt away from his sweaty body and fanning himself. He looked suddenly suspiciously excited, and I wasn't sure why until he said, "Here come the twins Herschel and Jenny right now this very minute!"

My best friend loved drama and he didn't feel the need to hide it.

Sutton's voice rose an impish octave as he grabbed another suitcase and rushed past us to the back staircase in the mud-room. The turncoat was leaving me to face Herschel, Jenny, and Abby alone while my only potential ally, Adrian, was staring at their phone like someone had died. I hadn't spoken to Jenny in weeks; I snuck around town like the Pink Panther when I wanted to avoid potential awkward encounters. Which was always.

"C'mon Cosmo," Jenny called as she and her shining blonde ponytail strode into the kitchen with my traitorous dog happily trotting along beside her. She wore perfectly crisp cargo shorts, a white tank top, and a forest green flannel shirt tied at her waist. Her muscled shoulders and forearms, I grudgingly admitted, looked amazing, one wrist wrapped by a braided, leather bracelet. Herschel, his short, damp blond curls sticking out from the back of his cap, lumbered in behind Jenny. He was also handsomely bedecked in cargo shorts, a white tank and a green flannel shirt. I wondered whether they had planned ahead to match outfits like they did when they were kids, but I didn't have time to think about how weird that was because I had to find something hospitable to say. I was the host. *Don't panic*, I thought, as Herschel swooped in front of Jenny to scoop up Noodle. No words were coming to my mind. Literally none, until suddenly something desperate inside me locked into gear.

"Well, I'm happy that y'all are here," I abruptly chirped, raising my arms Evita style and quickly slapping them down by my thighs. I smiled wildly and my teeth felt huge. "And how is your business going?" I asked Jenny, extending my hand to shake hers and immediately wanting Captain Picard to beam me away to a distant planet. My palm was sweaty, and I wondered if Jenny could feel my nerves buzzing in my hand.

"Business is good, thanks," Jenny answered, surreptitiously wiping her hand on her hip after shaking mine. She then folded her muscular tall body down to nuzzle Cosmo's fuzzy black and brown head. If I wasn't mistaken, Jenny was employing my own dog as a living shield between us. Point for Jenny. Maybe both of us were nervous? She waved at Abby, who briefly acknowledged her, then went back to studying her binder.

"I mean, the company is doing well." Jenny stood up and glanced again over at Adrian, who was still typing on his phone. "We are booked into the middle of summer for dock building jobs. Speaking of docks, I saw your dad's old dock was really getting hammered out there in the wind . . ."

I started to say that the dock had literally just been inspected when a phone repeatedly chimed to the tune of Dolly Parton's "Here You Come Again," interrupting us.

"Excuse me," Jenny said, unzipping her denim fanny pack to pull out her cell. Her expression changed from mildly uncomfortable—she was talking with me, her girlfriend's ex, after all—to disturbed. She pursed her lips and slammed her phone back in her fanny pack so violently that Herschel noticed from across the room. He loped over to me, the blonde curls of his mullet bouncing, and positioned himself between me and Jenny.

"Hey, Maggie," he said, extending his hand to shake mine while raising his eyebrows at Jenny.

Jenny walked over to Adrian, who was standing in the corner of the kitchen. I took Herschel's hand in one of mine digging my fingernails into my other palm to distract me from Herschel's clammy grasp. I tried to turn and see what Adrian and Jenny were doing, but Herschel pulled me into a bear hug and clapped my back hard, mashing my face against the moist chest hair peeking out over his tank top. I could smell the stale beer on Herschel's breath as his chest heaved. "Maggie, Maggie, Maggie," he exhaled into my hair. "Lance sounds like such an asshole." His barrel-shaped chest raised and fell like a bellows. I had forgotten how emotional Herschel could get when he'd been drinking.

I nodded and tried to extrapolate myself from Herschel's tipsy grip, but he squeezed me tighter. "I mean," he continued, painfully thumping my back even harder, "the cheating was bad enough, but like, you were *sick* too. And then you had to move back home all broke and stuff? And then your dad actually *died*? And then it didn't even work out with Lance after you guys *did that to Alice*." He squeezed harder. "That's so sad."

Herschel was never one to be delicate. He was more like a big, wet, well-meaning golden retriever. A muffled "thank you?" escaped me from the depths of Herschel's damp bosom. I threw back my head and took a deep breath, trying to escape the Axe body spray, before I grabbed a dried-out pastry to distract Herschel while I extricated myself from whatever this was.

"Catch, champ!" I threw the pastry at him and discreetly used my upper arm to wipe away tears. No one from here, not even Mia, knew that I had hooked up with Lance up north when I was supposed to be signing divorce papers. The still unsigned papers were sitting in my tiny log cabin on the property, mocking me like the pregnancy test I was too scared to take.

"Oh my gosh, Hersch. You didn't need to bring all that up now," Abby said. I was mildly surprised that Abby had come to the rescue. She picked a hangnail off and flicked it. She then brushed glitter off her light orange sundress and turned another page over in her binder. "I don't know if you remember," Abby said, glancing up, "but I went to your dad's funeral, Maggie. I think most of his students did. We're all so sorry."

I smiled a little, thinking about how Dad's funeral was standing room only, with his old students from his middle school physical science classes filling up the lobby of the Lakeside Funeral Home. Every kid had wanted to be in Mr. L's class, even giving up a lazy summer to go spelunking around the caves and digging for diamonds and crystals for school credit.

Abby snapped her binder shut, knocking me out of a lovely memory. "Hey Maggie, I almost forgot to ask what was with the coroner van nearby. Why was a police officer here earlier? Why was he 'testing' (Abby did air quotes) his car in your driveway?"

Uh oh. Out of the corner of my eye, Adrian looked up from their phone. Jenny's long ponytail swished around her head as her eyes jerked toward me. Even Herschel stopped chewing and looked up.

"My cousin Mark?" I tossed back at her, sure she couldn't have seen the coroner's van with Mr. Trembolt's car, which we'd hidden way off the beaten path on a side road. "Mark was over here helping us, um, move a dresser." *And looking for evidence in the freakish untimely expiration of my first guest while yelling at Sutton and me.* I definitely knew why I was nervous about the cops, but I was not sure why this group was weirdly interested in local law enforcement's comings and goings.

Mark's bellowing from this morning still rang in my ears. "I can't *believe* you put Regina and me in this situation." An angry red color had spread up from his white neck to his freckled ears. "You stuffed him in that car like a damn Jenga puzzle."

I had helpfully pointed that out Jenga was a game, not a puzzle, but Mark grew even redder and demanded that I keep Sutton's weak stomach away from his patrol car.

"So, the police were not here in any official capacity, right? Like the coroner van?" Abby asked. "I don't want anything to look like trouble here."

I shrugged my shoulders and raised my eyebrows in what I hoped would show how silly this conversation was. "Why would Mark be here otherwise?"

"Well, I don't know," snipped Abby, helping herself to a chocolate croissant that Heidi had dropped off earlier. "But if anything is off, Mr. Carlyon will find out. He just has a sixth sense about these things."

"Huh," was all I could manage. *Wait.* Abby and Mr. Carlyon couldn't possibly know about Mr. Trembolt, could they? Is that why she kept asking me? To catch me in a lie? My pulse raced and the telltale hot, itchy blotching started around my neck just like my cousin Mark's had. Abby was right. If any of the wedding party found out about a guest dying on the premises, Tamsin's dad would yank his money, and I would be foreclosed by next week. Would I go back to Lance? What if I really was pregnant? Lance swore to me he had changed, and my old boss had been trying to lure me back, sending me hints of tantalizing offers with more money than I had made before. I could move back into my home that Lance and I built together with the little nursery that I had decorated in a dinosaur theme. No late bills, no dead bodies. All I'd have to do was walk away from my friends and everything I'd built here.

"Jenny." Abby's voice pierced the silence. "You all are changing before the sunset cocktail hour, yes?"

Abby's laser sharp gaze turned to Adrian and Jenny, who were huddled together by the sliding glass doors, both still looking at their phones and whispering. "Hey, what are you two plotting over there?"

Adrian's and Jenny's heads whipped up and they stashed their phones away. I wasn't the best at deciphering facial expressions but just given the red coloring in Jenny's cheeks and neck and Adrian's furrowed brow, something was definitely up.

"Sorry. Just work stuff," Jenny answered, furiously twirling her ponytail. "I need to take off, actually. Good seeing you all." Jenny quickly waved at us and walked out the sliding door.

"Yeah, me too. Work stuff." Adrian's eyes followed Jenny until she was out of sight, then they asked for their room key. "I need a power nap before tonight's activities." Adrian bent down to give Cosmo a few pats on his head before taking their key from Abby.

After Abby, Herschel and Adrian went up to their rooms, Sutton magically reappeared.

"And where have you been, hiding like a coward?" I asked, taking a few precious minutes to sit with my feet up. Noodle was lying on my lap as we sprawled across the couch, while Cosmo happily chewed a dental stick on the braided rug.

An ice pack was nestled in the pillow behind my neck, cooling my tight muscles and nerves as half an edible was starting to hit. Thank goodness.

"In the bathroom and I blame you for it," Sutton said, plunking down in the old leather recliner. He pulled my grandma's crocheted blanket over him and leaned his head back.

"And how am I responsible for your toilet adventures?"

He pointed to the wall. "You took down our 'Drink Water & Take Your Medicine, Bitch' sign and I didn't remember to take my intestinal inflammation meds. Now I am reaping what I sowed." Sutton made a "pss pss" sound and Noodle jetted off my lap and onto his. "Mia also blames you cuz she didn't take her ADHD meds this morning when she was here. She tried to work when she got home, but she said it was like Mr. Bean Tries Accounting."

"Oh no, that's too bad. Oh hey!" I turned my head towards Sutton and readjusted my ice pack. "Weird thing happened. Jenny and Adrian were acting all mysterious with their phones. Weren't they a thing in school?"

"Uh, more like middle school. Jenny has dated exclusively women since ninth grade, so you can forget about Jenny cheating on Alice, especially with Alice's cousin." Sutton sat up straight in the chair and made full eye contact with me. "Speaking of hooking up and all that, would you mind telling me why you have been patting your stomach?" Sutton was quiet for a moment, then gasped. "WAIT. We haven't had our 'Maggie-has-PMS' all-day brownie dough ice cream and Lifetime cheerleader killer movies in quite a few weeks. Are you . . .?"

"I never have regular periods; you know that," I snapped. "And just who would be the father?" I threw a pillow at his head and laughed, hoping that the thought of me having sex with anyone right now was preposterous. "Back to the matter at hand, something was definitely up with Adrian and Jenny."

Sunset is the right bet for
cocktails and mixing with
friends old and new. Please wear
cocktail appropriate attire and
be sure to thank our gracious host
Maggie Livingston.

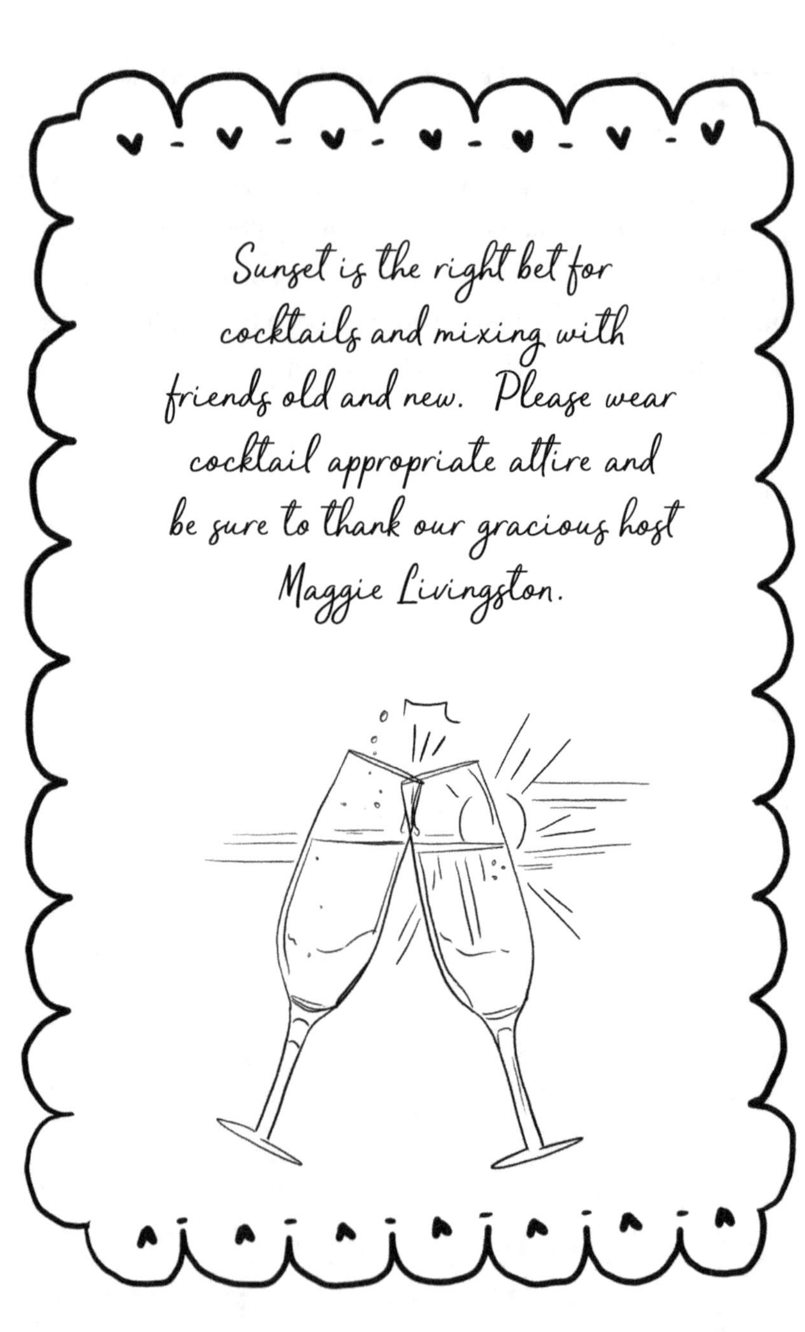

CHAPTER THREE
Mingling Under the Loblollies

"You could just go up to Alice and talk to her, you know." Sutton sauntered up to me and leaned casually, Cary Grant-style, against one of the oldest Loblolly Pines in my large, wooded yard. "The evening might go faster if you just get up and start mingling." Flicking a green needle off his new jacket, he sipped a Tom Collins and eyed a gorgeous woman in dark clothes standing out amongst our guests, who were mixing and milling about the property in a flurry of pastel-colored seersucker and silk.

"Damnit! Now you made me lose sight of her," I grumbled. "And no, I'm not spying on her." I shifted my weight as I perched precariously on my rickety arthritic ankles.

Sutton knew me well enough to guess I would be hiding in the bushes and looking for my ex-girlfriend while watching my guests' every move to see if they were enjoying themselves. Leave it to Sutton to forget this evening had to go off without a hitch if I wanted to earn my bonus. Plus, I had to keep an eye on the dock because it was listing to one side in the lake's choppy waves, while above us the dark grey clouds gathered. You never could tell what the chaotic weather would do in the mountains or if danger was just over the next peak. At least up north in the prairie you could see tornadoes coming from miles away.

"Sutton," I said, "I am keeping an eye on the weather, not just Alice. Also, I am learning things here behind my bushes. You might be interested to know that I saw Jenny and Adrian creeping across the yard staring at Adrian's phone again just like they were in my kitchen, and *then* they were staring for a long time at *Jenny's* phone. What do you think Herschel's twin sister and Mr. Adrian-zen-prayer-hands are so engrossed in their phones for? Also, where does Adrian get their silk scarves. That one they are wearing today is divine."

Sutton delicately blotted his forehead with his cerulean blue pocket square. He spotted me staring hard at the dock again and said, "That was five questions in one you just asked me, Mags. You should try to relax, honey. The dock is fine. Inspected and everything. The special champagne toast on the dock this evening will go great." He held his glass with his manicured fingertips and swirled it expertly. "As far as Adrian and whatever they are doing with Alice's girlfriend Jenny, how is that even your business?" He asked, before taking a sip. "Besides, I have some things to discuss with you."

Wow. I turned to look at Sutton and a blueberry branch hit me in the face with a "thwap." "Unbelievable," I said, my eyes flashing. I boosted my boobs and straightened my shoulders. I'd stuffed my ample décolletage and soft belly into this little black cocktail dress for this sweaty mess of a day, and now Sutton was coming at me with "something to discuss?" Granted, I enjoyed that my plump ass looked amazing today, but after hobnobbing with old bullies in the boiling heat, gently stashing my deceased guest, and getting grilled by my irate detective cousin Mark, all I wanted to do now was take a refreshing bath, gnaw through some gummies, watch *One Tree Hill* with Noodle and Cosmo, and eat a pizza that would definitely gum up my digestive tract. But *here I was*, all dressed up and squatting in the berry bushes with Sutton fixing to ask me if I was *pregnant*. His timing, as usual, was about as helpful as diarrhea at the airport.

I shoved away the branch so I could throw another bruising look at Sutton. "Gosh, Sutton. Do tell, would you next like an Old Fashioned, or perhaps a Harvey Wall Banger before we discuss my messed-up life here in the dirt?"

"I beg *your* pardon." He dabbed his neck, taking another sip.

"Sutton, I told you, I miss periods because of my endometriosis. Mia is pregnant; not me. No time. End of discussion." I waved him off and started looking for Alice in the crowd, but Sutton wasn't giving up.

He sipped some more and gave me the just-hold-on-and-listen look. "No, it's actually some of your unpaid bills. Your bigger creditors started forwarding them to my office because I'm your attorney. I tried to tell you the other day, and I wanted to tell you now before you got all the creditors' threats in the mail."

Not the pregnancy then. This was an entirely new awful thing that I didn't even *know* about. I stared at Sutton incredulously. "Well, this is a *fine* time to bring it up, at the end of this day, of all days, when everything is happening, and if this doesn't go well and I don't get my bonus from Bridezilla Tamsin's dad I'll lose my house!" A loud roaring filled my ears. My hands tensed and my mouth went on autopilot. "My god, Sutton. It would be so easy to just give up and move back up with Lance. It was better there and, I'm so close to—"

"Better there?" Sutton's eyes widened in tipsy surprise before Mia interrupted us.

"Why are we hiding now?" Mia asked loudly, cutting off our conversation, as she and Heidi walked up. Heidi crouched down beside us and then offered a hand to Mia, who was wobbling as she tried to balance her pregnant belly and kneel while handing us our little hors d'oeuvres plates. Mia looked gorgeous in a light pink halter top and skirt, her braids piled high on her head with little sterling butterfly clips. Heidi was also stunning with her blond hair in a chic French twist, a pale blue sheath dress and strappy wedges, perfect for the terrain.

Sutton had seen my eyes welling up and my hands clenching and unclenching, and he jumped in to answer Mia's question while I pulled myself back from the brink. It was just a few missed periods. Well, two. And a storm. Maybe. Or not. Plus, Alice, and the dock. And I didn't want to imagine the fallout with Abby if the party tanked tonight.

"Take your pick as to who we're hiding from, Mia," Sutton said. He gestured to the soirée happening on the other side of our yard.

Heidi and Mia must have noticed they had walked in on a serious conversation but blessedly they didn't ask about it.

"Mark has cornered me twice already," I said, "demanding more details about Mr. Trembolt. I thought we told him enough earlier today?"

"I mean," Sutton took another sip of his drink. "Mark has a point. Technically, you did—" Sutton cut himself off when I gave him a death-ray look.

"I'm well aware of what *we all* did," I snapped back, still feeling bad for putting Mark and Regina, and yes, Mia, Heidi, and Sutton, in a very compromising position. "Sorry, you guys, I'm exhausted, and the evening has just started." Whenever I shut my eyes, I saw Mr. Trembolt, wrapped up in a cartoon cat shower curtain, bouncing down my stairs. I shuddered and tried to concentrate on the vibrant pink crepe myrtle blossoms surrounding us. I breathed in the heavenly scent of the outdoors; in and out, in and out. *Trembolt died in his sleep. Totally natural. Everyone dies.*

Mia patted my arm. "And how are the *guests* settling in?"

I groaned and stroked the soft material of my dress between my index finger and thumb, trying to concentrate on the pleasant velvety sensation instead of stress. "So far, I've had complaints ranging from the beds are too hard to there are too many pine needles around." I motioned up to what my dad Henry used to call our "heavenly pine cathedral" with the trees swirling their branches high above our heads as they danced on the amber pine needle carpet beneath our feet. I roughly wiped away one audacious tear. "What the hell am I supposed to do about the pine needles anyway?" I grabbed Sutton's pocket square and wiped my neck and face before shoving it back in his jacket. The sweltering air was thick with moisture that clung onto my skin. "I swear," I glanced over toward the guests. "I keep getting flashbacks to when that group used to write 'RAINMAN' on my locker in permanent marker. Every fucking week. I hate being dependent on them now. I'm unravelling."

"Well, we all unravel sometimes, Maggie," Sutton said, sipping his drink. "*You* just can't unravel *this* week." He winked at me. "Hey, didn't they also tape a sign on your car that said, 'I'm an Excellent Driver?' I vaguely remember that."

"Nobody said they were original," Heidi said, rolling her eyes. "Hard to believe we all used to be so close." She nibbled daintily on her crostini and brushed back a pretty curl that had fallen from her French twist, then cocked her head. "But then the bullying just stopped," she said, the side of her mouth twitching.

"Right," Sutton said, "What did you put in the gas tanks of the expensive cars their parents bought them again?"

"No idea what you're talking about," Heidi said mildly, before she asked, "Did y'all see Abby keeps breathing down my neck about every food tray my servers bring out?" Heidi did her best imitation of Abby's sharp, loud voice: "Did they *really* wash their hands; was the meat cooked at the right temperature; why is the cheese sweating?"

Before Heidi could go on, a shriek and cackling caught our attention, and we turned to see a large group of guests congregating in the middle of the lawn. Our former classmates were yelling "CHUG! CHUG!" to Trig, the early arrival with Herschel from this morning. Trig's off-color signature baseball cap for today said, "YOUR DAD IS MY CARDIO," which was pretty funny, but Abby and Tamsin were begging him to take it off. Trig had been our high school quarterback and trumpet first chair, the supposed hero of our class. He now wobbled on a rented table, trampling mud on the white tablecloth, and downed a pitcher of beer. Trig caught us looking at him, his strong jaw jutting out and his close-set hazel eyes ever so slightly narrowing when he made eye contact with me. "Isn't he Noah's best man?" Heidi asked.

"Ah yes, the 'best dude' as he calls himself. Still don't know why or how Noah, who's just a great person, and Trig the beer-guzzling partier are still friends, but whatever," I mused, sampling the sweaty cheese. Noah and Trig were opposites in every way that mattered, so their enduring close friendship was a puzzle to many.

"Maybe they've all changed, grown up a bit," Mia mused.

"Most of them were bullies, and they certainly didn't spare you either when we were teens, Mia," Sutton said, eyes wide. "Are you defending them?"

"I agree with Sutton," I said. "They seem exactly the same."

"I haven't forgotten," Mia said. "But shouldn't we give them a little grace and time to see if they have changed? I mean, they were kids too back then." Mia shrugged and smiled. "And it seems like they have all made choices to change and make their lives better. At least we should give *ourselves* a little grace to acknowledge our own pain and the work we've done to move on?" She shook her head. "After I had kids, I got soft, I guess."

"No," Heidi said, smiling at Mia. "Choosing kindness and empathy is never weakness. If anything, kindness is strength. Speaking of strength, wow," Heidi said as she peered through the blueberries and spotted the spouse-to-be Noah talking with their parents. "Noah definitely takes after their parents' good looks," Heidi said. "Their luscious black curly hair . . ." She sighed as she popped a prosciutto wrapped cantaloupe square in her mouth.

"And those eyes. Are they brown? Gold? I just can't tell." Mia also sighed. "Remember how we would bribe our home room teacher to seat us next to them every year?"

I nodded. Noah stopped conversations when they walked into a room, their bright smile made anyone with hormones go a bit weak, and tonight's white shirt and tan pants set off their rich, brown skin. Plus, for as long as I could remember, they were always the first person to volunteer for a charity race, bake sale, or park clean up. It made sense that Noah made a hugely successful career building a consulting company that matched wealthy donors with worthy causes. I frankly wondered what Noah saw in Tamsin, who had been such a self-absorbed bully when we were young.

Noah walked away from their parents to talk with the collaborators, Jenny and Adrian, who had both finally joined humanity. I slunk down further behind the bushes and turned to Sutton, Mia and Heidi. "Ugh," I said, lowering myself even farther to the ground. "I'm just not in the mood to talk with anyone. But I know I have to."

Heidi picked a dead leaf out of my hair before blotting the sweat off my chest. "I think it's fine you take a break, Mags," Heidi said. "Abby should be satisfied with the evening and everyone's glow-ups."

I agreed. The twins Jenny and Herschel looked dapper in their matching slacks and light blue, button down shirts. A little odd to be matching again, but Jenny did look pretty, I had to admit. She could make any outfit look amazing. Her hair was pulled back in a tight ponytail that showed off her cheekbones. And her smile, damn her, appeared friendly and normal.

As if the drama gremlin Sutton could read my mind, he asked, "Hey everyone, where's Alice? I swore I saw her by the house a while ago?" He took a long swig of his Tom Collins and leaned against the pine tree, grinning behind his glass.

"What?" I yelped. "Is she coming this way?" Luckily, I didn't see Alice anywhere near us, and my breathing slowed to normal. This week was going to kill me. I calmed down by stroking the smooth fabric of my dress again and then a thought occurred to me. "Do you remember the last time we were all together in one place with these people? Almost to the day fourteen years ago?"

"Oh no, that's right." Mia checked her calendar. "Yep. That horrible night fourteen years ago coming up on Friday, which was also graduation night." She shivered as a strong gust of wind blew through her light dress. "I can still see Carl Gleet's truck going off the interstate bridge and crashing into the lake. Remember how we stood there until dawn watching the divers and the rescue boats?" We were all quiet for a moment, remembering when Carl, a quiet sophomore at our school, had gotten very drunk and run his pick-up through the guard rail.

We didn't speak for a while, lost in memories that we hadn't thought of for years. "Why were we all on Noah's dock that night in the first place?" Sutton asked, a bit tipsily, breaking the silence, and getting a glare from Mia. "Oh yeah, that's when Alice found out that Maggie cheated on her at that student government thing with sexy-senior-from-Minnesota Lance, and Alice was so mad she pushed our Bridezilla Tamsin in the lake because Tamsin was blabbing to everyone about it . . ."

"Wow, Sutton." I flicked some pine needles at him. "We don't need to bring *that* up." My cheeks burned with the memory of Alice's hurt, angry face. Lance convinced me to screw up, and a few weeks later I left to move up by him, tail between my legs. I had been planning to attend state university with my friends that fall, but after fucking up so badly it was easier to just go be with Lance. His version of a relationship was an all-about-Lance situation, but it had been predictable, and safe. Lance had, as he put it, heroically put up with most of my idiosyncrasies, plus he had supported us, so I never had to worry if some weeks I had to work less than others because of chronic pain. Truth be told, we had been really cozy up by the Great Lakes with the snow and the spruce trees, where I could avoid interacting with people for long periods of time. Up until I had found out about Lance's extra-curricular activities, that is. At the time I was sure his cheating was a deal breaker for me, but now?

Before anyone could say more, Heidi announced, "We've been spotted." She waved at Abby motioning to her by the food table. "Wanna help me, Mia?"

Mia nodded and they pulled each other out of their awkward crouching stance. Heidi and Mia left our little hideout to venture into the crowds toward Abby, as I caught a whiff of Sutton's drink when I stood up. "Wow, that is strong." My nostrils puckered up as I leaned on his arm for support. "What . . ."

"Get back!" Sutton suddenly pulled me back down behind the Loblolly.

"Is it Mark?" I said, flailing and frantically searching around for my cousin who had been looking for me all evening. After the terse afternoon conversation about illegally moving a body and making his job hell, not to mention how I was jeopardizing Regina's job as county coroner, I guessed that he had a point. I felt horrible about the whole ordeal, but Mark would just have to understand that right now, I had to concentrate on getting through this night. I grabbed onto Sutton's arm to steady myself while trying to balance on the balls of my sandaled feet. "I mean, I get why . . ."

Sutton clapped his hand on my mouth and pointed, silencing my next thought. "Look who's coming!"

Even though his hand smelled like salami, I didn't move an inch. For there, standing amongst the peonies merely yards before us, was the bride-to-be: Raven haired beauty, Tamsin Carlyon. Valedictorian in both high school and college, most dedicated volunteer at the Hugs-4-Dogs Humane Society, State Teen Princess two years in a row. Her hair still shiny, dark, and thick, cascading down her back like a frickin' Disney character's. Admittedly, I had a thing for textures, and I yearned to stroke it. Also enticing, her skin was still silky with a hint of natural rose blush covering her cheeks. Not a zit in sight. "Did you know that those lashes are natural?" I whispered, running a finger under my own stubby ones to remove the delightful combo of sweat and clumped mascara.

"And how, *how* could eyes be so blue?" Sutton asked, perhaps also experiencing a mildly revived Tamsin crush. "Shit! We've been spotted. Act natural." Sutton jumped out of his crouch behind our tree, his hip knocking me sideways into a blueberry bush.

"Maggie." Perfect Tamsin extended her manicured hand out to me, which I reluctantly took. "You haven't changed a bit," she said as she pulled me up effortlessly, of course. God, she was good.

Hadn't I? I looked down and saw my ample, and if I might say so myself, lovely derrière, now covered in leaf bits and pine needles. *Still curvy, still a mess,* I thought as I swatted Sutton's hand away from my butt and brushed off the last of the dirt and foliage.

Sutton tipped his straw hat and gestured to the cocktail party venue: my family's lake property decorated in twinkling lights that draped across pine and oak branches as the voices of Lady Gaga and Tony Bennett filled the little cove. Our old classmates and their parents congregated on the dock or on the lawn, while the sun contributed a gorgeous display of reds, yellows and oranges that slowly settled into the lake and behind the mountains.

"What a kick-off to your wedding week, Tamsin," Sutton said.

"Thank you, Stanley . . . Romanoff is it?"

"Sutton. Antonoff."

"Sorry!" Tamsin laughed and held up her champagne glass. "I really need to be more careful."

"Careful about what?" Abby the wedding planner and maid-of-honor nosed her way into our conversation. She'd put her blonde hair up and carried her rhinestoned binder, its white feathers contrasting with the cornflower blue and white cocktail dress that swirled around her lithe ballerina's frame.

Tamsin pointed to her champagne glass and faithful Abby held up hers. "Bottoms up," she said, and they knocked back their drinks, giggling when Abby spilled hers down the front of her dress. At that point, Sutton skipped off. I glared at him, but he was already sashaying toward Mia's parents who were happily watching the sunset from their Adirondack chairs.

"Here." I handed Abby my napkin when Tamsin wandered off to her parents' table, leaving a moistened Abby with me blotting at her bosom and her batting me away. "Is William coming tonight or later in the week?" I asked, having checked in his girlfriend Lena-Elise, another one of Tamsin's bridesmaids, earlier today, but without William.

"Oh, he's here already." Abby grimaced down at her dress and pointed to a tall man with light skin and dark, short hair talking with Trig. Abby waved William over to us when Trig spotted Cosmo and started playing tug-of-war with his hat, leaving William standing alone. He walked toward us with the same slightly stooped over stance as he did in high school. He also sported black glasses and a preppy style of pressed khakis, loafers, and a Polo shirt. He'd always been known as our school's 80's throwback, even standing up his alligator-shirt collars just-so. Made sense he was so organized. He was a therapist now, and back in the day was in most of our senior classes when he was only a sophomore.

"Hey, William," I said. "So nice of you to take the time off and join us this week."

"My folks still live here, and this past weekend they moved

to the retirement village a few miles away, so the timing worked out great," William said. "Incredible what you've done here for the party, Abby." He gestured around and Abby beamed. "And Maggie," William added, "your dad would have loved what you have turned the place into."

Wow, this guy. I tried to smile back, careful to count to three then look away. My dad and I had loved our quiet, solitary life at our lake home, anxiously watching fledgling blue birds making their way into the world and waking up early to find catfish on the yo-yo baits. Would he be okay with me turning our home into a rental party house? Well, I didn't have much of a choice if I wanted to keep our beautiful property.

I was going to jump into the conversation with Abby and William, when I spotted Alice darting through the trees, dressed up fancy, for her, in a dark green shiny shirt and slacks instead of her usual Game and Fish uniform. My heart and stomach square-danced, and I nearly threw up. Even my wrists betrayed me and felt numb at seeing Alice. I had so far mostly succeeded avoiding her in town by—and no, I wasn't proud of this—using Mia's phone app that still tracked Alice's location—yeah, it was bad. Knowing that I would be bumping into her soon enough, probably when she was being lovey dovey with Jenny, I just needed to pull on my big girl panties and make a move.

"Hey guys, have a great time tonight and I'll see you back at the house later," I said, trying to sound as normal as possible as my eyes darted to Alice and back. My fingers found my trio of tiny rocks in my pocket that I had forgotten about and twirled them around to calm my nerves.

"Sounds good," William said, but I could barely hear him because I was already moving quickly toward Alice.

I slinked around the left side of the cabin, past the outdoor shower to where Alice was standing with her back to me. I didn't know a clever way to start this conversation, so I blurted out, "Think you can avoid me all night?"

Alice jumped but quickly recovered. "Not avoiding anyone," she said sternly as something skinny and long slinked out the top of her shirt.

"Okay, what is . . . oh my god is that a *tail*?" I leaned forward to get a better look at a tiny kitten tail poking up from Alice's t-shirt. "Aww . . . you got a kitt—" then the non-kitten hissed at me with little, sharp teeth, and glared into my eyeballs with its own beady black eyes. "ACK THAT'S NOT A KITTEN." I quickly backed up against my cabin door.

"SHHHHH," Alice commanded, frantically looking around for anyone that might discover her weird secret. "I'm not supposed to have her here."

"No shit," I said. Manhandling a dead body in a bed and break-fast *was* probably worse than hiding a freaky little possum between your boobs, but I wasn't going to admit that. "Why? And . . . why?"

Alice petted her stowaway and made kissing noises with her pale pink, full delicious lips. "No one could stay overnight at the wild animal shelter, and Athena needs to be dropper fed every twenty minutes."

"Okay, so, why all the subterfuge? You just could have brought her home." I said the word "home" a little too provocatively as I leaned against the outside wall, peevishly imagining Alice and Jenny laughing and doing dishes together in their awesome kitchen. I was more tired and achy by the second as splinters from the ancient logs dug into my back.

"Jenny insisted that I come because she felt uncomfortable with all of our old classmates." Alice said in a decidedly irritated voice, rolling her eyes.

Oh ho, trouble in paradise? Good. "You could have used my house for an emergency; I thought you knew that." My voice betrayed my hurt. Fatigue was making it hard to act normal.

Alice tucked her chin length dark hair behind her ears that endearingly stuck out a bit. "Yeah, I *could* have, but then I would have to explain why I keep going inside the house, so I've been feeding her when no one's looking." She pulled out a baggie with a syringe looking thing and started feeding the creature. My heart melted at the tenderness.

"Wait, so Jenny doesn't know you have her here?" I was enormously proud that I said this without sounding too gleeful. Still, my mouth twitched ever so slightly, which I'm sure Alice noticed.

"Ahhh, no." Alice made some more cooing sounds before continuing. "Jenny has forbidden any more baby animals in the house, so I'm winging it with this one."

Don't smile don't smile don't smile. "So, what about . . ." I heard my name being called repeatedly by Mia. "Ugh. I need to go." I looked at Alice, her big, deep brown eyes were almost covered by her thick fringe of bangs. She gave me a little flirty half grin before she looked back down on her ward.

I was going to tell Alice that she could feed the little gray and pink demon as long as she needed to here, heck maybe even move in, when the spouse-to-be, Noah, called out, "Let's gather round for the special toast on the dock, everyone!"

From where we stood on my cabin's porch, we could easily see the dock, about thirty feet away, and Noah's mom Mrs. Allerton's blue and white caftan flowing around her as she moved across the lawn with her husband and son.

Mrs. Allerton waited for everyone to leave the dock before she walked on, regal, the gold clips in her locs twinkling in the fading sunlight. She then raised her champagne glass, smiling as the chatter died down enough for her to start speaking. "Welcome everyone!"

Alice, the tiny demon named Athena in her shirt, and I crept forward to better hear Noah's mother's toast. As Mrs. Allerton continued to orate to the crowd about Tamsin and Noah's upcoming union, I stood on tiptoes when I noticed Sutton, across the lawn from me, was trying to get my attention by frantically pointing to where Mrs. Allerton stood.

"Alice," I whispered. "Is the dock sinking, or am I seeing things?"

Alice looked up from her furry little companion and pushed a guest out of the way who blocked her view. "What the . . ."

At this point, more than just a few of us had noticed that loud, creaking sounds were coming from the dock as Mrs. Allerton grabbed onto the dock railing, attempting to retain her composure.

"My, my. Someone driving a boat didn't follow the No Wake Rule," Mrs. Allerton said, now holding on with both hands.

I looked around the cove and saw there were no boats around that could have made the floating dock move like it was going to . . . OH NOOOOOO!

A chorus of "Mrs. Allerton!" went up as she went down in a cloud of blue and white silk.

"Mom!" Noah, Herschel, and Trig jumped in and swam to Mrs. Allerton as everyone else lost their collective minds, screaming and pointing at the lake.

"Take Athena!" Alice tried to shove the baby possum at me.

"I will not!" I yelled as we ran to the dock, which was mostly in the water and sinking fast. "Seriously, get that thing away from me!"

"I can help more than you, and I need to see if anyone else fell in," Alice barked as she tried again to hand Athena over to me. "I'm a *game warden.*"

"You're seriously throwing rank or whatever at me while Mrs. Allerton is drowning in the lake?" I practically screamed as we dodged tables, landscaping, and other guests. "Move!" I shouted to a couple standing in the middle of the path.

Alice somehow managed to secure Athena with Mia's mom right before we got to the landing. She kicked off her Tevas and jumped in while I made my way to the scene of the crime.

"How did this happen?" I carefully stepped onto the part of the dock that was still above water.

Herschel, his spiky hair plastered to his head, looked up at me, a sopping mess from the water. "From what I can tell, these bolts must have come loose with all the extra wind and weight and the dock couldn't take it." He held up a metal rod and pointed to where the bolts used to be. "When was the last time you got this inspected?"

"Just a month, month and a half ago," I said, trying to keep the defensiveness out of my voice. True, I had skipped on a few items around here that needed money, but I learned from my dad to keep up our old dock, which had included yearly inspections. "Can this be fixed easily?"

Herschel pushed his wet hair out of his eyes and held up a part of the dock to see it better with the dock lights. "Well, I'm no expert—my sister Jenny is—but maybe I could sweet talk her and her crew to come out here tomorrow and take a look."

"I'd really appreciate it," I said, trying to force my face into a smile. I grabbed onto my emotional support rocks in my pocket and furiously rubbed them together. *This fucking day.*

"I'll drive your party barge over to your neighbors around the point. They've got an extra slip," Herschel said as he climbed the boat ladder.

Trig came down from the house with my boat key and saluted me before he joined Herschel.

"Who else needs a towel?" Abby called out, carrying a huge stack of bath towels. She placed a stack on the nearest table for Mrs. Allerton and the people who jumped in to save her. "We will need to do laundry tonight," a seething Abby warned me as she strode by.

I was so tired and achy already and the night was far from over. At least Mark was too busy making sure all the guests did not drown to be grilling me again over that little, tiny, inconsequential thing like illegally moving a dead body. *My god, that was just this morning.* I trudged toward my once quiet home. As exhausted as I was, I couldn't shake the feeling that something wasn't right about my dock "accidentally" falling apart.

Rise and shine!
Run at Tamsin's Hugs-4-Dogs 5K
or treat yourself to a spelunking good
time exploring The Old Treasure
Caves. Have a magical day!

CHAPTER FOUR
You Say Stalagmite; I Say Stalactite

"Okay, does everyone know what vans they are supposed to ride in?" Early morning sun streamed through my kitchen windows straight into my eyeballs. I was already counting down the minutes until my hungover guests left my property so I could clean the house in peace. Some blessed quiet this morning would be great even if I had to keep working. After that, I had to check out my dock and try to figure out what the hell had happened to the damn thing last night. I wiped sweat from my forehead. Thick moisture clung to the windows, and my dew laden peony blossoms were laid out on the path execution style signaling a sweltering day.

"They haven't gone yet, have they?" I turned to see a frazzled Virginia Hernandez trotting down the stairs in her shorts and tank top while hastily running product through her magenta tipped, black spiky hair. The only time our school's soccer team won state was when Virginia was captain, and I could see why. Muscular in her running attire, Virginia looked like she could still lead the team to victory.

"They won't leave without you, Virginia, I promise, but it is time to go now." I was outside the front door counting who was already in the vans and signaled for Sutton to wait. Half the group was heading to the Old Treasure Caves tour, while the others were running the 5K to benefit Tamsin's favorite charity, Hugs-4-Dogs. Sutton had graciously taken off a few days of work to help me make this week go as smoothly as possible. It helped that he owned his small law firm and didn't have to answer to a boss.

"Gonna run today, Sutton?" I called as I waved at my nosy neighbor Miss Vera, who was hurrying down the gravel road in a pastel-colored housedress with her old corgi Rebecca's short legs frantically trying to keep pace. Miss Vera stared toward our house as she pretended to get her mail. She had been a constant pain in my ass through this whole bed and breakfast licensing ordeal by informing the town committee of out-of-state renters that would overrun "our quiet cove." She even littered the village with flyers detailing how I, personally, was ruining our neighborhood. I waved again sweetly, and Miss Vera yanked poor Rebecca's leash and shuffled back inside her home.

Sutton leaned out of the open van window and ran his hand through his salon kissed hair. His blue button up was no doubt tucked neatly into freshly pressed shorts. "Yeah, no, I'm not running," he said. "I will, however, take every chance I get to offer my legal services to my little charges as I drive them around today."

"Please don't bore them," I said, waving at the people in the full van leaving for the cave. My phone buzzed again, and, without looking, my guess was another text from the power company warning me that if I did not pay the overdue bills, my power would be cut off. My billing cycle took me just through the wedding, so I wasn't worried about that. When I glanced down at my screen, my heart skipped. Lance had texted me, and maybe did want to talk, but I couldn't open the text now because Sutton was looking at me expectantly.

"Just don't bug them too much about how important it is to prepare their Last Wills and Testaments, Sutton. It's a wedding, okay? And you're a lawyer. Nobody wants that."

"Whatever," Sutton said cheerfully. "I should try to get *something* out of this, cuz no one is paying me. See you soon." Sutton made a rock 'n' roll hand gesture before pulling away from my gravel parking area too quickly to see the hurt on my face. I smiled at my departing guests until my face ached.

I knew Sutton didn't mean it, but I felt horrible enough that I'd had to rely so heavily on my friends since I returned six months ago. As I walked back to the house, I glanced at my little cabin nestled up to the lake's edge that Mia's husband James had fixed up for me. The house needed so much work that I couldn't afford that my friends had painted walls, sanded floors, and moved furniture while I handed out beer and rested my swollen joints. I constantly carried around guilt about how I could never repay everyone. My phone buzzed again, and I almost looked forward to connecting to Lance and hearing what was going on up there after all the stress down here.

I shielded my screen from the bright sun and opened my phone to a larger-than-life Lance "dick pic" titled "**wut up babe?**" with a heart drawn around the head.

Leave it to Lance to shove his genitals in my face at a time like this.

"**Gross**," I typed back. My stomach cramped and I walked back to the kitchen to pour myself a glass of water. The morning heat and humidity were making me dizzier than usual, which I attributed to, well, everything. My phone buzzed again, and I sat down at my kitchen island.

u luv it lol when r u coming back

I looked up from my phone and out the window at the lawn game remnants strewn around by my first group of official guests. My life plan had looked vastly different a few years ago when I still lived up north, before I got chronically ill, and before I found out Lance was having sexy time with my curriculum writing partner. After a few years of grueling infertility treatments, I'd started having trouble getting out of bed in the morning. My joints ached constantly, I had unrelenting headaches, nerve pain zapped through my body, and according to Lance, I stopped "being fun." He said that he could put up with my autistic "weirdness" and "mood swings" from hormone shots but drew the line at not being able to take our weekend north woods trips with his friends or stopping at the local brewery after work. This was around the time when he took up with Shelly. As soon as I found out, I packed up Noodle and Cosmo and moved to a quiet, small apartment that had a wonderful view of a lake. Cheating was a red line, after all. When I finally got an autoimmune disease diagnosis after years of limbo with doctors telling me I was just anxious or sad or needing attention, I was relieved to begin treatments and hopefully start to feel better.

Almost immediately after I left, Lance begged my forgiveness and tried everything to get me back. We had been together since first year of college and now it was like he had lost his comfort blanket. He showed up at my infusion days with snacks and rubbed my neck when the nausea was overwhelming. He watched Cosmo and Noodle when I had stays at the hospital, Face Timing me so I could see both their sweet, furry faces. At the time, it felt ok to be friends with Lance even after the gaslighting and cheating. I was still meeting with my divorce attorney, and my dad was helping me start a new life. Then dad died. The next time I saw Lance in person was a few months ago to talk about finalizing our divorce, then one thing led to another . . .

I was jolted back to the present by hot water squirting from my broken kitchen faucet on my swollen stomach. The period cramps would start soon; I just knew it. This had to be just retaining water from PMS and the heat. No way I could be pregnant after all those failed IVF treatments with Lance. I yanked the broken faucet handle and tried again to wash the breakfast dishes that I'd collected from the large, oak kitchen table as I made a mental note to buy a new faucet. I was concentrating on scrubbing out a stubborn oatmeal pan when Cosmo leapt up from his bed and started scratching on the sliding door.

I followed his focus to see Alice out on the lake, rounding my property in her red and gray Ranger. She shielded her eyes with one hand while expertly steering her boat with the other like a model in a sports magazine. My chest squeezed at the sight of her. The quiet portion of the morning was over, but this dock nightmare was bringing Alice to my doorstep, and maybe she could help figure out what happened. I looked down at my outfit as my stomach flip-flopped: Carhartt overalls and a flowered tank top, plus my grandmother's Norwegian rosemaled clogs. *Sexy.* I ran to the powder room to check my hair and ran just as fast out when I saw that most of my curls had escaped my poor excuse of a braid that I did not have time to fix.

I opened the door and stepped out onto my porch. "Jenny's not here yet," I called, covering my eyes from the sunlight beating through the tree branches. Good lord it was going to be an extra hot one for the runners, I thought, as Cosmo raced ahead and greeted Alice.

Alice Ambrosia Giannopoulos. Her Greek mom and dad had broken with the tradition of giving their daughter a family name and instead named her after her mother's favorite childhood story. I still remember a vintage *Alice in Wonderland* framed movie poster that hung in her bedroom next to a signed Lieutenant Worf photo from a Star Trek convention my dad took us to.

"I'm not here to see Jenny." Alice jumped to the front of her boat and secured a line to the dock post.

"Why then," I started to ask, but she put her hand up for me to wait until she hopped onto the bank to close the gap between us. She pushed back her blunt cut, dark bangs that were drenched in sweat and bent down to accept Cosmo's frantic kisses all over her face. Then she stood up and confidently strode toward me wearing her Game and Fish uniform—forest green shorts that ended halfway down her bronze thighs; a khaki short sleeve button down shirt that showed off her muscled arms; and hiking boots that gave her an authoritative quality that made me feel naughty. I also tried to stride confidently toward Alice, which was difficult in clogs on uneven ground with joint and nerve issues, but by golly I strode so fucking hard that I felt like a general meeting in the middle of a valley to accept my opponent's surrender.

"Have you seen THIS alligator?" Alice pulled out her phone to show me a picture of what looked like any alligator from Jack Hanna's reruns that I used to watch with my grandma.

"That *particular* one?" I pretended to think hard, resting my chin on my hand. "I mean, certainly there have been *so many* up here in our little mountain range . . ."

Alice made a disgusted sound and shoved her phone back in her pocket. "We think she's from that group of alligators that animal rights doofus set free into the lake last year."

"From Gary's Gators n' More?"

"Yeah." Alice walked past me and headed toward the half submerged dock, Cosmo trotting behind her like a traitor. "I mean, that 'petting zoo,' and I'm saying that in quotes," she looked back at me and motioned me impatiently to follow. "It should have been shut down years ago."

Just that fast I had lost any upper hand as I trudged after her, especially when I tripped over my own clogs. "I heard that," I said as I slipped on a moss covered stone.

Alice tried to hide a snort, but when we arrived at the dock debacle she quickly sobered up. "This is worse than I had thought," she said, lifting a low hanging oak branch and turning to me. "Someone could have gotten really hurt."

"I know," I said, sounding like a sulky teenager. "But the inspection was up to date so unless they botched that . . ."

"I knew you would at least keep up with the boat and dock safety," Alice said, making her way down the part of the walkway still above water.

"What's that supposed to mean?" I took offense to the "at least" part because I had been working hard to keep up with most everything here. I kicked off my clogs and gripped the railing, careful to stay away from the wall of cobwebs as I stepped onto the catwalk.

Alice, now knee deep in the murky water, leaned over to examine the part of the dock that had fallen apart. She glanced my way then back down. "I meant nothing by it."

I didn't want to slip, so I held the railing tight and craned my neck to see what she was looking at so intently.

"Hey, there's no rust on these bolts or on the structure." She turned to see them better in the sunlight, leaning in closer and squinting.

An obscenely large spider—more like a fruit bat with eight legs—brushed my hand, and I held in a screech as I tried to get a peek. "So?"

Alice reached over and gently guided the bloodthirsty arachnid away, then surprised me by grasping my arm. "So, it means that your dock didn't just crumble apart on its own."

The little hairs on my neck prickled my skin as Alice and I locked eyes. "But the wind . . ." I began, then trailed off as if my brain had just short circuited.

Alice stepped onto the sea wall next to the catwalk and hauled herself up. She glanced at the sunken dock, then back to me. "I don't think it was the wind." Alice looked like she was going to say more, but we were interrupted by a loud boat coming our way.

My phone rang as Alice waved over Jenny, who was maneuvering up the lake toward us on her construction boat looking like a total boss. Of course, Jenny, my ex-girlfriend's girlfriend was a pro dock builder here to rescue my sad clog-wearing ass. I waved half-heartedly to Jenny and answered my phone.

"You need to get to the hospital right away," a stressed sounding Abby commanded.

Alice frowned at my reaction. "What do they want?"

I mouthed the word "hospital," and Alice rolled her eyes. "What? Did Tamsin get a sliver?"

I put the phone on speaker in time for both of us to hear Abby scream, "LENA-ELISE HAS BEEN GORED!"

"Holy shit, what?" I began clog-running toward the house. Jenny could call or text me later with news of my dock. My gut roiled as I glanced back and saw Alice smile at Jenny and help tie up Jenny's boat. Bone-deep sadness brought me right back to the end of high school when I knew I'd lost Alice. I shook my head to shake off the grimace overtaking my entire face. "What's going on, Abby?" I asked, out of breath and trudging up towards the house.

"Lena-Elise, she fell."

I followed Cosmo through the open mudroom door, noting that even with a fresh coat of paint, the old gray wood showed through. "Uh huh," I answered, my mind flailing to remember where the shy, rather mousy-looking bridesmaid named Lena-Elise had chosen to go this morning. Did she go with her boyfriend, the therapist William? He had been dressed for a run, his dark hair puffed up at the top by an eighties looking, terry cloth headband. I could have sworn Lena-Elise was wearing a sundress and not racing attire.

"She fell on a stalactite," Abby said, her voice rising.

I was silent for a moment. "You mean a stalagmite."

"What?"

I held the phone away from my ear as Abby scream-barked orders to the EMTs while I tried to explain: "A stalactite hangs from the ceiling of a cave, so no one could possibly fall on a . . ."

"Oh my god, Maggie. A bridesmaid has literally been gored. Gored by the thing sticking out of the ground. Who the fuck cares! You're the same as you always were, Mags!"

"Stop saying gored." I sat down on a kitchen stool and grabbed my medicine bag, pushing everything else out of my mind so I could concentrate. "What can I do?"

"William is running the 5K, and I can't get a hold of him, so could you meet the ambulance at the hospital so Lena-Elise won't be alone without her boyfriend?"

"And you can't meet the ambulance because . . .?" I rummaged through my bag until I found ibuprofen and popped two in my mouth. Any hope I had of a rest this morning was vanishing fast.

"I need to drive the van and keep track of people, Maggie." Abby had a certain way of saying "*Maggie*" like my ballet teacher had when she used to catch me in the dressing room reading Pokémon comics instead of warming up.

I packed my standard day-out-of-the-house backpack with meds, a few muffins that wouldn't bother my stomach, and a travel mug of tea. I gave one last look to my quiet kitchen, its old wooden floors bathed in sunlight where Noodle splayed out, slightly wheezing as he slept. Cosmo curled up beside him, turning his tummy to the warmth. I wished that I could snuggle up with them as I grabbed my bag and headed out the door.

"I was walking just like everyone else." Lena-Elise tried and failed to haul her small frame off the hospital bed. She flopped back down, then brushed a few strands of her mousy brown hair from her face. Her normally pale complexion flushed red as she tried again to sit up in her bed, before falling dramatically back into the pillows.

I hadn't remembered exactly what Lena-Elise looked like, but when she'd first arrived, I placed her as a French Horn player in band. I looked at her puffy face now. She'd held some office in student council. Secretary? Had she been together with William while we were in school? No. I'd overheard Abby telling Sutton they started dating after William moved back to the state for his new therapist job.

Lena-Elise groaned and waved her hand at me, rattling her stainless-steel I.V. stand with a clang. "Maggie, I said . . ."

"I know you said you were just walking, Lena-Elise," I answered with a sigh. "It was the part after that when you got gored that was the problem."

Lena-Elise exhaled out of sloppy lips and shielded her eyes from the harsh, outdated fluorescent hospital lights, motioning for me to turn them off. Luckily, she didn't have any life-threatening injuries, but she would be hurting for a while. Through her morphine induced haze, she began to tell me all about her harrowing ordeal.

I nodded along, letting Lena-Elise's pain-killer addled words fall over my ears without entering too far into my brain. I clicked off most of the lights and repositioned Lena-Elise's bandage-wrapped sprained ankle before I finally sat in a folding chair next to the bed. As my aching legs hit the hard plastic, I wished there was a cushion to soften the nerve pain radiating down my back all the way into my calves. Lena-Elise cleared her throat a few times, so I handed her a cup of water with a straw.

"I'm not thirsty," Lena-Elise said, then leaned over to put her lips on the straw, head bobbing as she missed repeatedly and drooled. Her hair was pulled up in a haphazard bun, quite different from this morning when it was sleek and styled. Lena-Elise's light green hospital gown crinkled as she moved. I looked around for her pretty sundress and saw that it was hung over a steel cart, a rip and a small amount of blood marring the side of the dress. *More like a scratch than a goring.*

"Here you go." I held the cup steady with one hand while maneuvering Lena-Elise's chin over the straw. "So, who do you think pushed you at the Treasure Caves?" I joked.

After she sucked down half her water, she eyed me suspiciously over her straw. "It was an accident! And nothing to do with . . ." Lena-Elise's hand flew to her mouth. "I can't tell you."

"With what?" I inched closer to her face. "Or with who?" I hurriedly asked, intrigued and mystified at Lena-Elise's bizarre reaction. Why would she think that it was anything but an accident?

"Um," Lena-Elise mumbled, then shrugged her shoulders and giggled. "I can't remember. Must be the meds."

When it was clear that whatever Lena-Elise was going to spill was now off limits, I asked her how she thought the "accident" happened. *Was it like the dock had been an accident?*

"I was just walking like anyone else," she said again, her eyes crossing slightly as she rested her head. "Adrian was up by the tour guide, and so were Noah and their parents, I think." Lena-Elise focused on something on the wall and leaned forward, trying to grab it.

"Um," I said, gently taking her hand and placing it back on the bed. "Whatcha doing there?"

"Have to help the spiders line up." Lena-Elise squinted her eyes and made a swiping motion with her hand. "There are so many." I glanced at the wallpaper, off white with a tiny gray and black floral pattern. If I were drugged, I'd more than likely see small arachnids too.

I started miming lining spiders up the best I could while putting Lena-Elise's arm down again. "I'll take care of the spiders while you talk."

She leaned back on the pillows again. "We were in a line, about halfway through the tour, you know the part, when Gary of Gary's Gators slaps on a conquistador hat and talks in that horrible accent?"

I nodded, chuckling softly as she continued. "Well, he was reenacting burying the treasure right below me." Lena-Elise mimed digging a few times, then swatted the air. "Damn birds. Anyway, I turned to talk with Abby who just dropped her water bottle, and the next thing I knew, I was on the cave floor with this thing sticking out of me while everyone looking down on me screamed." She pointed to a bandage on the side of her abdomen where a small, thin stalagmite had pierced her skin.

I did not know how to ask the next question without risking her clamming up again, so I approached the subject very delicately. "So, right before you fell," I asked, holding her water up to her again, "was there something slippery on the ground, or . . .?"

Lena-Elise slurped the rest of her water up and then batted the cup away. "I don't . . . maybe? I remember Abby telling me that Sutton told her that you still have feelings for Alice . . . I saw you two talking at the party, by the way, and you still make an adorable couple."

I made a "move along" gesture while mentally noting to kick the gossiping hen Sutton as soon as I could.

Lena-Elise continued, "As Abby was talking, I reached for the railing, and then . . . blammo." Her head dropped back onto the pillows, then her eyes darted back and forth. "Where's my phone?"

"Here." I handed her the phone, not sure how wise it was to let her use it in her condition, but that wasn't my problem. When I fished my own phone out of my backpack I was surprised to find an extreme number of texts and missed calls, mostly from Sutton and Mark, and a text from my nosy neighbor Miss Vera. Shit. My first reaction was to throw the phone out the window, which I actually had done on more than one occasion because multiple texts and calls activate my panic center, but I had responsibilities now. I knew why Mark was trying to get a hold of me, but Sutton on overkill? That was not a good sign.

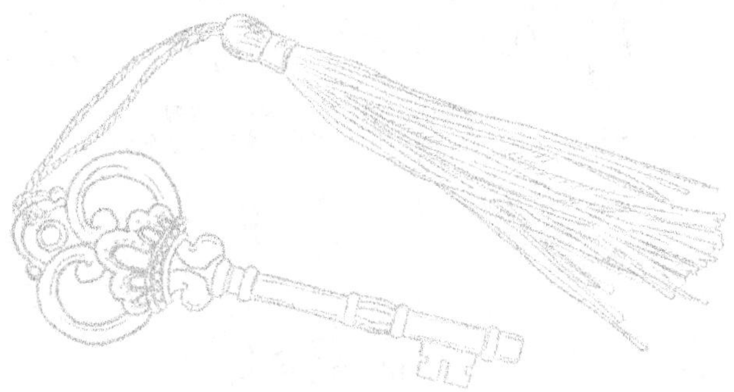

Next stop pure bliss as you rehydrate lakeside with cucumber eye wraps and the dulcet tones of Yoga Pat's Autoharp CD, on sale now at Patty's Bait and Tackle.

CHAPTER FIVE
It's Tough When You're in the Closet

I shifted in my uncomfortable seat beside Lena-Elise's emergency room bed as Lena-Elise pawed clumsily at her phone.

"WHERE HAVE YOU BEEN?" Sutton wasted no time on niceties when I called him back.

"Well, hello to you too. I haven't been doing much, you know, just sitting here at the hospital with Lena-Elise who JUST GOT IMPALED."

"Wha . . . okay, I don't know what to do with that information. But we have a problem. A *huge* problem." Sutton was trying to keep his voice low, but it kept rising to shrieking levels.

I groaned. Then Lena-Elise groaned also, like it was a competition. I stepped out of the room and asked what was happening, even though it was barely afternoon, and I was already aching and on sensory overload.

"Old Man Trembolt didn't die in his sleep," Sutton whispered urgently. "He was murdered."

"*Murdered?*" I practically screeched. Several heads popped up over the nurse's station, suspicion all over their faces. I made an "all good here" gesture as I darted into the nearest supply closet and immediately regretted my choice, overwhelmed by a strong antiseptic smell.

"That's impossible, Sutton. Mr. Trembolt died peacefully of old age." I rambled on, making my way through the supply closet's rows of shelves overflowing with bed pans, sheets, and other hospital supplies. "Mr. Trembolt must have had a heart attack after he woke up, because he was dressed and . . ."

"He never went to bed, Maggie." Sutton said. "Regina told Mark *in confidence*, who also told me *in confidence* that he died from an overdose of Xanax, some sort of sleep drug, and an opioid."

"Well, how is that murder then?" I sputtered, upset that Sutton was overblowing things as usual.

"I'm not *done* yet," Sutton retorted.

My phone buzzed, startling me, and I hit my head on a low pipe. "Damn it!" I rubbed my sore head. Mia texted that she was "**PARKING NOW**." I sat down on the cold tiled floor and texted back.

Me: **in supply closet by Lena-Elise rom**

Mia: **WTF**

Me: **don't let nurses see u4 reasons will explain when u get here**

Mia: **watever**

Me: **here into the closet**

Mia: **don't want to know**

I was going to text Mia more information, but Sutton broke in: "Regina also looked at Mr. Trembolt's medical records . . ."

"I shouldn't even be listening to this," I said.

"Regina also looked at Mr. Trembolt's medical records and saw that he was not prescribed any of those drugs." Sutton had ignored me and kept going.

"But that's not enough evidence to prove –"

"Also," Sutton continued, "the drugs were not in Trembolt's system a few weeks ago for a comprehensive blood test."

"Seriously, how does an overdose equate to murder, though?" I asked. "I mean, I get that we could be in trouble for failing to report an overdose, but . . ."

"And, Maggie, there were NO PILLS in his stomach contents." Sutton took a deep breath. "So, Trembolt either drank a liquid concoction, or it was delivered intravenously, but there were no needles, bottles, or anything left in the room that could have delivered the drugs. So maybe we can't call this an official murder yet, but it's starting to look difficult not to call Mr. Trembolt's death a murder."

"Fuck that it's a murder," I said. "Why would Regina tell *you* any of this? That's not even legal." I insisted while stuffing pee pee pads from the hospital supply shelf under my butt for some cushion.

"Well, we've gotten to know each other through all the cases we have worked on over the years, and she is a fantastic golf partner. So, I think she's trying to protect us because of our . . . involvement with the case?" Sutton took in a deep breath. "Which leads me to my next point."

Before Sutton could continue, Mia busted into the supply closet. "I have no idea what you're doing in here, but you are never going to guess what I just found out." She plunked her pregnant body down beside me and leaned back on the shelves while patting her ever expanding belly. I subconsciously started patting my own and quickly stopped before Mia noticed, I hoped.

"What?" I asked, covering my face with my hands.

Mia hissed, "Mr. Trembolt is really Mr. Gustaffson!" before Sutton got his first word out.

"I wanted to tell her," Sutton said loudly in a pouty voice. "What are you even doing there at the hospital, Mia?"

Mia grabbed the phone and held it to her mouth. "I'm here, instead of managing people's money, which is my job, because I, along with you and Maggie, could be complicit in covering up the suspicious death of Maggie's first ever official guest." Mia slapped her hand on the cold concrete floor with each word for emphasis.

"Honestly he was just passing through," I said. "Not a big deal."

"How did you know about all this?" Sutton asked Mia.

"Regina came by the office to . . ."

"Hold up. Mr. Trembolt was Mr. Gustaffson . . . our old high school *janitor*?" I had just registered what Mia had said, and I looked up at her, then at the phone, so confused about what was going on. How could Mr. Trembolt be Elias Gustaffson, the janitor who retired after we graduated? Then I remembered Mr. Trembolt's thick, black hair, beard, and mustache. "Mr. Gustaffson was bald and had no facial hair," I said.

"Fake facial hair," Mia said.

"And a hideous wig," Sutton helpfully added.

"But why?" I was dumbfounded, thinking about the time he'd spent at the house, puttering around, reading in the library, walking along the lake wall. I wasn't even going to let him stay as a guest. "Oh, but I knew your dad," he'd said with nostalgia-filled eyes. "It means so much to me to stay here before you officially open."

I returned to the present. "Why would our school janitor lie to me and disguise himself like a frickin' Scooby Doo character?"

"Are you going to answer Mark's call?" Mia held my phone up, showing that Mark was trying to FaceTime me.

"Shitballs, I should. Mia, could you FaceTime Sutton so he can be present for this flaying my cousin is about to give us?" I hung up on Sutton and answered Mark while Mia FaceTimed Sutton. I instantly wished I hadn't answered Mark's call when his angry ruddy face filled the screen. His small, piercing blue eyes bored guilty holes right into my soul. I checked for my support rocks, but my pockets were empty, so I settled for fiddling with the patient gown ties that were hanging off the shelves. After repeatedly running my fingers up and down the soft, fuzzy strings, my breathing finally started to even out.

"Hold me up, Mia. All I see are rows of enema kits." Sutton's voice grew loud as Mia turned up her volume and tried to maneuver her phone screen up to mine.

"Trust me, Sutton, your view is better than ours." Mia grimaced as she took in Mark's angry aura.

"Y'all think this is funny?" Mark barked. "Is Sutton hearing this too? Do y'all even *know* how much trouble you are in? Turn the phone to Sutton. NOW."

"I'm good with my current view, thanks," Sutton said. "Not necess . . . oh hi, Mark." The phones now faced each other.

"You are the lawyer in this situation, and you know damn well how serious this all is. Tampering with evidence, interfering with an investigation, tampering with a corpse . . ."

"Well, that sounds awful," Mia's voice quavered. "Maggie, are you listening?"

"Maggie is trying desperately not to have a complete breakdown in the hospital supply closet," I said, then sighed. I let go of the gown ties and turned my phone so I could see Mark. "*I'm* the one who did the corpse thing and moved evidence around. Just me. Okay?" I sniffed loudly and wiped snot on a nearby bed pad.

Sutton soothed, "Mark, look, I know this *looks* bad, but the official coroner's report is not due for a few days at least, right?"

Mark grumbled as Sutton plowed on. "So, we will all keep our ears and eyes open for what could have happened to Mr. Trembolt, I mean, Mr. Gustaffson, while you and Regina *please* keep our names out of the official investigation for now, okay? For your little cousin Maggie?"

A pause. Then Mark finally spoke. "I believe that you weren't responsible for the man's death, but I can't keep your involvement quiet for long, maybe a few days, tops, while we're writing the final reports." Mark tried his best to turn his glare on each of us to get the message through.

We thanked him profusely and promised to tell him of anything suspicious that came up, which satisfied him enough to say goodbye.

"Well, that went better than expected," Mia said, holding up Sutton on her phone, who was contorting around in the driver's seat of our rented van.

"And why is my skin *itching* like this?" Sutton blurted out as he squirmed.

"*Sutton*," Mia scolded. "Bigger problems. Like possible JAIL." She pulled out a muffin from my bag, ripped it in half and gave it to me, then crammed the other half into her mouth. "Thank the gods you brought your muffins," Mia said through her full mouth. I handed her my tea and she winked at me.

"Oh no," I said, muffin crumbs falling down my overalls. "When Tamsin and Noah's family finds out about Mr. Trembolt, they are going to move their people out of my house and I'm sure that they could get out of paying BECAUSE THEIR HOSTESS KILLED A GUEST." I started rocking back and forth while shoving the rest of the muffin in my mouth.

"They're not going to find out just yet. You could still get paid. The bonus too," Mia said, thinking aloud. "Remember, Mark told us he would wait a while to release any information. Isn't that right Sutton?"

When Sutton did not answer, I yelled, "HEY LAWYER OF OURS."

"I'm sorry! But there is something terribly wrong with me." We could hear Sutton furiously scratching his skin through the phone.

"Sutton, pay attention. What is wrong with you? The focus of this moment should be murder or suspicious death in my very own home!"

"I don't know! I have not been this itchy since we went to that sleepaway camp twenty years ago," Sutton wailed.

"When we all got poison ivy?" Mia asked, gulping down more of my tea after finishing off her muffin half.

"Yeah, but . . ." Sutton was quiet for a moment. "I was in some greenery helping Mrs. Carlyon after she tripped and skinned her knee. I swear she is aging backwards; I *must* get her plastic surgeon's name . . ."

Mia interrupted. "There is no poison ivy on the 5K path. Park management regularly gets rid of any south of the highway. They kill the entire root system." She pulled down a pillow from one of the shelves above her and sat on it.

"How do you suddenly know so much about park management's trail clearing habits?" I asked.

Mia raised one brow. "Oh! James' friend is the Parks and Rec manager. The other night he showed James plans for a new housing development that James' company could bid on. It's right by the park by the 5K path."

"But the route was north of the highway, going through Baker Trail," Sutton said. "What should I do for this rash?"

"Heyyyy," I said. "I'm sure the 5K route is super fascinating, at *any other time,* but . . ."

"Baker Trail?" Mia said, surprised. "That's the area marked for a butterfly and bee sanctuary, no spraying allowed, and all natural plants. There's barely a running trail there at all."

"Right? The trail was barely visible through the growth," Sutton said, then continued with his scratching. "Ugh! What if I scar?"

"OMG WE ALMOST CERTAINLY ARE GOING TO JAIL WHO GIVES A FUCK ABOUT YOUR ITCHEES?" I could not take it any longer. I stood up and threw a few pee pee pads on the ground, which did not have the robust dramatic effect I was hoping for. "How and why aren't we figuring out a plan to find out what happened to the old man janitor? And have we considered that an unknown, violent murderer of weird old men could easily have broken into my home?"

"Maybe it was a sex thing," Mia suggested. "Because of the disguise. Like roll play?"

Sutton stopped scratching to speak: "Let's take a cool down on the sex stuff with the dead janitor—what the hell is this? I'm suffering here."

Mia closed her eyes, mumbling about being a respectable mother and business owner.

"Look," Sutton continued, "*If* someone nefarious somehow got through your security system and was in your house, you were far away in your cabin with your ferocious guard dog."

Cosmo was ninety-nine percent goofball, but that other one percent was pure protection. I started to feel a bit better about my safety, but not about what Mark had said. "How on Earth are we supposed to figure out what happened to Mr. Gustaffson in my home, while keeping our little investigation on the down low?"

Mia offered me a hand to get up. "I don't know if we can keep it on the down low because there is that *teeny tiny* part about a funky *murder* happening in *your* home." Mia brushed the crumbs off her protruding belly and replaced the pillow she had been sitting on to its shelf. "Should we be scared? I've got this little one and two more to consider."

"I mean . . ." I struggled to articulate my swirling thoughts. "I guess if we were the targets, which would be totally bizarre, we'd know by now, right?" I asked.

Mia nodded and Sutton grunted to the affirmative.

"So," I continued my morbid thought. "If my guest was already helped along to his death, we don't have to worry, right? Because we're not the targets? Right?"

"I guess," Sutton said. "Nothing else hinky has gone on at your house since then, so I'm good with thinking that our old janitor died under majorly messed up circumstances that had nothing to do with you, and if we find anything along the way this week to help Mark's investigation, great."

I couldn't even follow what Sutton had said just then, but his tone suggested the plan was solid.

He continued: "And that leaves enough time for the wedding to happen and for Maggie to get paid without the guests knowing anything."

Other than my dock possibly being sabotaged. I remembered what Alice had said. *Was that just a few hours ago?* I held the door open for Mia as we stepped out into the emergency room hallway. Whatever was going on, I just needed to push through until Saturday when I got paid and could save my house. The dock had to be a coincidence, I convinced myself. And no one else was in danger, I thought, as we snuck past Lena-Elise's room, where William was inspecting her stalagmite wound. I was going to bring up Lena-Elise's weird reaction when I asked her what happened in the Treasure Caves, when Sutton interrupted my thought.

"Speaking of guests, a whole bunch of runners are coming back to the van," Sutton said. "And I can see them scratching from here. I don't think I'm the only person who got into something bad, so you had better get back home to greet us."

I rolled my eyes. *Who cared about itching at a time like this?* "I'll pick up some Calamine lotion on the way," I said, before I hung up. How was I going to keep the maybe-murder and the dock debacle under wraps for four more days, while also keeping my sanity intact?

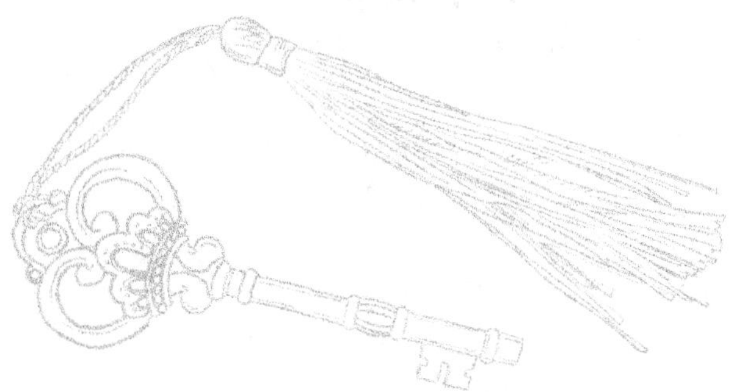

What fun we're having!
Enjoy the views in our picturesque
village as you stroll the
cobblestones and leisurely peruse
our many fine boutiques.

CHAPTER SIX
Pass the Calamine

"No, I can't see it at all," I lied, leaning away from the angry, raised rash beginning to form on Virginia's normally clear light brown face. "Maybe a bit more cover-up?"

"You're right," Virginia agreed. "I'm probably imagining it." My old classmate nodded vigorously and returned to her face reflected in the silver and gold diamond patterned framed bathroom mirror. I picked up a pile of dirty white towels that lay in a heap by the claw foot tub.

"Hey." I looked up at Virginia while trying to retrieve a washcloth that was wedged underneath the hamper. "How is Missouri treating you?" Sutton had told me that Virginia and her kids moved from Fayetteville to Kansas City after her divorce.

Virginia paused mid eye-liner application. "I love my job at the hospital there. I just got promoted to the head of physical therapy for the whole campus, and I can't complain about all the benefits that have come with it."

"And are the kids settling in okay?" I peered up at the shower, looking for cracks as I talked. Luckily, the third-floor bathroom had still been in very good shape before I turned my home into a bed and breakfast: the old black and white hexagonal tiles sparkled under an art deco light fixture; a new gold shower head jazzed up the subway tiled shower; and the faded, floral wall paper had been replaced by a delicate lake pattern with the Loch Ness monster roaming about.

"Oh yes. Diego loves his soccer team, and Alex is in the accelerated program at his school, which is only a few blocks away from our house." Virginia held her mouth in an "O" shape as she applied another coat of mascara.

"That's great." I smiled at her as I threw the towels down the laundry chute. Trig jumped out of his room when I walked into the hallway, still sporting his tiny running shorts. He whipped his leg up on the oak railing with a "thud!" and pointed to raised, red looking skin on his inner thigh.

"What do I do?" He wailed. "I think it's spreading!" He pointed upward towards his pelvic area.

I made every effort not to stare at his not-so-little friend poking out from his shorts. "Ah. Ehhhh . . ." I reached into my pocket and held out my last bottle of Calamine lotion. "This is all I have, buddy. But if the area above . . . that is to say . . . if it travels . . . uh, up, then you might need to get that area checked out." I made circular motions over my own groin with both my hands.

"No, no, no, no, no." Trig grabbed the bottle out of my hands and ran back into his room surprisingly fast considering his condition.

Herschel yelled for the lotion next. *Did all the runners get poison ivy?* I couldn't think about it now. "Hey Adrian," I said as Alice's cousin came rushing out of their room, looking very dapper in a silk blouse and a long, velvety skirt.

Adrian jumped back and banged into a framed picture of my grandparents. "I . . . I didn't see you there." Adrian grabbed onto their satchel and held it closer as they visibly panted.

Weird.

"I'm so sorry, Adrian. I kinda snuck up on ya there." I put my hand out to steady myself on the railing, but Adrian took it and held on while we walked down the back stairs. Pushing back my aversion to random touching by people I didn't know well, I distracted myself by looking around. The fresh coat of paint that we put on the wainscoting was already starting to show wear, and the old hand railing was splintering and needed to be replaced. Well, mortgage payment first, and then hopefully I could start on repairs. *Don't try to solve everything today*, I heard my dad's voice in my head.

"I'm sorry," Adrian said. "I'm just tired from all the events and on top of that, I didn't get much sleep," they explained, looking a tad sheepish as Abby strolled by, watching us pointedly as she went.

Hmmm . . . had the hook-ups begun already?

"Well, hopefully you can rest after a robust meal from The Magnolia," I said as we entered the kitchen. The aroma of strong coffee wafted through the air as I caught sight of the sink, already filled with used mugs and plates from a late afternoon of caffeine and muffins. My body ached just looking at the mess I was going to have to clean up.

Adrian gently squeezed my hand before they let go. "And how are you doing? I've been meaning to call you after your dad's passing."

I tried hard to maintain Adrian's tractor-beam like eye contact but cheated a bit and stared at their nose. "I've been okay," I said, nodding. "And you? Memphis sounds right up your alley."

"Oh yes. The music scene is fabulous, and my day job in investments allows me to indulge my love for live jazz most nights of the week." Adrian briefly smiled and then glanced down at their cell. They mumbled something about needing to make a phone call before we left for the village and strode quickly to the sliding door, ignoring Abby's raised eyebrows.

I shrugged. They were all adults and would have to sort out whatever was going on. "Vans leave in twenty minutes for fun in town, people," I yelled. "Let's Go!"

I was blasted with steamy air as I fast walked to my little log cabin on the lake, trying to avoid fallen branches and milky quartz sticking up from the clover and pine needle covered ground. As I stepped onto my covered front porch with its cushioned wicker chairs and hanging flowerpots, I marveled at the amazing job Mia's husband James and his crew did fixing up this once dilapidated structure that was now my cozy living space. I opened the front door to a little kitchen and table on one side of the cabin, and a comfy couch, easy chair, and TV on the other. Lining the back wall was a bathroom and a queen-sized bed, with a long closet and wall separating the two. Perfect for just Cosmo, Noodle, and me. Though by popular demand, Noodle stayed in the main house last night because the guests fought over him.

Cool air greeted me inside the cabin, and I was very tempted to curl up on the slip covered couch with my grandmother's handmade quilt and a bowl of popcorn in my lap, an ice pack on my neck and my feet soaking in a warm foot spa. But I had to push past my pain and social anxiety and work to keep this place going, so I reluctantly walked past my cute little sitting area to get dressed for the evening. I threw on some wide legged linen pants, a soft sleeveless blouse, and a pair of sandals that I hoped wouldn't give me blisters.

As I put in some earrings, I flashed on the ominous events of the last two days: a dead body appeared on the same day as someone messed with my dock. For the millionth time, I thought about what my dad would do, and then quickly shut that down, because he would have done the right thing and gone straight to the authorities. But if I did that, then I could say *good-bye home.*

Whatever was going on, the wedding party could not find out until after the wedding, *after* I got paid, and hopefully got that bonus. Then there would be plenty of time to do the right thing. Jenny wasn't answering my texts, so maybe she would be at her parents' bookstore tonight. I completed my outfit with a Norwegian necklace of my grandmother's and loosely clipped my hair back to keep my curls from sticking to my neck in this humidity. I swallowed down an extra prednisone and two extra strength Tylenol to get me through the evening and walked toward the big house.

My little group was waiting for me outside, faces already sweaty. Clad in various summer dresses and slacks and nice tops, my guests cleaned up very nicely, apart from the blossoming rashes. Some of them were scratching theirs while others were swatting the itchers.

"You'll scar. Do you want that, Virginia? On your face?" Abby demanded.

Virginia glowered at Abby's verbal attack but lowered her hand.

Damn Abby. Although, she wasn't wrong. "Doors are all unlocked. You all are with me, and Abby's going to pick up Tamsin and Noah and their families at the other houses," I said, getting into one of the vans Tamsin's parents had rented for the week. I hoped they hadn't heard anything about the dock. Or the janitor, for that matter.

After we all got settled in our vehicle, I started my little prepared speech. "Hey y'all, I know some of you moved away and haven't been back to the village for a while . . ."

"Pussies," Trig uttered, already tipsy or high, or maybe both.

He flipped his trucker hat around to reveal the embroidered phrase, "Moister than an Oyster" and took a swig from his flask.

"Thank you for your, uh, input, Trig," I said, catching his eye in the rearview mirror. "Anyway, we will have about an hour of time to explore before dinner at The Magnolia, so be sure to check out the stores. Many are staying open later."

I waved at Miss Vera. She didn't wave back, just stood by her mailbox on the side of the gravel road clutching onto her mail, glaring at us as we drove by. I hadn't answered her text in which she complained about the amount of traffic caused by my guests, so she was probably smarting about that.

"Hey." Herschel, with his perfectly coiffed mullet, wiped his mouth clean of whatever was in Trig's flask. "My sister Jenny said that something hinky happened with the dock," he said, then clapped a hand over his mouth. "Oops. I wasn't s'posed to say anything." He offered the flask to Adrian, who first politely shook their head no, then reconsidered and slammed it back.

I glanced back at a guilty Herschel, hoping my expression was nonchalant. "Really? I haven't heard that." I steered the van down the gravel road towards our little town center, furiously chewing my gum to keep my stress levels down. Old landmarks guided me through the forested area: the chipped metal *Gary's Gators n' More* sign that stood crooked in the ditch, partially covered by the shiny new sign for the Black Forest Inn, the skinny dirt road entrance to the Blue Cloud Trailer Park, a freshly painted arrow pointing to the turnoff to the Old Treasure Caves, and up high on a cliff soared The Majestic Hotel, looming over the lake like a gigantic bat. The Victorian Gothic spindles and high rectangle windows were lit up from below, welcoming visitors to its haunted rooms and grisly ghost tours.

"Nah," Trig said, joining the dock conversation. I jumped at his sudden presence in the conversation. He scratched his face, which was turning red and bumpy. "Lots of docks fall apart, especially if you're not taking care of them."

Virginia turned around and forced Trig's hand away from his face. "Don't do it; it will only spread. And I'm sure Maggie has done all the safety things for her new bed and breakfast." She waited a few seconds for my answer, and when I did not say anything, she asked, "Right?"

Well, this was quite the conundrum. If I said that I didn't get it inspected, I was liable for anyone getting hurt. OR, if people knew that I had the dock inspected and it was in great shape, the guests might freak out that someone had tinkered with it. I gave a non-committal "of course," then changed the subject. "Random question," I said as I pulled into a parking place in front of the Nguyen Family Hardware Store. "Anyone remember Mr. Gustaffson?" I hoped that my voice and face correctly conveyed an "innocent" question, because I was terrible at acting. I twirled my small, smooth rocks in my pocket to keep myself calm.

"The janitor?" William ducked his head getting out of the car. The beginnings of the poison ivy rash on his forearms were smeared with pink Calamine lotion.

"Didn't he move away?" asked Virginia. She grabbed Lena-Elise's crutches and handed them to her as William helped her out of the front seat. We all were concerned that Lena-Elise was pushing it coming with us to dinner, but she insisted that she was feeling much better.

I was wondering how long poor Virginia's slathered-on foundation and powder would hold up under this heat and humidity when she turned to me and asked, "What made you think about that old dude?"

"I was just randomly thinking about him the other day, you know . . . just wondering," I said weakly. *Activate mildly curious smile.* I lifted one side of my mouth.

Adrian climbed out of the van and pulled their black hair into a low ponytail and said, "I still remember that janitor creeping around the girls' locker room. How he remained employed is beyond me."

"Now that you mention him, I thought I saw him fishing between you and the Jablonskis' two weekends ago when I was helping Jenny with Mr. J's dock," Herschel said.

Trig shook his head. "I doubt it."

"You weren't there." Herschel took another swig of the flask. "How would you know?"

Trig was silent for a second before responding with a non-committal, "Whatever," and then announced that he, Herschel, and Adrian were going to the Black Forest Inn to grab a beer, and anyone else was invited to come.

I didn't have time for the tension that seemed to be building between Trig and Herschel. Why had Mr. Gustaffson fished by my cove before he stayed with me, *without* his disguise if he was going to come to my house later with a disguise? *Bizarre.* I watched my guests limping along down the cobblestone street and wondered if all the injuries were more than coincidence. The slightest shiver of unease crept up my spine. I tried to shake it off. The town was as it had always been—adorable, and with nothing bad going on. In fact, I was going to enjoy myself and the fact that no cars were allowed in the large multicultural square and surrounding side streets. The cobblestone roads were dotted with bistro tables and wicker-backed chairs, carts of Mexican pottery, racks of imported Norwegian sweaters, and colorful Nigerian wrap skirts and stacks of books. Decades back, when gambling was outlawed, and thus Majestic Springs' biggest money maker disappeared, the town rebranded itself as an international village showcasing food and goods from around the world. Honestly, it *was* wonderful to have grown up here.

And yet, I never made time to just take an afternoon to enjoy myself. Perhaps I was addicted to drama. On cue my stomach cramped and I took a deep breath just trying to enjoy the famil-iar sights. These past six months had been a whirlwind of work and stress and pleading with banks and the power and water companies. There had been so many days where I asked myself what the hell I was even doing. Not to mention having no time for properly grieving my father, who died a few days before Christmas from a heart attack.

As I walked by the tiny gelato shop, remembering getting the tiramisu flavor with my dad and Aunt Mary on Sundays, I ran right into Noah and Tamsin, holding hands and looking adorable in linen pastels. "Hey spouses-to-be!" I called, my voice coming out artificially high. I counted to three staring at Tamsin's forehead. If Tamsin and Noah could sense my social discomfort, they didn't let on, which was nice since I was so tired of masking. Good thing I'd been doing it for so many years, so the masking was automatic, albeit exhausting.

"Hey girl," Tamsin said, giving me a side hug, her perfume burning my eyes and tickling my nose. "We're heading over to the Inn for a drink, wanna come?"

"Thanks, but I need to run an errand before dinner." I stole a peek at Tamsin's tanned, rash-free legs and arms. "Hey, so did you get the dreaded poison ivy too?"

Noah laughed and slid their arm around Tamsin. "Luckily, she decided to help with sign-ups and handing out beverages at the last minute." Noah gazed at Tamsin adoringly, while Tamsin fidgeted with her necklace. "The 5K raised over four thousand dollars for dog food, beds, and toys for Hugs-4-Dogs."

"Everyone was so generous that it was the least I could do to help out," Tamsin said, looking around her. "We'd better not be late, honey."

"Hey Noah," I said before they could get away. "Did you see what happened to Lena-Elise?" I noodled my pocket rocks around to ground me as I tried to act nonchalant.

Noah shook their head. "It was the weirdest thing. I heard a noise behind me on the narrow path by where the treasure was supposed to be hidden, you know the one where Gary wears that Spanish hat . . ."

I nodded.

"Yeah, so Gary started his monologue and then I heard something behind me and when I looked down a few feet below, there was little Lena-Elise, lying there on the cave floor, clutching her side."

"Did anyone see, maybe someone next to her . . ."

"They're waiting Noah." Tamsin pulled on Noah's arm and waved at me. "Bye Maggie. See you soon."

As they sauntered off towards the biergarten, I sat down on an old wooden bench to rest my aching legs. I couldn't shake an odd feeling so I turned around. Tamsin was staring back at me, with an expression that said *back off.*

Stunned and chewing on Tamsin's dirty look, I almost missed Sutton making a beeline toward me, holding his phone up to his face.

"Look at me!" Sutton wailed, dapper in a lavender silk shirt and light-colored pants.

I peered closer at his freshly exfoliated and moisturized face. "Not seeing a problem, honey."

"I know the pus-filled blisters are coming. I just know it." Sutton took another look at his phone and then jammed it into his leather side bag.

I raised my hands up in frustration. "The rash isn't even on your face, so it's very doubtful blisters will show up." I peered down at his forearms slathered in anti-itch lotion. "Just wash all the clothes you wore so you don't spread the oil from the plant, and don't touch your owies."

"I'm burning my clothes in the backyard as we speak." Sutton was going to take my arm for walking, but I stepped back in alarm.

"We can't even promenade!" I yelped.

"Maggie and I can." Mia hooked her arm around mine and I pointed to the book store Jenny's family owned, hoping that Jenny would be there so I could find out more about my dock and confirm what Herschel told me. Mia's multicolored skirt flowed around her as we marched along the street, passing the Nordic Emporium with its window display of carved wooden trolls, Melkesjokolade bars, and wool sweaters, while the sweet scents of fenugreek, cinnamon, and cardamom wafted from Habiba's Ethiopian Restaurant.

"Heyyy," I said. I didn't know exactly how to broach this topic, but I thought I might as well jump in. "So, Alice was over this morning . . ."

Mia and Sutton stopped abruptly, and I ran straight into Sutton. "Ow!"

"What happened?" Mia asked at the same time Sutton asked. "Are you and Alice getting back together?"

"Wow. No, we are not getting back together because she is dating beautiful wood-chopping Jenny, and also because she never will forgive me for cheating on her with Lance." I glanced over at Sutton and absently patted my stomach. "Before we go in, I need to tell you something. Alice thinks the dock might have been tampered with, plus, Herschel let it slip that Jenny also found something weird, so we need to get the info and then try to stop it from getting out." I stood up from our huddle only to be pulled right back down by Mia. "What's wrong?" I asked.

"What's *wrong*?" Mia whispered loudly. When I did not answer, she continued: "What's wrong is that not only did someone die suspiciously at your home, but your guest-filled dock collapsed into the water, *on purpose*." She pasted on a smile and waved as her little family James, Brianna, and Shaun walked towards them, then glared at me again.

James, easily recognizable by his tall height and shiny brown head, was holding hands with two of the cutest little kids ever (though I could have been a bit biased since they were my godchildren). Eight-year-old Bri's multi-colored bracelets glittered in the waning sunlight as she frantically waved at us while Shaun, age five, dragged his ever-present stuffed elephant along the cobblestones.

"Yeah," Sutton chimed in while giving Bri air kisses as Mia and I waved goodbye. "I'm now changing my accidentally dead janitor theory to stone cold murder, since there have been other bad things happening that you neglected to tell us about, meaning the dock," Sutton said, pointing a finger at me.

"It is starting to look that way," Mia agreed, as the street lanterns came on and the town's limestone buildings glowed a soft gold around us.

Sutton held up his Calamine-covered arm. "Hold it—the poison ivy! The route was changed this morning to a bad trail, on purpose, just like the dock."

"Oh, come on," I whispered. "You think someone switched the route to expose the runners to poison ivy?" But then I thought about my interaction with Tamsin. "Way out of left field here, but Tamsin really wanted to change the subject when I pointed out that she wasn't suffering from a rash like the other runners were. In fact," I closed my eyes to help me remember our conversation. "She didn't run in the race *at all.*"

Sutton looked up from examining his growing rash. "That's odd. She never passes up an opportunity to shine."

Mia held up her phone. "I'll have James text his parks friend to see where the 5K was supposed to take place."

"While we wait, I guess we find out what happened to my dock, *discreetly,*" I said.

We walked into Books on the Square, Jenny and Herschel Clark's parents' store. In the sunny front window perched Guinevere, the very spoiled bookstore tabby cat. Most of the buildings downtown, including this store, had been built in the 1800's from limestone, making the structures resemble castles, and lending a fairytale atmosphere to our village. The bookstore's oak shelves overflowed with first editions, framed by dimly lit lanterns and local artwork. We made our way to a cute little sitting area with slip covered chairs and a wood burning fireplace, where Jenny just happened to be sitting with her mother, Mrs. Clark. Hopefully Mrs. Clark didn't see the automatic grimace that appeared on my face whenever I saw or thought about her daughter. Mrs. Clark waved hello, apparently oblivious to my discomfort, then sped off in her motorized wheelchair, her lap filled with new releases to shelve.

"Hey Maggie, I was just going to call you," Jenny said.

I sat on a chair next to Jenny and her pretty, no-makeup face. She looked like a Peloton instructor in a cute little athleisure number. "The dock didn't collapse by accident, did it?" I asked.

"I can't say definitively," Jenny said, lowering her voice. "I'm still gathering the broken parts of the deck to see what really happened. But soon I'm going to have to give what I've found to the police."

"Ah, yeah." I scooted closer to Jenny. My fingers found the rocks in my pocket, smoothing them over and over as I tried to keep my panicky feelings down. I glanced over at Mia, James, and Sutton, who were watching this little show from behind books they were pretending to read, although Mia's was upside down. "Look," I said, "you would be doing me a huge favor if you kept this to yourself as long as possible, at least until the wedding is over."

Jenny leaned in, scooting a lantern lamp out of the way to see me. "Aren't you worried that someone is trying to harm you or the people staying at your house?" She lowered her voice to say, "You have a good security system, right? And Cosmo is a big dog, so that's good. I guess I can keep it on the down low a little while longer."

I was touched that she cared so much about my wellbeing until I remembered that her brother was staying at the house too. "Jenny, nothing else sketchy has happened at the house, so honestly," I crossed my fingers behind my back, "I think it's fine to wait until you're fully done looking at all the dock stuff."

She regarded me for a long moment. "Okay," Jenny said, finally. "But if I find something that shows definitively who or why someone damaged your dock, I will have to go to Mark." She stood up and put out her hand to help me up, which was nice because I was struggling to stand; a serious autoimmune flare would be coming on soon no matter how much prednisone I took. "And if you suspect anyone messing around with your house, or guests or *anything*, you can tell me, okay?" Jenny searched my face and I looked away. "Be sure to tell me."

"Thank you," I said, my face and eye muscles twitching with fatigue from all this socializing. "Are you going to The Magnolia?"

Jenny looked a little embarrassed. "Yes. I'm bringing Alice."

"Well, she needs to eat too, so . . ." I pumped my fist in the air awkwardly, but then luckily Mia's kids Shaun and Bri rescued me from further embarrassing antics.

Bri was jumping up and down with excitement to show me her books, the little purple and green beads on her braids making clicking sounds. "Ooh! Look at these!" Bri held up a collection of drawing books and I oohed and ahhed over each of them, then I did the same to Shaun's picture books that he was showing to his stuffed elephant. I was just going to sit down with them on the comfy couches to read and rest, when my phone lit up:

when the fuq u getting here?? no servers. Disaster :(

It was Abby. Time to go.

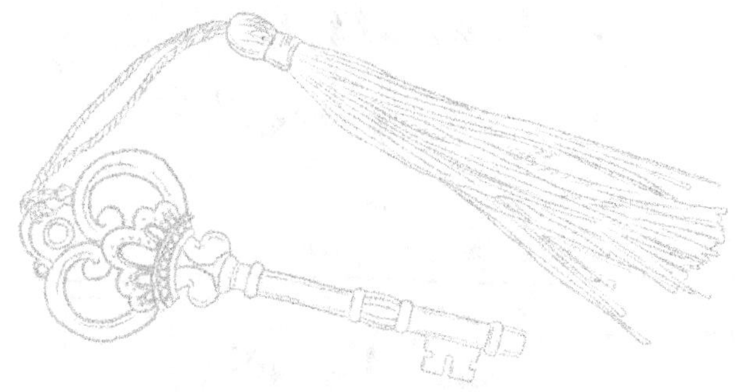

Bring your appetite and enjoy fine
dining and friendship at
The Magnolia Restaurant,
proudly owned by the Hernandez
family since 1975.

THE MAGNOLIA

CHAPTER SEVEN
I Got You, Babe

"Mama called and said that all the servers who ran in that 5K have a rash, so they can't work the wedding party tonight," Mia said. James, Sutton, Mia, Bri, Shaun and I started heading over to The Magnolia.

I was in no mood to hurry and go serve the wedding party their dinner, even with Abby's insistent texts—I'd had enough of her picking at me, and the day wasn't even over. I was also stuck on wondering why Jenny was so insistent that I inform her about any new information I learned. She was just supposed to fix my dock.

"I'm out for serving, unfortunately," Sutton said, raising his arms showing his red bumps. "People won't want to eat anything I'd serve."

"Hey kids," James said, as the children ambled beside him. "Want to eat dinner in Grandmama's office and watch Bluey with Uncle Sutton while Aunt Maggie, Mommy and I wait tables?"

"Baked mac and cheese?" asked Bri, stopping to pet a pair of wire-haired dachshunds on the sidewalk with matching plaid bows on their collars.

"And brownie sundaes?" asked Sutton, who got a huge grin from Shaun.

"Yes, to both," James said, taking both kids' hands and swinging them.

While James and the kids skipped ahead, Mia and Sutton swarmed me. "Well, what did Jenny say?" Sutton took out his phone again, surveying his face for a rash.

"She said that there *might* be something to the fact that the dock disaster had some help." My voice petered off as I pretended to be extremely interested in a carved wooden statue of a cheetah sitting outside the Nigerian Marketplace store.

"*Might* be something?" Mia stared at me until her attention was diverted by the Cheetah. Mia's attention span was always easily captured with anything cat. "Oh, this is beautiful." She held it up and examined the expert craftsmanship, then shook her head and put it down on the shelf. "Maggie, come back here."

I turned around, trying to arrange my face to look innocent. "Jenny doesn't know anything definitive, and neither did Alice, so . . ."

"So, we are planning to keep the fact that someone most likely tampered with the dock to ourselves?" Mia asked. "Plus, the very suspicious 5K route change?"

"Let us not forget about the body we moved. *Illegally*," Sutton added. "Come on, we've got to serve dinner to Tamsin and her followers." He made a move ahead gesture.

"What do you two want me to do?" I stood firm in the middle of the cobblestone street, garnering the attention of a few pass-ersby. Panic and desperation were slowly taking over rational thoughts as I spoke, which was happening far too often these days. "You both have homes with no extra bedrooms. You both have incomes. I have a huge mortgage payment due by the end of the week, *with money I don't have yet*, or else I'm homeless." *I mean, unless I want to forgive Lance and move back in with the cheating bastard.* My arms started flapping around in the air and my voice rose. "Is what I am doing a bit morally ambiguous? *Maybe.* But I have no parents or brothers or sisters or families like you all do . . ."

Sutton raised his hand. "Not to get technical, but I don't have brothers or sisters either."

I sighed. "Yes, I know, Sutton."

"In fact," Sutton continued as he guided us to a quiet nook by an alley. "I'd argue that my home life story is far more tragic than yours."

"It's not a competition dude," I said, smiling despite myself.

"True," Mia said, adopting a British accent. "Sutton's mom ran out when he was but a wee one, and his dad died not much later, leaving his grandfather to raise him all on his own while running the family law firm."

Sutton rested his head on Mia's shoulder. The golden hour was still upon us, and the waning sun streamed through cracks between the buildings, casting a warm glow around us in the alley. "Well, not all alone," Sutton said. "I practically lived at your house on the weekends, and on the weekdays we all did our homework at The Magnolia together." He looked at me. "The *three* of us. Which means that you *do* have siblings, even if you don't like it."

We began walking slowly again, arm in arm, making our way over the cobblestones toward The Magnolia to serve the wedding party's dinner. Sutton was right. I remembered how my dad would pick me up from The Magnolia at the end of his work days after I'd sat in a booth with Mia and Sutton completing our homework with tummies full of fruit and biscuits. We spent holidays with Mia's and Sutton's families, and of course, they were my family. That just made me feel worse about involving them in all this. "You don't have to get further dragged into this mess," I said. "I can get through this week on my own." Even saying that made me feel more exhausted than I could imagine, both from the thought of physical work and the emotional labor.

We paused walking and Mia and Sutton looked at each other. "Even though he's pissed, Mark promised he's going to keep us out of trouble with the whole disturbing the crime scene and moving a dead body thing," Mia said, wiping sweat off her forehead. Even though the sun had just set, the air still felt soupy.

Sutton added, "And we don't know the reason why someone would tamper with your dock, which is very concerning, but we can keep it under wraps for a few days while we discreetly ask around." We had stopped in front of an herbal store that sold natural remedies, and a pleasant patchouli aroma wafted out.

"We just need to be very careful and make sure that you are not in danger yourself," Mia said, taking my hand.

I gripped her hand tightly, grateful that Sutton and Mia knew that I needed to review the facts over and over to calm down before we went to The Magnolia. "I promise that I will tell Mark the second that anything else suspicious happens or if we find anything that shows who did what. In the meantime, we keep our heads down and try our best to make it to Saturday, which is payday, and hopefully bonus day." I tried not to think what my dad would say to me in this moment. I could not lose my home, no matter what. For the first time in my life, I was taking care of my own home and my own bills (kind of). If my home was sold, I'd not only lose the most important connection to my family, but also I'd lose this new independent person I was becoming. I took a deep breath, my mind a little clearer, and linked arms again with Sutton and Mia, signaling I was ready to head to The Magnolia and face the wedding party.

We walked the rest of the way in companionable silence, waving to the neighbors and shop owners we had known all our lives.

"Hey," I whispered to Mia an hour later as we were acting as impromptu servers and liberally refilling the guests' wine glasses.

"Don't look now . . . I said *don't* look!" I lightly kicked Mia's ankle behind Mr. and Mrs. Carlyon's chairs.

"Everything okay, dears?" Mr. Carlyon, dashing, with a white-haired mane, million-dollar smile, and deep blue eyes that had either an unnerving twinkle or bored into you when you spoke to him. Right now, they were doing both.

"Yes, thank you for asking," Mia smoothly answered. "Do you need anything else right now, Mr. Carlyon?"

"Someone to pay this bill," he laughed, pointing at different people at the table.

Everyone at the table laughed appreciatively including Trig, who pointed back and knocked over his wine glass for the second time.

"Easy does it, Trig." Noah quickly mopped up the wine while Virginia giggled and fondled Trig's hair that was sticking out the bottom of his trucker hat. "You're drinking like you're back in high school."

"Oh wow, speaking of partying. Remember when Noah's parents were out of town, and we sunk their party barge out by Parrage Island?" Lena-Elise giggled and mouthed "*Sorry*" to Mr. and Mrs. Allerton, who shook their heads in mock dismay.

Herschel, red-faced from heat and too much alcohol, finished off his wine and pointed to Noah. "Our best parties were at your lake house. Like that rager we had on graduation night after you-know-what happened . . ."

"I'd like to make a toast," said Abby abruptly, for once not carrying her feathered binder. She stood up and expertly brushed back her long curls with her manicured hand, smiling as though she was back on that pageant stage accepting first prize for talent again. She benevolently looked down upon Tamsin and Noah, both giddy with happiness and several glasses of expensive wine. "My dearest friends, since, gosh, how long has it been?"

While hanging around to listen to Abby's riveting speech was tempting, I was far more interested in the goings on in the basement hallway. I slowly backed out of the dining room and glided along the restaurant's deep oak trimmed walls, stepping quietly on the stone floor. The wide, lantern lit hallway had carved-in conversation nooks, which was where Jenny and Adrian were huddled in deep conversation, sitting on two red leather wing backed chairs. Their expressions were angry, possibly scared, their voices low, but I could hear a few words.

"This is wrong, and you know it," Adrian whispered, flipping their long hair and scowling.

"No one will find out," Jenny said, before she saw me looking at them and motioned Adrian to shut it.

I tried to quickly go back into the main dining room but tripped and banged into a wall while trying to locate Mia to tell her what I'd seen.

Alice caught my eye as I rubbed my sore shoulder and called me over. She had not touched her slow-cooked ribs, collard greens and potato salad. "You look tired," she said, taking in the dark bags under my eyes and me holding onto the back of a chair for balance. "Can you go home and rest before your guests go back?" She said "guests" like "cockroaches."

I *was* tired. My feet and hands were stinging with inflammatory arthritis, and the glands in my face were starting to swell up. I was already taking way more prednisone than I should, but I was going to have to take much more to get through this week, which would make my rheumatologist very unhappy. Even though I was a week away from my next infusion appointment, I felt like I needed it today. I had been tired from an autoimmune flare before, but honestly, this felt different. *Like a pregnancy?* When Alice's golden-brown eyes met mine, I instantly felt a rush of warmth and shoved all thoughts of Lance's possible baby out of my mind.

I mumbled, "Aren't you hungry?"

It was Alice's turn to look embarrassed. Her eyes darted to the hallway. "I ate before. I gotta go." She shot up from the table but was stopped by Trig before she could exit the dining room.

"Aww, you two having a former lovers' spat?" Trig took up most of the space under the archway, blocking us between him and the rest of the dinner guests, who were watching us with interest. Trig took a long swig of his beer and wiped the side of his mouth, his arm stretching across the archway. "Maggie sure did a number on you, didn't she?" He said to Alice.

Alice stood tall, calmly pulling her hunting knife from its sheath and holding it close to her thigh.

"That's enough, Trig. Jesus." Adrian shoved Trig into the side of the arch, leaving room for Alice to slide the knife slowly back into its leather pocket. She strode through the dining room, her eyes trained on Trig as she wound her way around the tables. All eyes were on me as I stood there, alone, sure everyone was thinking about how I'd cheated on Alice. It didn't matter that I had betrayed her fourteen years ago; the white-hot pain in my chest was almost as fresh as that night when her tear-stained face flashed stark white in the lightning on Noah's dock.

Tamsin had grinned wickedly that awful night when she told Alice I had cheated. Gesticulating wildly, her hair blowing around her face in the storm, Tamsin had pointed at me. Alice turned around, her face a mixture of anger, betrayal, and most of all, hurt. Even in the pouring rain, I could see that Alice was crying, her body contorted in rage. Before I could say or do anything, Tamsin leaned over and whispered something in Alice's ear, and to everyone's surprise, Alice had shoved Tamsin into the lake.

Mia approached, snapping me out of the memory. "What was that all about?" Mia whispered, balancing a tray of pitchers on her shoulder as she sailed into the dining room. She looked around the silent room with everyone's eyes on me while handing out the fresh water pitchers. "Oh dear." Correctly assessing that I needed a Hail Mary, she handed me an empty pitcher and motioned me out of the room.

Relieved to stop thinking about the past and get out from under everyone's gaze, I followed her out of the room and up the back staircase towards the kitchen. On the way up lantern sconces lit up beige and gray stucco walls and the original exposed brick. Old framed black and white photos of gangsters posing with politicians and entertainers hung here and there, showing the colorful history of Majestic Springs. I concentrated on those pictures to get all the judgmental faces out of my mind. "Did you see Jenny and Adrian all cozy in the hallway a bit ago?"

"I think I did." Mia set her tray down and unloaded the dishes. "Yeah, I did. I was surprised they weren't with the group." Mia handed me a new pitcher of ice water while she got a tray of assorted pie slices. "Poor Alice was just sitting alone, and you know how she feels about that wedding party."

I grabbed a large glass bowl of whipped cream and a silver serving spoon and walked carefully back down the stairs, feeling each step throb in my swollen knees. "Jenny and Adrian were obviously not happy and talking about how 'this is wrong,' and 'nobody will find out,' which obviously means that Jenny is cheating on Alice."

"Um, I think that's a stretch." Mia ate a cherry that had slipped out of a piece of pie. "Or maybe wishful thinking?" Mia looked like she was going to say more about Jenny, but stopped when she saw my pained expression. "Maggie, it's obvious your joints are hurting. As soon as you serve the desserts, why don't you go home? I'm sure that you need to get some house stuff ready for the guests, and then you can rest."

"What about you? Don't you have clients in the morning?"

"I took the rest of the week off. A few clients moved their appointments, and the rest I easily rearranged. With the extra people in town, I want to help Mama and Daddy here and the tips are exceptionally good. I'm also a lot freer to help with wedding stuff."

"Are you sure?" I felt so guilty already.

"Honestly?" Mia leaned up against the wall, absently rubbing her baby belly. "I'm getting so bored with accountant work. I've been percolating on something about your lake property. I've been talking with James about costs and going over some legal stuff with Sutton, and I think that we have figured out . . ."

Tamsin interrupted, calling Mia into the dining room.

"Duty calls," Mia said. "I'll explain the rest, later."

An hour later I climbed into bed with snacks, Cosmo, and One Tree Hill on the TV, hoping to put this entire day behind me.

Cleanse your body and spirit
at Sunrise Yoga with
our own Yoga Pat, owner of
Patty's Bait and Tackle!

CHAPTER EIGHT
Midnight Madness

"WHY IS YOUR PENIS IN MY FACE IT'S ONE IN THE MORN-ING!" Bright light seared my eyes as Sutton's goods waved in front of my face. I thought he had been sleeping up at the main house—what was he doing here now? Cosmo barked and leapt from my bed, knocking a naked Sutton to the ground.

My friend looked around as he jumped up from the floor. "My sheet must have fallen off when I was running down here from your house. I didn't even grab shoes," Sutton said, brushing pine needles and tiny pebbles from his feet.

I rubbed my eyes and tried to process what was happening. Sutton ran to my dresser and grabbed a pair of old beige sweatpants from Patty's Bait and Tackle Shop. He hopped on one leg pulling the sweatpants on. "You *have* to get up to the house, now!" He stumbled back to my dresser and threw me another pair of Patty's Bait and Tackle jogging pants, this time in mint green (how many pairs did I *have*?).

I was still too rattled to compose a coherent sentence as I got dressed, so all that came out was, "Whaaa?"

Sutton took my hand, and we stumbled up to the house through the pine trees lit only by a flickering security lamp. Sutton wore my grandma's clogs and I my ever-so-alluring Crocs. As Cosmo ran through the open mudroom door, I was going to yell at Sutton to shut it, because the house would be a humid bug hotel if he left the door open, but then I heard it: the RETCHING.

Three levels of retching in my home. The home that my great, great, grandparents built with their own hands was now filled with the sounds of vomiting. And oh god, the smell! Sutton knew my abhorrence to bad smells and silently handed me a face mask, then put one on himself. I stood in my mudroom, trying to control my own gagging before heading in.

"How much did you dipshits drink?" I stepped around Adrian who held Abby's hair and a wet dishrag on her neck as she threw up in my white porcelain farmer's sink. The white really set off the colors, I noted. "Hey Adrian, you okay?"

Adrian wore their long black hair—so much like Alice's—up in a bun and sported only a pair of low riding jogging pants and a nice ab six-pack. Adrian nodded their head. "I'm fine, but Abby's been going at this for about twenty minutes now. Sorry about all that." They pointed to a pile of dirty towels.

I gave Cosmo a toy to keep him from disturbing the sick guests and then carried the towels back into the laundry room where I found Sutton.

"The weird thing is," Sutton said, frantically gathering clean washrags and towels from the dryer, "other than a glass of wine or a cocktail, none of us really drank much. We sat on the screened porch for a while, talking about high school stuff and whatnot, and then we all went to bed."

"And where was bed for you, Sutton?" I asked, throwing the soiled towels in the wash. An unpleasant feeling of FOMO washed over me when I heard that everyone had been enjoying themselves, reminiscing about all their cool times in high school while I was sleeping alone in my bed cradling Cosmo and a messy bag of Cheetos.

"Long story, gotta go." Sutton patted me on the head, which he knew I hated, and booked it upstairs to deliver more towels. Was Sutton flirting with anyone last night? I was trying to remember when my cell phone rang. I recognized the number.

"Hey Mr. Jablonski. What are y'all doing up there in the middle of the . . .?"

"I see your lights on," he said without preamble. "Are any of your guests sick too?"

I looked out my window and sure enough, I could see Mr. Jablonski's multistory log home lit up across the cove where the Carlyons and Allertons were staying. "What's going on?"

"Best I can figure is food poisoning," said Mr. Jablonski.

"Well, that's ridiculous; we all ate at the same place but not all of us are sick," I said. "I have never heard of food poisoning caused by The Magnolia, ever, and besides that, I ate a quick dinner with Sutton and Mia's family in the office before serving, and Sutton and I are fine." I felt defensive of Mia's parents' restaurant, especially since I'd brought this nightmare of a group there. "I need to go, Mr. Jablonski, I'll check in later."

"Let me know if you find anything out." Mr. Jablonski hung up right as a text from my neighbor Miss Vera flashed across my phone:

YOUR LIGHTS ARE BOTHERING RICHARD LOOK AT HIM

Vera attached a photo of her African gray parrot, whose feathers were admittedly a mess. I chose not to respond to the text from Miss Vera, just as I got a middle-of-the-night text from Lance:

hey send a closeup of the boobs but not the face

There was no time for any of this.

I texted Mia: **Are u up??**

Mia: **yah Mama just called me. just going to call u**

My phone rang as Mia called to discuss, and I answered as I handed a fresh, wet washcloth to Abby, who was now lying on my kitchen floor in her SpongeBob nightgown with Adrian rubbing her back.

"Who's sick at your house?" I asked Mia.

"No one!" Mia answered. "My mom and dad aren't sick either and they are checking in now with the staff."

I sat heavily on a kitchen stool. Getting only two hours of sleep did not improve the nerve pain shooting through my legs, and my joints were more swollen by the minute. "But I know we all ate the same food." I lowered my voice when Abby groaned. "From the same kitchen."

"I can't figure this out," Mia said. "Mama's already gotten a terribly upset call from Mr. Jablonski on behalf of the Carlyons and the Allertons, who were all too busy yakking to complain themselves."

Noodle bumped his furry head against my arm wanting pats. I scratched his ears with one hand while holding my head up with the other. "Well, there's nothing for you to do now and it's two o'clock in the morning. Can you go back to sleep?"

"I'm gonna try." Mia whispered something to James. Then, back to me, "I suppose you need to stay up?"

"Yeah. I'll try to nap later today. Love you and I'll text if I learn anything."

"Sounds good." Mia hung up.

"I'm heading upstairs to check on everyone," I said.

Abby rallied and gave me a thumbs up from her prone position on the floor. But as she reached for her vomit bowl I hurried away with a quick "I'm sorry" so my gag reflex wouldn't be triggered. As I hobbled on stiff knees up the stairs, I heard Adrian soothing Abby that it would all be over soon. I hoped so as I entered the upper floor hall and found what looked like a staging area for a zombie movie. The bodies were even strewn through the hall. I stepped over Virginia who was sitting on the floor propped up against a wall. Her perspiring face was covered in oozing, poison ivy blisters, and her once spiky hair stuck damp and flat to her head. She curled up around her pillow, moaning.

"Virginia's down here because Trig is using the bathroom upstairs," William told me as he stepped out of a bedroom, mopping his brow with a washcloth. Luckily, his rash had been contained on his forearms and legs as far as I could tell. "Virginia," he said softly, leaning over. "Bathroom is free when you need it."

"Who's all sick?" I whispered as I carefully tucked a towel under Virginia's head.

"Well," William motioned me to the little sitting area between my dad's and my aunt's rooms. "I woke up to Herschel making a racket next door." He pointed to Aunt Mary's room. "Then I heard someone, I think Sutton because I saw him bringing up towels a bit later, go downstairs. By that time, my stomach lurched, and I was throwing up right after."

I sat down heavily in an old armchair, shifting around until my butt wasn't getting pierced by a rogue spring. "Okay, so you, Abby, Trig, Herschel, Virginia." I counted on my fingers, trying to think of other people.

"Lena-Elise and Adrian," William said. "Ugh, hold on." William scooted off to Adrian's bathroom because Lena-Elise was still in his.

Adrian. They must have been sick before I got here. At least Adrian could take care of Abby, who was in bad shape. I cracked open Aunt Mary's old door, the same room where Mr. Gustaffson, aka Mr. Trembolt, died just two days ago, a fact that I pushed right on out of my mind. "Do you need anything, Hersch?"

There was a sliver of light coming in from the bathroom. "I washed off the bedspread, but it's gonna need to be cleaned," Herschel said.

"No problem." I spotted the patchwork quilt in a heap by the bathroom door and carried it with me as I headed out. "Anything else? I asked.

"No," Herschel mumbled. "Some Gatorade or something later, but nothing now. Oh, you could kill me. That would be great."

"I'm so sorry," I said, closing the door quietly behind me.

"Maggie," Sutton hissed from somewhere up above me.

Looking around, I spotted Sutton and Noodle looming above me from the top of the stairs on the third level. "What's going on?" I loudly whispered. I dropped the bedspread down the laundry chute and crept up the stairs as quietly as I could in case anyone up there had mercifully passed out.

"It's like a TB ward around here." Sutton had found latex gloves, which paired well with his face mask, Camp Rock shirt and the bait shop jogging pants. "Trig is back in the bathroom. It's coming out both ends."

I felt the remains of my own dinner trying to make it back up my esophagus and painfully swallowed it down. "I do not need to know the details, but I gotta know, is Trig, the rich lawyer and class bully, the reason you were sleeping over here at the house?" Noodle did a figure eight around my legs, purring as he went. I picked him up and carried him as I peered into Abby's room and sure enough, there was a pile of dirty linens by the bed. I exchanged the cat for the sheets and blanket and met up with Sutton in the hall.

Sutton looked a bit sheepish as he took his mask off. "You know we hooked up a few times in high school, and don't give me that face." Sutton slingshot his mask at my squinched up expression, which missed me by inches. "Anyway, whatever. He's cute and I haven't gotten action in a while."

"Since that doctor guy?" I asked, remembering the heated relationship that just as quickly burned out, ending with Sutton squatting in my house for a whole week eating nothing but pizza, chips and ice cream while watching Love Island on repeat.

"Yep."

"Well, then, you deserve some sexy time so go on and get some," I said.

"It means literally nothing," Sutton clarified, "but I still feel obligated to be Nurse Nightingale." He tilted his head toward the door.

"That's your business," I said, massaging my aching wrists.

"I know, but I don't want you thinking I'm a slut for bad boys." Sutton flipped his hair out of his eyes and winked at me.

I laughed and was going to make a dirty comment when Mia texted me:

I couldn't sleep so I'm at the front door with supplies

"Oh, thank goodness, reinforcements," I said.

Later that morning when the whole group was convalescing in my living room, all our phones buzzed at once.

"Is that group over at the Jablonskis' fucking kidding?" Herschel asked from his throw-pillow lair on the cool kitchen floor. "Weren't they all sick too?"

Even perky, rule-following Abby threw her phone and wedding planning binder on the couch cushion beside her and groaned. At some point, she had changed from her nightgown to a light pink terrycloth jumper with rainbow ribbing and braided her hair in two blond plaits. "Yes, they were sick," Abby said. "But somehow Tamsin and Noah are going to be here very soon for sunrise yoga with Yoga Pat, which . . ." We all followed her gaze looking out the sliding glass doors to the already hot, humid, and very sunny day. Yoga Pat of Patty's Bait and Tackle had been notified to come later than scheduled and was setting up on the lawn. "Well, I guess now it's almost midday yoga."

I surveyed my kitchen sitting area. Most everyone had found their way down here in the last few hours for group comfort. Mia had brought electrolyte drinks, more Calamine lotion, ice packs, portable barf bags, Advil, Tylenol, Pepto Bismol, Tums, and a few stuffed animals you could throw in the microwave so they doubled as squishy heating pads. Sutton was hugging a warm lavender scented hippo and curled up in the oversized chair by the fireplace. Virginia snuggled into the other side of the couch, her short black and magenta hair matted now in clumps, and her face covered in lotion that I hoped would bring her blisters down. Adrian, Trig, and Herschel spread out on the floor, flopped on various cushions and blankets from the living room. Veronica Mars quietly played on the large TV with subtitles on.

"Hey, where did Lena-Elise go?" Herschel asked.

William, looking the sportiest in an orange polo shirt and khaki shorts, took a sip of his lemon ice Gatorade. "She had to go to the drug store for tampons. I offered to go, but she felt bad making anyone else suffer riding in a bumpy car."

"Oh shoot. I'll put period products on the list of things I need to stock here." I made a quick note on my phone and was disheartened to see how long that list had grown. A new text appeared from the water company demanding their past due payments. They sent at least one text a day warning me what would happen if I didn't pay, and even though they were supposed to have a generous grace period that should last me until after the wedding, I was still worried. I must have made a face because William pushed the oat milk toward me and poured more coffee in my mug, which I raised in thanks.

"How are you doing?" William's skills as a therapist were evident in his comforting way of asking. I envied his clients.

"I know I need some sleep." I held up a finger as I gulped down half my coffee.

"Yeah, but beyond that. It's barely been half a year since your dad Henry died and from what I understand, you have not slowed down." He raised his eyebrows when I shrugged.

I teared up—maybe because I was sleep deprived and in pain. "I don't know what other choice I have. This is my home, and I'm proud that I've found a way to keep it going, but . . ." I wiped my wet face with my sleeve. "I feel so guilty, all the time."

"About what?"

I gestured around. "Everything. When my dad died, I found out that he heavily mortgaged our family home to pay for my medicine infusions."

"You didn't have insurance from your job?" William sipped his coffee, watching me over the rim of his mug.

I stacked some decorative napkins into a pewter holder, focusing my eyes on the napkins rather than on William. "I had good insurance when I had my job, but I had to quit when I got sick. I finally got on other insurance, but it doesn't remotely cover everything."

"So, your dad stepped in, like any dad would do if he could. You do know it must have felt good for him to be able to help you, right?" William got up and let Cosmo in through the sliding door. Hot, steamy air wafted in, bringing the scent of lake water, burning leaves and pine trees.

I nodded, brushing a tear from my eye. "God, I miss him so much." I reached down to stroke Cosmo's velvety ears as he licked my leg. "Every time I pick up rocks by the lake, every time I watch a sunset from our chairs on the dock, the pain is still so raw. At least I still feel him here, you know? But honestly, I don't know if I can keep all this work up."

"What about Minnesota?"

"Going back?" I sat quietly for a moment, picking at a piece of paper towel and painfully aware of William's and Herschel's eyes on me. I wanted so much to confide in someone about the possibility of leaving Majestic Springs. My hand went to my abdomen as I thought of the little Tudor home in Minneapolis I'd shared with Lance, where I didn't have to constantly clean for others, dodge bill collectors, and seethe with envy every time I saw Alice with Jenny. But I couldn't risk any hint of this getting back to Sutton and Mia until I'd made my decision. "I've been working so much I haven't been able to think about it," I shrugged.

William said, "I've been learning that it's okay to let go of things that are not serving you. And honestly, have you considered whether Majestic Springs is the healthiest place for you, if all you're doing is working and not taking care of yourself?"

I nodded politely but scrambled to change the subject. "Are you happy coming back to the area?" I was surprised to learn that William had moved back from California, where he'd gone right after he graduated a couple years after we did. "Here, Herschel." Herschel was looking a little green, so I handed him another fruit punch Powerade.

"Thanks," Herschel said. This is the only thing I can keep down right now." He retreated to his seat in his grimy white undershirt and cut-off sweat shorts.

"Stop scratching, Herschel," I said and then had to laugh when he flipped me off and kept scratching. "Hey, how's Jenny?" I asked, secretly hoping for an answer about Alice as well.

"Don't know. She hasn't texted back." Herschel looked at his phone again and stood up, reading something intently, his expression changing from mildly amused to troubled. *Interesting.* I tried to discreetly watch Herschel, but he had turned the other way.

Meanwhile, William had been considering the question I asked him. "Yes. I'm happy to be back here. Very happy, now that I've found Lena-Elise." He raised his Gatorade to Lena-Elise as she entered the house and tried to sneak up the front stairs, which turned out to be impossible on crutches. Wow, she was really shy. "The new therapy practice is going great too," William continued. "My practice partner and I are able to discuss tough cases, and he's been in the area for a long time. He has some interesting patients too."

"Do therapists talk about each other's patients?" I had not thought about that before. Did my therapist do it? My pulse hammered at the thought.

"I think most do, but we keep names and identifying details private when we consult with each other about patients."

"Hmmmm." I considered the many things I'd said in therapy and which other therapists in the area she could have consulted with. The dryer alarm sounded for the hundredth time, and I gave a "What can you do gesture" to William and got up.

"Sutton, could you help me with the beds?" I asked.

Sutton's head popped up from his chair, hair sticking up in places and flat in others. He reached for his tortoiseshell glasses and put them on while searching for his shirt. "Yeah, hold on."

As we were moving toward the stairs, we heard hushed voices in Herschel's room. Sutton made a frantic "stay back" move and we both flattened ourselves against the light olive painted wall. I carefully peered around the corner to peek in and saw a very tense looking Abby and a frowning Herschel standing on opposite sides of my aunt's four poster bed. I leaned in as close as I could.

". . . I swear it wasn't me." Herschel was saying. He took off his hat and pushed his sweaty blond hair back, then plopped the hat back on again.

"What's happening?" Sutton hissed, dropping the laundry basket by our feet and poking my arm.

I batted him away and leaned closer.

Abby was busying herself with making Herschel's bed. As she jammed the pillows into flowered cases, she said, "I didn't think you would do this to yourself, Hersch, but then who did it?" Abby plumped up the pillows and placed them on the bed, then started working on the top sheet. "Straighten that side."

Sutton pushed my face up and snuck in under my arm, so our heads were stacked on each other. "Oh my god you smell," he whispered.

I rolled my eyes and shushed him.

"I didn't see Adrian sick at all, is what I'm saying," Herschel said. He grabbed the blanket from the basket and tossed a side to Abby. "Did you?"

Didn't I see Adrian sick? "Did you?" I mouthed to Sutton who had a quizzical look on his face. I tried to remember. When I came in at death o'clock, Adrian was taking care of Abby. I peeked into the bedroom again. My body hurt from head to swollen ankles, and I wondered when my next dose of ibuprofen was due. I could even sneak in another dose of prednisone, which my doctor was very much against if I wasn't in an active autoimmune flare, but I'd accepted that flaring was inevitable; I might as well start medicating for it.

"Well," Abby straightened the blanket and then started working on the bedspread, strands of hair trailing out of her braids as she furiously worked the wrinkles out. "Now that you mention it, I don't remember Adrian running to the bathroom or anything, though they *said* they were feeling terrible."

Sutton's sculpted eyebrows shot up at this.

My legs were rubbery, and it was getting harder to stand in one place, but we needed to stay put and listen. I bent my knees, trying to get blood to my feet and pointed to Sutton to massage my calves. *What were they getting at?*

". . . now I gotta deal with this thing tonight," Herschel was saying.

"I still don't know how we are going to . . ."

"Don't worry about it; I got a plan."

"Need help, guys?" Lena-Elise had come limping out of her room and was looking at us curiously, me leaning forward comically on the wall and Sutton rubbing my legs. *Crap! How long was she standing there?*

"Just resting a tic before we go upstairs," I said, pulling Sutton by his shirt to a standing position. "Thanks though!" I could feel Lena-Elise's eyes on our backs, and when I stole a quick glance, I saw her entering Herschel's bedroom.

We ducked into Virginia's sky-blue room, and I wheeled around at Sutton. "Shit! Is she going to tell them we were spying on them?"

"Okay, Okay." Sutton patted the air with his hands, trying to regulate us both. "What have we learned?"

I crawled on the bed and wrestled the pad down on one side while Sutton secured the other two corners. "What have we learned?" I repeated breathlessly, resting for a moment after wrestling with the bed linens. "Um, I just don't know. Were Herschel and Abby talking about the food poisoning?"

"Here." Sutton waited for me to finish the fitted sheet before he flicked the blue and white striped flat sheet in the air and let it float down onto the bed. "Maybe they were talking about the food poisoning. I think so. Herschel said something like it wasn't him. Which means . . ."

"Which means that the food poisoning wasn't accidental." I finished Sutton's thought. "But why would someone do this deliberately? And why did they mention Adrian?" I asked.

I sat up on the bed and started stuffing pillows into their butter yellow cases. "This could be important. Adrian and Jenny were talking in a heated way at the restaurant last night. I thought that they might be in some sort of romantic tangle."

"You *hoped* that was the case that Jenny was cheating on Alice," Sutton said.

Ouch. "I know understanding 'the people' is not in my wheel-house," I said sardonically, "but I saw what I saw. I guess that it's possible that they were just talking about poisoning their friends, cuz that makes *so* much more sense."

We unfolded my grandma's soft old blue and yellow bedspread and laid it on the bed. I fluffed the shams and centered them against the iron headboard while Sutton folded down the sheets to make it all look pretty.

"What if Jenny and Adrian were trying to make the wedding party sick?" Sutton asked. "And if so, *why*? Also, I hate to bring this up, but what if this has something to do with the dock and our janitor's overdose?"

"Don't forget the mystery of the changing 5K route." I sat down on the bed. "Jesus. Why *would* these goobers be trying to hurt each other?"

"And let's not forget Herschel saying that 'he had a plan,'" Sutton warned.

"Fucking super. I guess *we* need to be extra vigilant until Saturday so these clowns don't burn my house down. If we say something now to the cops, I can kiss any money goodbye and might as well start packing today." I thought about how maybe if I could keep my head down and just do my job this week, that would be enough. But I just couldn't stop thinking about the "why's."

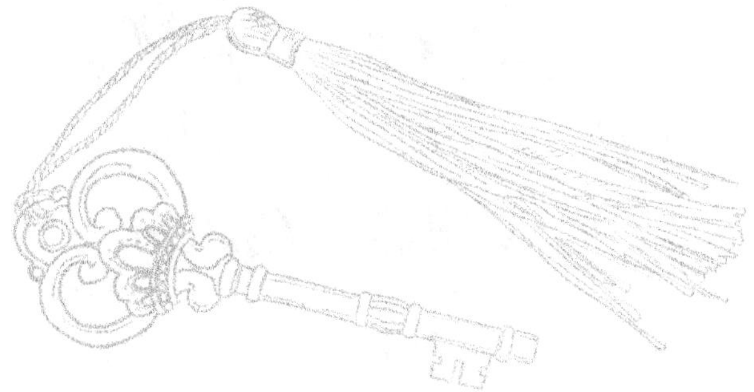

Who's ready for fun
in the sun? Grab your
swimsuits and your paddles—
It's time for the Cardboard
Boat Making Contest!

SUNTAN
LOTION

CHAPTER NINE
Who Remembers Mr. Gustaffson

"My god, did *everyone* throw up? *Everywhere?* And then they did yoga with Yoga Pat? That's amazing!" Mia lifted her flowered prairie skirt and stepped gingerly around the blast from my hose washing vomit through gravel and crab grass. She was in her second trimester and was starting to waddle a bit, which was an adorable comic foil to her strong physique.

"I know," I said. "You have to admire their dedication."

"How are you going to pull off this cardboard boat-making contest in this mess?" Mia asked. "Does anyone even *want* to do it? And are you *sure* they want to take that boat tour this afternoon?"

"Abby has commanded everyone to 'stick to the schedule, or else,'" I said. "It's almost frightening the way she insists we stay exactly on task. I guess she was always like that."

Mia sighed at me. "It could be that Abby just wants her friend's wedding to go well, Maggie."

"Fine, but she could let up a little. Anyway, it was entertaining during sunrise yoga with Yoga Pat to watch Tamsin repeatedly swallow her barf during tree pose." I sprayed off my flip flops, careful not to get my rolled-up overalls wet. I'd taken another dose of prednisone, and it was finally starting to take effect, so hopefully I'd have less pain and swelling for the rest of the day.

"Wow," Mia laughed. "You talk about people not changing since high school, but you sure haven't changed much either . . . oh, no Cosmo!" Mia tried to stop Cosmo from sliding right into the puke river, but to no avail.

I laughed. "Mia, you're one of the very few people who gets to call me out like that and get away with it. Anyway, don't worry about the mess and Cosmo," I said, aiming the hose at Cosmo's paws. He twirled around and around trying to bite the stream of water while splashing in the swill. Jumping in the lake sounded heavenly to me, but I had no time for that, so I settled for a handful of cold hose water on my sweaty neck and face.

Mia shaded her eyes as she surveyed the mounds of flattened cardboard boxes, assorted colors of duct tape, and large Tupperware containers of scissors, knives, and squeezable paint bottles in every color imaginable. "I can't believe that people are up to making cardboard boats in this heat after last night. At least they can cool off in the water."

I stopped watering my vomit yard and motioned for us to sit under a large live oak that provided wonderful shade at this time of day. "Here." I handed Mia a covered mug with iced tea.

"Homemade?" She brushed off the dirt and dried leaves so she wouldn't get her skirt messy.

"Of course," I said. We clinked our mugs together and leaned back in the Adirondack chairs my dad had picked up decades ago from a guy up in the hills. "We're under a heat advisory today, but apparently nothing can keep these dinks from following Abby's itinerary." My cell phone lit up, and as soon as I saw it was a dick pic, I rammed my phone back in my pocket. No way I wanted Mia to see that I was texting with my ex. This was the third dick pic that Lance had sent this week alone. *Why* had I slept with him again?

"Speaking of your lovely guests, here they come!" Mia lowered her voice as the guests began shambling toward their boat-making stations. Mia nodded hello to Mr. and Mrs. Carlyon as they walked by, arm in arm, looking amazingly healthy and not like they had pulled an all-nighter yakking up thousands of dollars of food.

James walked up to us and grabbed a chair.

"And also speaking of the guests, my sleuthing husband James here found out something very interesting about some of them." Mia blew James a kiss as he plopped down beside her.

"I sure did," James said, looking very Key West cool in his parrot patterned button down shirt and cargo shorts.

"Hey there." I handed James an iced tea. "You took off work to watch this circus?"

"Abby offered me a gig judging the cardboard boat contest," James said. "I think she did it because I'm a contractor, and therefore I must know the ins and outs of cardboard boat making." James rolled his eyes and nodded at Virginia, who was carrying a crate of the special stainless-steel water bottles they had made specifically for the wedding party today. After Virginia looked away, James pulled one of the fancy water bottles from his bag and took a slug.

"Oh no you didn't," Mia laughed. "Abby will kill you if she sees you with one of those; they are only for the wedding party."

"I don't know nothing about nothing," James said, tucking the bottle out of sight with a wink. "Besides," he added, "they're cute; each one has a quote on it for what makes a good marriage, and I love *our* good marriage, so I wanted one."

"Awww, I love you, boo," Mia said. "God, what this wedding week must have cost." She shook her head. "Ooh! Tell Maggie what you heard last night at the Drunken Oar."

"Yes, tell Maggie, but *quietly*," I whispered as Herschel, Trig and Adrian began furiously cutting up their cardboard boxes near us. "And hurry up because they are moving fast and then we have to get things ready for the boat tour when they're done."

We all leaned in to hear what James had learned at the Drunken Oar.

"I still don't know what to make of it all." James gulped down more of his stolen water and wiped his forehead on his sleeve. "So, I was talking to my buddy Trevor, who is with Parks and Rec, and I asked him about the sudden route change for the

5K on Tuesday that led everyone afoul of the poison ivy patch." James looked up to make sure we were all listening. We were listening, so he continued. "Alright, well he got real quiet, which is so unlike Trevor, you know?"

"Start over." Sutton swooped in and perched on my lap.

"Oof, you're heavier than when we were eight!" I gasped.

James laughed and said, "Okay, rewinding for you, *Sutton*. I grabbed a beer with Trevor last night after work, and when I brought up the 5K debacle, he got quiet, *then* changed the subject."

"Oooh," Sutton purred. "The plot thickens."

"Did Trevor look guilty of something?" I asked, as Sutton leaned back into me.

"Yeah, I'd describe Trevor's demeanor as guilty, even shifty, come to think." James had to raise his voice because Tamsin's boat-making group was screaming as they squirted paint all over each other.

Mia picked up a tennis ball that Cosmo had dropped at her feet and threw it away from the guests, who had begun congregating by my old swimming dock for boat judging. Jenny's crew needed another day to get my main dock up and running again, so that wasn't available.

"James," I said, "does Trevor know any of these jerks?"

"I wouldn't have thought so, since many of these jerks moved away," James said. "But Trevor must know Adrian from somewhere because I saw that Adrian texted Trevor while Trevor was in the bathroom at the bar."

We gasped and leaned in closer.

"What did the text say?" I asked, bracing myself on Sutton and nearly toppling him to the ground.

James looked a bit embarrassed. "I didn't mean to read it, but it just flashed on his screen."

"And?" We all asked in unison.

"The text read, '**Venmoed. Now we are even,**'" James said.

We all leaned back and sat silent for a moment, sipping our tea and swatting away the occasional mosquito.

Finally, Mia spoke. "Adrian was in a heated conversation with Jenny the other night. Is that suspicious when you combine it with the text with Trevor?"

"I've been thinking about this morning," I jumped in. "Do you remember it didn't seem like Adrian got sick."

"Oh my god, that's true," said Sutton, and he bobbed back into my boobs with excitement. "Adrian didn't seem like they were ill."

"Uff," I said, cringing at the tenderness in my chest. Either I was going to get my period soon or Lance's little critter was growing inside me; my boobs were *sore*.

"I came later this morning, so I wouldn't know for sure if Adrian was in the bathroom," Mia said. "But how would any of us know for sure if Adrian was actually throwing up? Plus, people were still barfing afterwards at yoga—something I'll never understand—and how does that fit with Abby's and Herschel's bizarre conversation?"

"Maybe they were suspicious of Adrian not being sick?" James said.

Sutton jumped in: "What about Herschel and his weird comment about tonight's party at the roller rink. He said he had to deal with a problem there but not to worry because he had a plan." Sutton turned to get a better look at the boat-making shenanigans on the water as he mused, "What kind of plan would a dude like Herschel have?"

Herschel looked ridiculous now flailing and bobbing around on a sinking cardboard craft. Most of the guests were either in the water trying to keep their boats afloat or climbing into the two pontoon boats, also known as party barges, that we had docked nearby.

"Well," Mia said, "who knows? But thankfully, I don't see how anyone could screw up today's boat tour. Then, tonight a roller-skating party will be impossible to ruin because it's in the town square and so public. Who would dare do anything there?"

"That's true," I said. "It's under the big tent in the square, yeah." That was a relief. And now I could relax a little bit because Abby had blessedly gotten the coolers and snacks packed for the boat tour. I sat and watched the guests board the party barges with their towels and water bottles. Everyone seemed wonderfully enthusiastic for the tour and someone had cranked up some music, causing the boats to rock with the group's spontaneous dancing. Just then, Mrs. Carlyon unbuttoned her silk blouse and swung it around her head while Mr. Carlyon made whooping noises and jumped back and forth, rocking one of the boats harder. Wow, if this was how the Carlyons partied, I was glad the Allertons were busy in town.

"Um . . . guys," James interrupted me. "Have you noticed the guests are having an *exceptionally* good time?" James gestured to the wedding party.

Admittedly, the Carlyons were really going for it, but they were the ones paying my bonus so if they were happy, I didn't care. "As long as they are having a good time, James, I'm fine with it," I said.

"True," James admitted. "But still, shouldn't we try to figure out what is really going on with these incidents? I mean, look at these people. They should be scared, or at least subdued, but they're all laughing and getting along like nothing happened. But *someone* re-routed the 5K to a poison ivy patch; *someone* managed to make the whole group sick. Why aren't they reacting to it?"

"Don't forget about Maggie's dock," added Sutton. "And now they are acting like nothing's happened."

"Assholes." I muttered. I wouldn't even begin to know how to file a claim on dock sabotage, so the repair money would have to come out of a non-existent stash that I would first have to build up.

"And, even though I don't see how, we need to think about how old man Gustaffson's death enters in here," Mia said, pouring all of us another round of iced tea.

"I literally forgot about old man Gustaffson," Sutton said, shaking his head. That seems like years ago. "Does anyone know why he would pretend to be Mr. Trembolt?"

"Didn't you say that he was the school's janitor when y'all went to high school?" James asked, leaning over to grab his new water bottle. "Couldn't that be a link?"

"Yeah," Sutton answered. He took a long swig of his tea before continuing. "But I thought he retired years ago and moved away."

"Yes, outside Little Rock, I think." I paused with my tea in hand, then took a few sips. "But again, what does a janitor's hinky death have to do with a wedding party trying to mess each other's shit up?" I gestured to the boisterous antics of my guests on the pontoon boats. "And WHY would anyone do these things to their supposed best friends? Are these supposed to be jokes?" We were no closer to the truth than we were when we started talking.

"Shouldn't we discuss all this with Mark?" Mia asked. "Whoever is pranking people is taking it way too far and I know we'd feel horrible if someone, including any of us, got really hurt."

"Well, if we're thinking that Mr. Gustaffson was offed when he was pretending to be Mr. Trembolt, then someone already did get hurt," Sutton said. "And what was up with that wig and fake beard thingy?"

"Truthfully, with all this stuff happening," I waved my hand in the direction of the guests now yelling at each other and throwing the cardboard boats in the air, "I forgot how bizarre it was that Gustaffson was lurking around in disguise." I had a sudden memory of walking into the kitchen and finding him crawling under the table. I assumed he'd dropped something. Now, thinking back, had he looked sheepish? "But if we tell Mark before Sunday and I get shut down, then no bonus for me, and then no more guests ever because who would want to stay in a place where someone just publicly died?"

"I just . . . I know that you'd be screwed without the money," Sutton began.

"Sutton, don't go there now," I threatened. "I can't call the police now, you know that."

Sutton continued anyway, "Maggie, isn't there a point where you have to do something for all our safety?"

"I suppose there is," I snapped. "Sorry you're friends with an unfeeling bitch." I pushed Sutton off me abruptly and tried to get out of my chair, which unfortunately did not achieve the huffy exit I wanted because I got stuck.

"Need a little help?" Sutton offered his hand.

"No!" I shook him off and stormed away as best I could despite slipping in the barf slush on my lawn. This had gotten out of control. I squinted through tears, not daring to look back at what were likely disappointed looks on my friends' faces. I knew that they were discussing me now, and how I could be so heartless, but I honestly had forgotten about Mr. Gustaffson. Or maybe I shoved the whole "secretly removing a dead body from my home" out of my brain because if I didn't, then I could not keep juggling all these balls in the air to keep this place afloat. I hated the fact that Herschel was sleeping in my beloved aunt's bed, and that other former classmates that used to tease the shit out of me were now living, albeit temporarily, in the home where my father and I should be reading our books and drinking coffee on the porch.

I slammed the sliding door shut and walked straight into a slightly frazzled William, who was opening and shutting my kitchen drawers, probably looking for something to help Heidi with the catering. Thank goodness Heidi was hired to do the catering, because there was no way I could have handled the food on top of everything else. "Sorry," I mumbled, wiping my tears with my sleeve.

"Hey, what's going on?" William asked, handing me a tissue, and pulling out a kitchen stool for me. Lena-Elise was so lucky to have this dude, I thought as I blew my nose. I laid my head down on the cool kitchen island and exhaled.

Heidi patted my shoulder as she pushed the food cart to the door. "I heard about last night. What the hell?"

I raised my hands up in a "I know, what the fuck" gesture.

"I want to hear more, but I gotta get all this out there. Love you." She waved and went outside, heading to the swimming dock where the pontoon boats were tied up.

"I honestly don't know where to begin," I said, sniffling. "I just yelled at my friends and stomped off like a toddler. And they were right about . . . what we were talking about." I didn't want to say too much to William, but it felt good talking to someone who didn't think I was a ghoul. "I . . . sometimes when I have to do something, something important, I get hyper focused on that, you know?"

William nodded. I felt a wee bit like I was taking advantage of the fact that he was a professional listener, but I was too over-whelmed to stop. "And when I just focus on one very important thing," *like saving my home*, "I sort of put out of my mind the other stuff around me." *Overdose, food poisoning, dock sabotage, murder.* William nodded again and I just verbal diarrhea-ed ahead. "And I thought I could handle having these people in my home for a week and just grin and bear it, you know?"

"They caused a lot of hurt for a lot of us," William said. "But that was a long time ago. At some point, we need to remember that we were all kids, and we all fucked up." William pulled out a veggie and fruit plate that Heidi left in the fridge and unwrapped it. "I seem to remember a certain graduation night when Alice found out that her girlfriend had cheated on her." He popped a strawberry in his mouth, his eyebrows up.

My stomach dropped. "Thanks for that reminder. That was such a messed-up night, right?" Alice's horrified face loomed in my head as Tamsin gleefully told her that I had sex with a hot guy—Lance—from up north. Tamsin had gotten me back for beating her to one of a few spots for the regional conference, which I regretted attending. If I hadn't gone, maybe, just maybe Alice and I wouldn't have broken up. No, that was a lie. I was looking to break us up, to get over with what I thought was the inevitable outcome. I just couldn't believe that wonderful, hot, smart and sexy Alice would be dating me, so I sabotaged us. "William," I said abruptly. "Were you there the night Carl Gleet's truck went off the bridge after graduation?"

"Well, I wasn't at the actual grad party because I was two years younger than your class, but of course I got tons of texts and calls as soon as it happened," he said.

"Oh, that's right," I said. "You didn't graduate with us, but you were such a smarty pants you were in most of our advanced classes."

William blushed at this and took a long drink from his new silver water bottle, inscribed with "Marriage is like vitamins: We supplement each other's minimum daily requirements." He held it up and smirked when he read the trite quote.

I ate a piece of cantaloupe, then another. I realized that I had not eaten all day and was starving. "Is there any meat in there?"

As William rummaged in the fridge, I thought about what he'd said, that we were all basically the same, the demon classmates and me. Was their bullying any worse than what I did to Alice?

I rolled up a few salami pieces and wolfed them down. "They were ruthless to you too, William. I remember those pictures of you dressed up at a renaissance festival that were so cute but they doctored them up and plastered them all over the school and everyone teased you about it. Are you telling me you can just kumbaya that shit away?"

William laughed. "It's not as simple as that. I'm just choosing my happiness over wasting my energy wanting them to suffer for things they did when they were literally kids."

"Can't we have both?" I asked, semi-serious.

"I mean, maybe?" William looked around him. "Hey, there is something weird going on, right? I cannot be imagining all this."

I leaned towards William and lowered my voice just in case someone was upstairs and could hear us. "Yeah, but honestly, I still can't figure out what. Has Lena-Elise mentioned anything to you about some of the wedding party not getting along?"

"No. But she has been acting . . . different lately, these past two weeks. I think she's been nervous about seeing everyone. She was never an instigator in school, you know. Just a follower, and I think that she doesn't know how to act around these people now." He looked out the sliding glass doors where we could see some of the wedding attendants dancing with Tamsin's parents on the boats. "She's been jumpy around the others, I've noticed. Especially after her fall at the cave."

"Um, did she mention anything, or *anyone*, being near her when she fell?" I asked.

"Well, she told me that Gary and Adrian were walking in front of her and Abby, who dropped her water bottle a few seconds before she fell. But that's all she could remember." He packed up the food tray and put it back in the fridge. "She was talking about it with Virginia last night before dinner, but I think she was embarrassed because she changed the subject when I caught up with them."

"This is getting way out of hand," I mumbled.

William took another drink from his bottle. "What is?"

I breathed in deeply and blew out slowly. I didn't want to involve William in this mess, but I really wanted the chaos to end. "I think that someone is pranking the wedding party, and it has gone way too far."

William was quiet for a moment, thinking this all through. "I knew something was going on, like with the food poisoning, the weird rashes. Any ideas who it is?"

"No, and I think someone may have tampered with my dock, which could have seriously hurt people."

"That seems in a different class from pranks," William said. "Very different."

I nodded. "Yeah, I thought so too. I just don't know. Maybe someone who doesn't want Tamsin and Noah to be together? A jealous past love? And will they keep escalating to cause trouble?" I knew that Tamsin and Noah had dated other people before getting together but I couldn't remember who at the moment. "Anyway," I said. "I think it's time to get help."

"Yeah, it seems someone has not grown up as much as the rest of us. Do you want me to call Mark?" William reached for a napkin and blotted his perspiring face. "Man, I feel kind of light-headed."

"Are you hydrated?" I asked. "After all that puking, I'm surprised any of you are up and about. And don't worry about Mark. It should be me if I decide to do it." I thought about my friends who were also trying to convince me to call Mark. "Well, I better make my apology promenade and then see if my cherished guests need anything."

William smiled and nudged my arm with his fist. "They're your friends, and they'll forgive you. Trust me, you always want to make it right, no matter how much it stings now. Hey, you might want to check the air conditioner; it feels hot in here." William left the house and walked toward the party barges where all the wedding party guests had gathered.

I sat in my quiet kitchen, enjoying the peace and ruminating on how long I could have my home back before the next guests arrived. Could I really do this? Run a bed and breakfast full of demanding guests every day when all I really wanted to do was walk around the property with my dog and find rocks to add to my collection? *Not every group I'll have here will be as weird as this one, right?*

The sound of yelling signaled that my peace was over.

You've never seen the lake like this!
Float through nature's paradise
on a guided boat tour while you
sip cocktails, mocktails, and nibble
a sumptuous tapas spread,
courtesy of Heidi's Café.

CHAPTER TEN
The Naked Now

"JESUS CHRIST WHAT DO YOU MEAN THE WEDDING PARTY IS FLOATING AWAY?" Hands on my thighs while catching my breath, I was amazed I still had enough volume to yell. I had attempted to run off my porch and out onto the lawn, but nerve pain shot up my legs like I'd been shocked, and my swollen joints gave out on me. I sank into a lawn chair right as I heard Sutton screaming my name.

"It's bad. *Really* bad! The wedding party got super drunk and floated away on the pontoon boats!" Sutton was both talking to me and already texting someone else at the same time.

"*Who* are you texting?" I already sensed who he was texting, and my voice was loud and shrill to my own ears. But this *was* bad, and it made no sense. I quickly scanned the lake cove for the rogue boaters, but none were in sight. *Shit!*

"Uh, Game and Fish?" Sutton dodged me as I tried to grab his phone.

"Don't you DARE text Alice!" I tried at getting Sutton's phone again, but with my stellar balance, I missed and fell into a short leaf pine. "NOW I'M BLEEDING."

"Just your face." Sutton made a face of his own as he tried to clean the blood off with his shirt. "Oh dear."

"What?"

"Your face. It's . . . shredded a bit." He blotted lightly as he talked.

The pressure stung and I shooed his hand away. "Whatever." I got hold of his phone and saw that the text to Alice had been sent:

HELP ROGUE PARTY BARGES GUESTS MISSING GO GET THEM

"Really?" If looks could kill Sutton would have melted.

"Look." Sutton lowered his voice. "Would you rather I alert the police? You made it *noticeably clear* that we have to lie low . . ."

"Ugh, I'm sorry I freaked out, okay. But this . . ." I flailed my arms in the general direction of where the party barges had floated away. "They could be ANYWHERE ON THIS HUGE LAKE."

"And not in their right minds," Mia added, approaching behind us. "And James is with them." Mia's normally calm face scrunched with worry and she was wringing her hands together.

I took her hand and squeezed it. "Do we have *any* idea how this happened?"

"Heidi!" Mia waved Heidi over from where she was standing on the sea wall. "I saw Heidi talking with Mr. Carlyon before he got on the boat."

"How much alcohol did Mr. Carlyon drink?" Mia asked Heidi.

Heidi held up a hand for a second to catch her breath, pushing her blond hair off her dripping face. "Mr. Carlyon didn't have any alcohol," she said, stretching her calf muscles after jogging over to us in her strappy wedge sandals. "At first I thought it was the food, but how could food make everyone so loopy?"

I squinted hard, trying to see any remnants of the pontoon boats on the lake, but all I saw were a few old fishing boats and a kayaker. "Wait. If it wasn't booze, then what the fuck is happening?" I asked.

"I have a theory," Heidi said, tying her hair up in a haphazard bun. "Sutton, did you get a water bottle?"

Sutton had run to my cabin to get a new shirt and was now sporting my "Live Ugly; Fake Your Own Death" possum t-shirt, which revealed his midriff. "No. I kinda wanted a water bottle, but Lena-Elise was very clear that they were for the wedding party only."

"James snuck one when Virginia wasn't looking," Mia said. "Why do you ask?"

Heidi turned to us. "Mia and Maggie, did either of you drink from those bottles?"

We both said no, but then I remembered something. "Wait," I said. "William was drinking from one, and then he got all sweaty right before he left the kitchen." The terrible realization dawned. I put up my hand. "Are you telling me . . . that my wedding party . . . that Mr. Carlyon, the man who is supposed to pay the bill for ALL of this . . . are you telling me these people have all been ROOFIED?"

"Roofied might be a bit strong." Heidi scanned the lake for the wedding party. "They weren't catatonic, so I'd say it was more of a club drug that acts fast, causes a loopy mood . . ."

"A club drug," I repeated, stunned.

"Like Molly?" Mia asked. "What's the fancy name, DNR? No wait, that would be like Do Not Resuscitate. That's not it."

Sutton *tsked* her. "The drug is MDMA. Otherwise known as Molly. Are there any bottles left for Mark to test?" He looked at me for agreement.

"A club drug?" I asked, as I scanned the horizon for the wedding party.

"I think I've actually got some of it, you guys." Heidi pulled out a little plastic bag with a few white pills in it, along with a piece of torn paper. "Look." She held up the clear bag so we could see a pill with a little butterfly carved in it. "I found these in the water bottle crate. Nic told me some teenagers came into the ER last weekend acting like, well, our friends on the boats." Ah, Nic Giannopoulos. Alice's impossibly handsome older brother who was an Emergency Room physician and Heidi's adoring boyfriend. Nic was a widower and had two daughters that Heidi doted on. I had heard rumors of an engagement soon, so my fingers were crossed.

"How long were they affected?" Mia asked, looking outward toward the lake.

"Not long, thankfully. A few hours, and Nic said it didn't hurt them." Heidi turned over the plastic bag, examining the pill further. "Even before I found this bag with the water bottles, I thought there might be something weird going on with everyone. You don't normally see adults acting like over-sugared six year olds at a birthday party."

I blinked away sudden tears that threatened to fall then cleared my throat. "I need to say something." I took a breath. "I know—I know we need to call Mark." I nodded soberly at Mia.

"I agree," Mia said. "This is serious, and we need to involve the police."

I exhaled and my arms gripped my stomach. We did need to contact Mark, but once the police got involved, my dead guest, the dock, and the mysterious food poisoning would all come to light, and I would be shut down. Maybe this was a good thing? The decision would be made for me to move away. Just the thought made me want to cry more.

Sutton patted my back absentmindedly with one hand while he looked at his phone with the other. "Okay, Alice is already on the hunt for the party barges out on the lake. I'll call . . ."

I was wiping my wet face when my phone buzzed. "Maybe it's one of the passengers," I said hopefully. "Hold on." As I dug my phone out of my pocket, Heidi's and Mia's phones chirped too.

"Wait!" Heidi yelled. "Don't call the police."

We must have gotten the same text!

IF YOU CONTACT THE POLICE SOMEONE IN THE WEDDING PARTY WILL DIE.

★ ★ ★

Everyone was dead silent.

"Shit," Sutton finally uttered. "What do we do?"

"Since we started this week off with a dead body, I think we should take this threat seriously," Heidi said, staring at her phone.

"How, HOW could all these things be related?" I searched my phone for any other threatening texts or emails that I might have missed.

"James is on one of those boats," Mia said, trying desperately to call his phone. "Why isn't he picking up?" Her voice rose with every word as she paced the ground. "What was in those water bottles and what if it was worse than MDMA?"

"I don't know," I said. "But we certainly can't involve Mark now." I wrung my hands together, rocking back and forth while I tried to think. "Sutton, get Alice on the phone. We have to get those boats back without calling the police."

Sutton glanced up at me and saw that I was dead serious, so he put his phone on speaker as he dialed my ex-girlfriend. "Hey Alice," Sutton said when she answered, the noise of her Ranger in the background. "Heidi, Mia, Maggie, and I are here."

Alice said, "I've just heard from another warden that the boats in question are floating down Bayou Bay."

"What?" Mia leaned into the phone. "Can those party barges even get through there? It's so shallow at this time of year."

"I don't know." Alice shouted over the roar of the Ranger engine. "I'm going there now; should be there in about five minutes. I'll call you when I find something out."

"One more thing, Alice," Sutton said. "Um, please don't bring Mark into this, or any other police, or Game and Fish, or . . ."

We could hear the boat slow down. "Out with it."

"You gotta trust us, Alice," Mia pleaded, grabbing onto the phone.

"I DO trust you, Mia, but if no one else is coming, y'all better get on Maggie's boat right fucking now and meet me at the Bayou. I'm not dealing with these shitheads myself." The thrum of Alice kicking her Ranger into high gear drowned her out before she hung up.

Sutton ran up to the house for the boat keys while Heidi, Mia, Cosmo, and I headed for the boat. "Careful of the otter poop," I shouted at them. "And I'm pretty sure there's a new wasp nest under the table." A collection of moans went up as everyone slipped in pungent poop and swatted at huge spider webs while picking their way to my old boat.

"Sorry, so sorry!" I kept repeating as we pulled out of my neighbor's dock, since mine was still half submerged in the water.

"I just don't see how they could get through this," Mia said as she stood in the boat, holding a seat for support, while Heidi and Sutton used wooden oars to push us through the shallow, skinny inlet. Damp leaves whacked my face as we squeezed through the dense foliage that draped over the water.

Alice's motor was a low spitting rumble as she trimmed her motor and followed along behind us. "It should get deeper very soon," she called out one of the many times we got stuck.

My phone vibrated in my pocket, and I snuck a look in case it was from Lance again.

"Any thoughts as to who is fucking with us and who would threaten us if we call the cops?" Sutton grunted and braced himself against a seat as he pushed us off the lake bottom with an oar.

I waved at several people who were leaning out of their windows and watching us from the shore before answering: "The guests have all been acting weird, but none stands out as a murderer. I see a lot of pairing up and whispering, like Herschel and Abby in the bedroom, Adrian and Jenny at The Magnolia . . ."

"Something freaked Trig out last night, too," Sutton said.

"Your hook-up? How so?" Mia asked, moving to the other side of the boat to hold a branch back. She had changed into a swimsuit top with tropical board shorts and her strong brown shoulders shone in the sun while she tied her braids up on top of her head.

"Well, I was lying down beside him, almost asleep, when he jumped out of bed and ran out the door. A few minutes later he sort of tiptoed back into the bedroom," Sutton said.

"Did you ask Trig about it?" Heidi asked, grunting as she pushed us back from the shore.

Sutton thought for a moment as he paddled with the oar. "I was going to, because he seemed really stressed, but then he rushed to the bathroom and started throwing up, and then the whole house was up. That's when I woke you up at one a.m." When I didn't respond to Sutton, he nudged me. "Maggie?"

I nodded, half listening. My body felt both numb and jangly, like a panic attack was coming on. What was one supposed to do when a stranger texted your phone and just casually informed you that they are down for murdering you if you call the police? As I practiced my breathing exercises taught to me by my long-suffering therapist, I stole a look at Alice and my breathing deepened with desire. She wore her professional forest green shorts but had taken off her button down and sported just her black sports bra. Her tanned collar bones were magnificent, even from where I stood, and I had a lightning bolt flashback to tracing them with my tongue. It wasn't helping that Alice was standing with one very muscular leg hiked up on the Ranger's ledge. The shade from her faded blue baseball cap hid most of her face, but I could still see Alice's high cheekbones and her ridiculously perfect, plump lips. She waved and smirked, knowing full well that she'd caught me staring.

"Watch out for that dock." Heidi pointed to a large hound pacing the walkway. She held onto Cosmo's collar as we slowly passed a compound with a burnt-out hummer squatting in the middle of the dirt lawn. The hound watched from his vantage point, giving a slow, steady growl that had us all on alert as Cosmo whined.

"So, has anyone received any more threats?" Heidi asked when we finally passed the menacing dog.

"Not me," Sutton said.

Mia checked her phone again and put it back in the holder by the console. A wasp zipped out of a crack in the plastic and Mia calmly waved it away before continuing. "Nope."

"I haven't either," I said. "How are we to the left? Any logs over there?" In the past, I'd been a very lazy boat person, preferring to snuggle in a blanket and lie back looking at the clouds as my dad drove our little party barge around the lake. But as I piloted my dad's boat now, with its squirrel-nibbled bimini top and otter-pooped on seats, I felt a little sense of pride creeping in, side-by-side with a tiny but growing sense of dread. Someone had just threatened to kill my guests. They were not exactly top tier people, more like middle-tier people. But they were *my* middle-tier people, and I didn't want them dead. Some of them had even grown on me. Like Virginia, with her spikey hair, always smiling despite a bad poison ivy rash on her face that was constantly covered in chalky Calamine lotion; or Abby, who annoyed me a bunch, but was so eager to help me with everything. And William, who was being so sweet, and Lena-Elise, good naturedly hobbling along on her crutches after being impaled.

"Hey," Alice shouted. "Turn right at the next bend and watch out for a log sticking up."

"Okay," I yelled back. I steered our boat while Sutton peered over the front, making sure that the water was deep enough to keep gliding through. I heard laughter and splashing through the thick foliage and turned right.

"James!" Mia cried.

James, sans most of his clothing, waved enthusiastically at Mia from where he stood in the water. "Hey baby!" He slurred. "Get in here." He clumsily walked toward the boat holding up Trig, who was pale and wobbly but smiling way too big for the circumstances.

Heidi jumped out of the boat and met up with Trig, who was holding up his arm with a nasty gash on it. "What happened?" she asked, carefully examining his cut.

Trig yelped in pain and cradled his injury. "Don't know." He pointed to a cliff up the hill. "Probably when I jumped off that."

"Okay then, boss." Alice rolled her eyes and nudged her Ranger closer to Trig. "Hey everybody, I'll take Trig to urgent care while you wrangle the rest of them. I can't even."

She and Heidi hoisted a giggling Trig up onto Alice's boat. I could not hear all of Trig's words through his incoherent yammering, but I could have sworn he slurred, "This got way out of hand."

Alice looked at me in my boat as I pulled it up beside hers, and I shrugged. "Remember, no involving police . . ." I raised my eyebrows in what I hoped was a firm and serious manner. Alice had no reason to trust me, but at least she trusted Mia and Sutton.

"I hurt my dick, Alice," Trig said as she held up a towel while he clumsily got into some clothes. "Wanna rub it and make it better?"

Alice patted her hip. "I have a taser, Trig. Want me to rub it with that?" She gave me a look and shook her head. "You're going to owe me for this," she said, trying not to laugh.

I smiled back at her from my boat which was now bobbing gently beside hers.

"Hey, Maggie, where's the ladder on this thing again?" Sutton banged on the side of my boat.

I pointed to a carpeted panel as Sutton approached.

"Come on, big guy." Sutton unfolded the boat ladder and reached out a hand to James who was clad in just his possum printed boxer shorts and making moony eyes at Mia. "Let's get you up here safe and sound," Sutton said, grunting as he boosted James up over the side of the carpeted swim dock.

After several unsuccessful attempts to cover him up with a towel, Mia handed James a fresh, undrugged bottle of water. "Drink," she commanded.

Meanwhile, Heidi, Sutton, and I made a plan to round up everyone and ferry them back to my house.

"Sutton, can you drive the Jablonskis' party barge, and Heidi, can you drive the other one?" My phone scared the bejeezus out of me vibrating in my pocket but luckily it was just Miss Vera complaining about the noise and not another scary warning or wiener portrait curtesy of Lance.

Heidi waded over to where Herschel, William, and Jenny were playing naked Frisbee and chatting to Virginia and Lena-Elise, who were clothed and sitting on one of the boats. "Come along children," Heidi yelled. "Time to go home."

A chorus of "awwwws" rose up amongst the happily unclothed, who trudged to their prospective boats. Whatever they'd taken, it clearly wasn't poison.

"Hey, where are Tamsin's parents?" I looked around, then Mia pointed to a naked couple writhing heatedly on a nearby dock. *Oh my.* "Tamsin," I yelled. "Can you, um, gather your parents?" She and Noah were too busy kissing in the water to heed me, however, as were Adrian and Abby. "Adrian and Abby, sorry to break things up, you two, but we gotta go," I called. They reluctantly waded to the boat now piloted by Sutton.

"Are we missing anyone?" Mia asked, trying to count everyone in various states of undress. "Stop drinking from that water bottle, William."

William waggled his eyebrows and downed the last of his Molly'ed up water.

"Hey, if everyone could please stop drinking their water, we'll get you fresh cold water at home," I said loud enough for even the forest creatures to hear. We were lucky that no one seemed sick from the drugs, but I didn't want to push it.

Sutton grabbed Mrs. Carlyon's bottle out of her hands. "No, you don't Mrs. C."

Mrs. Carlyon pouted and then attempted to pull her cigarette pants on over her head.

"Everyone ready?" I called out.

Sutton and Heidi gave a thumbs up and off we went creeping back through Bayou Bay and then into the broader lake back home.

James had fallen asleep with his head propped on Mia's lap, covered up with an old beach towel. She was rubbing his shoulder while looking through his phone. "I can't find any texts or emails that threaten anyone, so it seems that James is just an unfortunate civilian bystander," Mia whispered.

Everyone was so out of it we probably didn't have to worry about anyone calling the cops.

"What should we do?" I asked Mia.

She shielded her eyes as we cruised along, the sun peeking through the hole-filled bimini top that shaded my old boat. "It could all be a big joke if we don't think the janitor's death had anything to do with this and the dock carnage, I suppose."

"You mean like if someone in the wedding party is pulling obnoxious pranks and they don't want the police involved, so they scared us into not calling Mark?" I considered this. "A few questions," I said. "One, why would anyone in this group do this shit to each other? That makes zero sense. I know that these fools are not model citizens, but some of these 'pranks' could have gotten someone hurt or killed, not to mention shutting me down. And two, what if the janitor and the other stuff are connected?"

"He was our janitor when we were in school, so there *is* a connection." Mia shielded James' head from the blazing sun as he slept. "And I think we talked about this before, but maybe someone in the group doesn't want Tamsin and Noah to get married or at least wants to mess up their week."

I handed Mia a Gatorade and we both sipped one to stave off dehydration. "I've seen the wedding attendants grouping off, whispering to each other almost like they are making secret alliances like on Survivor."

"So, we could be dealing with more than one saboteur, even several groups," Mia said. "Again, why? What's the point of all this?" She swept her hand back indicating around to the boaters who were passed out in the boats.

"I just don't know. But if that text is serious, we can't tell the police, just in case," I said.

"So, we keep acting like all is normal," Mia said, tenderly patting James' tummy as he giggled in his sleep. "And at the same time, we need to watch out for nefarious activities and be ready for anything."

"Agreed." I slowed down as we approached my property and navigated toward the neighbors' dock. The other boats were going to unload at the Jablonskis'. "Plus," I continued, "I don't see any reason to be worried. Now that we know something strange is going on, we will be able to spot danger before it happens, right?"

No one answered me.

By now you're accustomed to just how seriously we take relaxation here at Henry's Point. Enjoy a peaceful rejuvenating afternoon siesta comfortable in the knowledge that all is well and there's so much more joy to come!

CHAPTER ELEVEN
Cat Squids and Mermaid Bears

I am a calm, serene, mermaid-bear. No, a horse-fish. "What am I again, Bri?" I lifted the blue and white checked dish towel off my eyes and looked around for Mia's daughter Brianna. She was busy covering my guests, who were sprawled out in the living room and kitchen, with various linens.

"You are a cat-squid, Aunt Maggie. Lie back down." I did what I was told, re-covering my face, and closing my eyes to take advantage of this gift of a few quiet minutes to try to calm my nervous system. Keeping secrets from Mark had always been funny, but now I wanted nothing more than to tell my policeman cousin Mark everything that had happened. I couldn't do that because I would be endangering everyone. For the time being, we decided that the best way to watch our little band of drugged wanderers was to let them rest here until the drugs wore off. Mia's dad had already planned to drop off Bri this afternoon, so somehow, this was all working out very nicely.

I forgot how much I loved my cozy living room as I nestled into the soft, off-white cushions I had stolen from the couch and lay down on the cool, worn oak floor. I pulled my dad's favorite micro fleece blanket to my chin, relaxing as I moved my hand over the material in slow circles. The afternoon sun glinted off the crystals and geodes that rested between stacks of books and my grandmother's tea set on the large coffee table. Cosmo and Noodle found a warm patch on a braided rug and were curled up beside my aunt's knitting basket, permanently housed by the fireplace.

"And I'm some sort of bird, right?" Herschel was lying beside me, our heads resting on a shared couch cushion and his big jock body lazing by the wicker basket of firewood. He was closest to a wall of shelves, and while we played the game with Bri, he was fiddling with my family's flotsam of hurricane lamps, framed pictures, candles, trolls, and books, lovingly collected over the years. Herschel held up a carved Norwegian troll with a butterfly perched on its nose, examining it closely.

"A rare elf-bird," I whispered, helping Bri out. I could tell she was getting annoyed with us for not following the rules of knowing which animal you were and staying quiet for "animal rest time." Bri had been playing this game of covering up her stuffies and any human who would agree to lie still for a few hours, for as long as I could remember. It was really sweet that Herschel volunteered.

"We've started calling it 'Morgue,'" Mia had said when I had walked into their family room one day and found it lined wall to wall with what looked like a few dozen doll autopsies.

"We could also go with 'Battlefield at Dawn,' but Morgue works too," I'd said, getting comfortable on their recliner for my turn. This was also around the time Bri got diagnosed with autism. When I was diagnosed in middle school, I was placed in a special pull-out class that emphasized sustained and painful eye-contact along with torturous non-parallel play. It wasn't enough to happily play with your own stuff side by side with a friend who was happily playing with their stuff. You had to demonstrate "taking turns" and "resist stimming" for praise, and since these things were nearly impossible for me, I rarely got good reviews from teachers. I don't know about the other kids in my class, but I had melted down at home every day after those difficult days in school, even if I held it together during class.

My hand went automatically to twirl my hair, bumping Herschel's head in the process. "Sorry," I mumbled as I pulled one of my curls straight, then with my thumb, middle and forefinger, twisted it up into a knot. I sighed contently, feeling a release of stress as I repeated this motion.

Happily, times were different now, and Mia and James were formidable advocates for Bri to be as comfortable and happy as she could in school. Bri had even taught me a few things that she learned in her life skills class, like how to set boundaries with people and where to stare if you need to look like you're making eye contact (bridge of nose, forehead). Speaking of foreheads . . . I turned slowly until I was on my side, facing Herschel's sunburnt face. "Hey," I whispered. "How are you feeling?"

Herschel opened one eye and smiled lazily. "Not my worst day, if I'm being honest." He glanced at his phone and quickly put it down again before Bri noticed. "Just checking in on the fam."

"Where are you guys at these days?"

"Little Rock. We have a few acres right outside the city." He lowered his voice when Virginia shushed them from her perch on the couch. "The kids are loving all the extra room to run around out back, and we even have a few chickens." Herschel chuckled, then cleared his throat. "Hey, I've never had sun stroke before. Wild, right?"

"Yeah," I nodded, wide-eyed. We told a little, okay a *big*, white lie to the wedding guests, that they had been collectively struck by a combination of dehydration and sun sickness.

"If anyone found out that they were drugged, they could call the cops, and you know what could happen then," Sutton had said, reminding us about the text threat.

So, we lied our asses off. Lena-Elise, a physician's assistant, was the only one we were really worried about exposing our deception, but she remained quiet, which reinforced the idea that she might have had something to do with this mess. The idea that mousy Lena-Elise somehow procured illegal substances and drugged her friends was beyond rational comprehension, but honestly, so had been much of these last few days. Heidi was still over at the Jablonskis' house keeping a close eye on the elder Carlyons, while we did our best to slowly revive our troops here in my home. "Just keep drinking the Gatorade and rest, okay?"

"No problem there." Herschel put his hands behind his head and closed his eyes, breathing deep and slow until a soft buzzing sound emitted from his mouth.

I was just starting to doze off myself when I felt a sharp tapping on my shoulder. Abby was on her stomach, arms and legs spread eagle over another living room couch cushion. From the corner of my eye, I had seen her scooting over to my side of the room, carefully avoiding sleeping frog-owls and ant-beavers all covered up with throw blankets, towels, sheets, and dish cloths.

"What?"

"Just, um, checking on things." Abby propped her head on her hands, elbows on the cushion. "How's your new job going?"

"You mean being a bed and breakfast host to a group with the worst luck ever? Super well, thank you for asking." I moved the dish towel from my face so I could see her. "And how is your job treating you?"

Abby swiped away a strand of hair that had escaped her blonde braids. "I have two new accounts, one for that new natural foods chain in the state." I had heard Abby was at a marketing firm, making good money and working tons of hours. "But I don't know how much longer I'll continue there," she said. "I've been doing some event coordinating for a while now, and I like being my own boss and setting my own hours." She absently rubbed one of her wrists while she talked, grimacing a bit.

"Besides weddings, what other stuff have you done?" I asked.

"A few anniversaries, some kids' birthday parties that blew my mind how much they cost. My commission was great on those! I even organized a birthday party for a seventeen-year-old dog that went over a whole weekend, including renting out an entire resort." Abby laughed softly, then was quiet for a second before talking again. "Speaking of events, when we all go out tonight, you, know, to the roller-skating thing?"

I pulled my blanket farther up my chest to counteract the air conditioning chill and turned to fully face Abby. "Yeah?"

Abby glanced around her before speaking, her eyes stopping at Bri. "Yeah, well, maybe leave the kids at home tonight."

I jerked upright, enlisting a groan from Herschel and a "tsk" from Bri. "What do you mean by that, Abby?" I hissed, signaling with a wave to Bri that I was settling back down. Sutton noticed the current drama going down and tried as best as he could to clandestinely roll from the kitchen over to us in his burrito blanket.

"Are you aware of something going on tonight, Abby? Anything you need to tell me?" I didn't want to ask her outright if she had also received a threatening text just in case she hadn't and would then blab to the police. But I was starting to jump at small noises and see bad people in shadows, so I needed to figure out who the actual "bad guys" were before I went fully paranoid. "Ow, Sutton." Sutton flopped his head on my legs, glaring up at Abby.

Abby shrugged her shoulders. "I just meant, like, with the heat index up and everything, I just don't want the kids to get heat stroke . . . like we did. We should all be careful." She leveled her gaze at me.

"Yes," I answered back, holding her icy stare. "Heat stroke, like you all had."

"What did we all do?" Herschel asked, groggy from sleep.

"Say, Hersch," Sutton poked his stomach. "Question for you, big guy: You can't think of any reason for us to be worried about tonight, can you?" I guessed either Sutton was thinking back to the conversation that we overheard earlier between Abby and Herschel, or he'd overheard us just now.

Herschel was suddenly very interested in his phone again. "I gotta bug out for a bit before tonight, to . . . get some presents for my kids," he said quickly.

I yanked Herschel's shorts as he got up to get his attention. "You didn't answer the question, Herschel."

He looked down at me with a sad but determined expression. "I . . . don't know anything about all that. Just stay in a group and try to watch out for each other, like you'd normally do," Herschel added after he averted his eyes from mine.

Magic awaits you at the Majestic
Springs' Town Square Disco Night!
Enjoy all the food, shopping, and
activities our international village has
to offer, but don't get too stuffed, because
come dark it's time to boogie.

CHAPTER TWELVE
I'll Stop the World and Skate with You

I finished off my second bowl of rice pudding from the Nordic Emporium food stand after demolishing the Mediterranean Café's four kebabs and a bowl of tzatziki. I must have worked up an appetite running around for my demanding guests, because I was suddenly ravenous all the time. Was this because of more movement, stress, or a pregnancy? I needed to take a few minutes out of this batty schedule and just take that damn test.

"Oh, thank goodness, a breeze." Mia lifted her face to get relief from the oppressive heat bearing down on us at our picnic table. "Why do we have to sit outside again?"

"The perfect vantage point to watch over the safety of our little charges, and so far, so boring." Sutton had also been engrossed in his rice pudding and I reached over and brushed a sticky white glob from his lip. "Thanks. Okay. Anyone seen anything suspect?"

We had decided to heed Abby's warning: Bri and Shaun should stay home with Mia's parents because of the dicey situation. Mia sat with us at our table, along with a much recovered and clothed James. Heidi and her boyfriend, TV-handsome ER doctor

Nic also joined us. Heidi had sworn him to secrecy so we would have reinforcements looking for any signs of foul play.

"I still don't know what we should be looking for." Nic pushed his sweaty, albeit still nicely coiffed black hair back from his forehead. "And I'm not happy about Alice being caught up in all this just because she's dating Jenny . . . but don't tell her that her big brother is worried about her, because you know how she will react to that."

"Alice knows what's up," I reassured him, while also reassuring myself. "She'll pick up on anything weird." I patted my perspiring head and face with my napkin, wincing when I touched my cut-up cheek. I had put Neosporin all over it and then caked on some make-up, hoping I'd done a better job than poor Virginia.

James pointed to himself. "Yeah, I'm not convinced we'll be able to stop the saboteurs." I glared at him, but he went on. "I did not notice someone slipping me a mickey in a bespoke water bottle that said, "Love is the flower: You've got to let it grow." He took a big bite of his sopapilla sundae. "At least the drug was out of my system by the time I woke up from my nap at Maggie's. How did the others do?"

"Same. After we got to the house, Bri got everyone to lie down and rest, and people slept about two to three hours before getting ready for Disco Night," I said. "No real lasting effects except a little dizziness and fatigue."

Nic adjusted the umbrella to shield us from the late afternoon sun that was surprisingly strong at this time of year. "Since this looks like a similar drug that I've seen lately in the hospital, I wasn't too worried about the long-term effects, but I still checked out the elder Carlyons, who, other than suffering from massive embarrassment, are just fine."

"But do you think that they also bought the 'acute dehydration and sun stroke' story?" James asked.

"Weirdly, yes," answered Sutton, swatting away a pesky fly. "It is not all that far-fetched, I guess, when you think about the heat, the sun, and all the throwing up the night before. Coupled by the fact that deep thinking doesn't seem to be a priority with these people."

I was still hungry and helped myself to a bite of James' sundae. "Sutton's right," I said. "Remember they also barfed all day while they did yoga with Yoga Pat and they just kept on going."

"I still can't get over the puke streaming through the grass," Mia said, taking a bite from James' sundae. "And Yoga Pat's t-shirt that said, 'Ya Gotta Earn It!' really made the scene," she laughed.

I took another bite, as James gave up eating and scooted his bowl over to me. "Hey, have we thought more about who would do this?" I asked. "And a follow up question: are they the same people who broke my dock, poisoned the food, changed the race route and mollied the water?"

"Don't forget dead Mr. Trembolt who was also Mr. Gustaffson," added Heidi.

Mia took a large swig of Sutton's coke. "Yeah, and I don't know how, but maybe Lena-Elise's fall was not so accidental?" She took another sip before Sutton wrested the plastic cup back from her. "I know it sounds kinda out there, but now I am scrutinizing and re-hashing everything from the last few days because I'm getting scared."

We were all silent for a minute, pondering. I kept my mouth shut about the fact that I had already thought about Lena-Elise's "accident" not being so accidental, because I didn't want a group freakout. "Let's do this in order," I said. "Was anyone standing by my dock before it fell apart?" I tried to think back on the last week, but everything was a blur of washing sheets, cleaning floors, and vacuuming.

"You missed the janitor," Sutton said, pouring some more coke from a pitcher at the table. "That was first."

"Ugh. Okay, all we know is that Mr. Gustaffson, according to Herschel, didn't know he was spotted fishing near my dock before he disguised himself as his alter ego, Mr. Trembolt for some reason, and stayed with me for a week for unknown reasons." I took the last bite of James' sundae, enjoying the sugary wonder of the fresh fried dough and chocolate with vanilla bean ice cream. "And he was acting weird, inspecting every room, crawling under the table. I thought he lost something."

Mia swiped Sutton's coke again and held her hand up in his face while swigging some down. "None of us saw anything in his room that explained how he got all those drugs in his system," she said. "Because remember, Regina the coroner didn't find any remnants of pills in his system."

Sutton gave up on getting his coke glass back from Mia and started drinking straight from a bottle of wine. "Nope. Moving on, I *do* remember Trig and Herschel were playing with Cosmo down by the dock late Monday morning."

"Oh yeah," Heidi said. She turned to Nic. "That's when I first got to the house with the trays of food, and when I had to help move the . . . you know, the janitor." She made a gesture that showed lifting something heavy, then drew her finger across her neck with an impressive imitation of a death gurgle.

"Adrian Venmoed someone in the Parks and Rec office, and then Adrian texted '**now we're even**,' whatever that means." James made air quotes as he said this.

Mia jumped in, excited. "*And* Adrian and Jenny were whisper-ing to each other at the restaurant, *not* eating. Come to think of it, Alice wasn't eating, either."

"My little sister Alice wouldn't have anything to do with this," Nic said, throwing his hands up in the air.

"Of course not," Mia said, patting his arm. "But someone, like her girlfriend, could have told her not to eat."

"Maybe," I said, then changed the subject from Alice so my heart would resume its natural rhythm. "And none of us saw Adrian sick that night. So, I suppose that Adrian could have been responsible for both the poison ivy debacle *and* the food mishap, but why?"

"And Jenny could have easily been involved with the food poisoning, but I don't remember Jenny or Adrian being near the bottles like Lena-Elise and Virginia were," Heidi said, fixing her lipstick with the help of her phone. Nic brushed her hair back and kissed her cheek, making Heidi giggle.

"Lena-Elise and Virginia were fully clothed on the party barges and didn't look out of it like the others," Sutton added. "And don't forget the weird conversation that Maggie and I overheard between Abby and Herschel."

"What did they say?" Nic asked.

"That '*they* didn't do it,' and something 'happening' tonight, which is why we're all here, making sure that no one gets hurt." I closed my eyes and leaned back, feeling the breeze on my face. I was so tired and full that I just wanted to hide in my cabin for a month, alone, without thinking about why a group of people would inflict such miserable pranks upon each other. I also was starting to get the jittery shakes, an effect of the extra prednisone and sugar. I just wanted to slip under my weighted blanket. "So not only do we have possible multiple saboteurs who have unknown motives, we also now have a person who may or may not be a threat."

"I think we have to take this person seriously, and as much as I'm freaked out about this, let's not tell Mark yet," Nic said.

He put on a fake smile and waved to a nice family passing by as if we weren't plotting crimes.

We all nodded our agreement and sat quietly for a few minutes, absorbed in our thoughts.

After a brief time when we all finished our food and drinks, Heidi gestured toward the huge white tent set up in the middle of the town square. "When does the roller-skating extravaganza start?" We all turned toward the crowd starting to gather at the skate rental booth, young and old people picking out their sizes and finding places to try their skates on. "Um, where is everyone?" Heidi stood up to get a better look.

"I see Tamsin and Noah looking just as ridiculous as we do," Sutton said, pointing to the couple walking arm in arm in matching striped bell bottoms and vests. The theme was the seventies, and everyone, including us, had to dress up. "But no sign of the rest of the wedding party."

"Great. Just great." I started to pick up our dishes so we could finish up fast and go looking for the missing links. "I am not enthused about walking around town in this." I gestured to my rainbow embossed tank top and a ratty looking jean skirt. My hair was huge and frazzled, channeling Janice Joplin's, and I was already itching to put it up.

"Oh, come on, this is definitely your decade." Mia laughed. Easy for her to say as she looked perfect in her bright pink shorts onesie that zipped way down, showing off her cleavage and the top of her pregnant belly. "Grab these cups." She handed the rest of the garbage to James, who wore a complementing purple track suit. As soon as the table was cleared, we were off.

"When you spot any of the wedding party, try to herd them to the rink as soon as possible so we have everyone in one place," I said, giving up on my hair and putting it up in a bun.

"I don't know if I want to walk beside Nic and Heidi," Sutton said loudly enough for them to hear. "Their sequins alone are blinding me."

The setting sun was still bright enough to reflect off Nic and Heidi's sequined tops and red hot pants, making them all shimmery as they strode through the groups of people wandering around the square. Pig-tailed Heidi sashayed her hips and linked her arm through Sutton's, who was clad in a baby blue crocheted vest and white bell bottoms. "You're stuck with us," Heidi said to Sutton, smiling.

Mia, James, and I walked to the opposite end of the square, then down a narrow side street, passing by the old patchouli scented herb shop that had been here for ages, its tattered awning rustling in the wind, and then under a limestone archway situated by the Mediterranean Café. Three people were sitting with their backs to us partially hidden by the stones. I put my finger up to my mouth to indicate that we should be quiet as we inched closer to Virginia, Trig, and Lena-Elise.

". . . Just two more days and then he said it would end, right?" Virginia said, nervously scratching her face.

"For the last time, Virginia." Lena-Elise pushed Virginia's hand away from her head. "Now that we know everyone got these texts, can't we go to the police . . ."

Trig, wearing yet another colorful baseball cap that now said, "Gargle My Balls," waved his bandaged arm in the air and then grimaced in pain. "No. You know we can't do that, or else everyone will know the truth about what happened."

The three of us all leaned in closer to the group, eyes wide and ears open.

"Maybe they *should*," Virginia said shrilly.

"*Keep your voice down.*" Lena-Elise looked around frantically as we flattened ourselves against the stone wall. "You know that would be bad for all of us, especially for . . ."

Lena-Elise's voice petered off and we couldn't see if she was pointing at anyone. James rolled his eyes in frustration and indicated with his head to sneak into the herb store for cover. But before we could get all the way in, we were spotted.

"What are you guys doing over here?" Trig barked.

"Uhh, looking for you all." I did some sort of jazz hands move because I had the social grace of an aardvark. "It's roller-skating time!" I hoped I didn't look completely bananas as I attempted to smile through the fear. I couldn't put my foot on it exactly, but certain people had started to give me the heebie-jeebies and Trig was up at the top of the list.

"That's right," Mia said, sounding equally unnerved. She moved forward, cautiously sliding by Trig and grabbing Lena-Elise's and Virginia's hands. "Let's go."

James stepped in between us and Trig, who shrugged and started walking back to the town square.

Ten minutes later we were the last people in the wedding group to put on our rental skates and get out on the skating floor. "I think we all safely made it, yeah?" I asked, holding hands with Sutton as we skated along by the wall. My head swam with mild dizziness, probably from all the heat and the stress and whatnot. Surely that was all. I should be more watchful of my fluid intake, which my doctors were always on my case about.

"Seems so," Sutton answered. "Hey, I wonder if I can still do 'shoot the duck?'"

I shrugged and grabbed the wall while Sutton glided past me going down on one leg, his butt almost touching the floor as his other leg shot out like a stick. I laughed as he fist-pumped the air and shouted, "I'm doing it!" Then frantically called for someone to help him get back up.

James raced around me and scooped Sutton up by his armpits, and then they hooked arms and danced to Donna Summer's "Hot Stuff." I was too busy watching everyone boogie to notice that Alice had scooted up next to me until she said my name.

I startled.

"Hey," Alice said, looking too adorable in denim cut offs and a rainbow t-shirt like mine. She started to say something else when the DJ announced that it was a special couples skate and for everyone to find a partner. Alice pointed to me, then to the skating floor.

I wasn't a good skater, and I clutched the wall for support. "Are you sure that Jenny would be okay with this?" I asked.

Alice's eyebrows shot up and she nodded, reaching her hand out to me and waiting.

I hesitated, feeling very fine exactly where I was at my safety wall and not wanting to let go.

Alice moved a little closer to me and I could feel her breath tickling my neck as she said, "Don't you remember when we used to do this? I never let you fall."

I took a breath and let go of the wall, briefly suspended in space before Alice took both my hands in hers and the world stabilized. Alice expertly skated backwards while holding me up as I skated forwards. Her hands felt so natural on my hips, and I tried not to strangle her as I wrapped my arms around her neck for balance. Alice still smelled of baby powder deodorant and clean sweat. I tried not to be obvious when I inhaled deeply as we glided—Alice glided; I was doing more of a Clydesdale hop—through the other people skating in pairs.

"In all these years, you never learned how to skate properly up north?"

Wow. We were actually talking about real things. "No," I said. "College and grad school kept me so busy, and Lance . . ." Shit. I said "Lance." I tripped and Alice shot one arm around my back and the other gripped my hip tighter preventing me from falling.

Karen Carpenter's "Top of the World" started playing over the tinny old speakers. The overhead lights went dark, replaced by colored lights shining on a large disco ball that slowly began spinning around to the music, reflecting a glittering rainbow pattern all around the skating rink. Alice was a few inches taller than me, and she looked down into my eyes as Karen sang about "such a feeling coming over."

"It's been over a decade, you know," Alice said, steering me around the corner. "And from what I've heard, he's completely out of your life."

"Absolutely out of my life," I said, crossing my fingers behind her back. I snaked my arms around her neck tighter and rested my head on her shoulder. This gift was not going to last, and I was going to take full advantage of my stolen time with Alice, even if I had to lie my ass off.

Alice expertly steered us around a curve, still keeping a firm grip on me. "I'm glad to hear it. I'll never understand why you chose him over me, but that's water under the bridge now."

"I'm sorry. For everything." More than several excuses were swirling in my mind: that I was young, it was a time to explore my sexuality, I was scared to be hurt, I was scared to be dropped by Alice for a cuter, not as weird, funnier girl so I hurried up and sabotaged my relationship before she could. I didn't mean to hurt anyone. But none of that mattered, because I'd hurt Alice.

"Yeah, you fucked up," Alice whispered into my ear. "And honestly, I'm still pissed." Alice leaned back so that I was looking at her again. "I will never get out of my mind when Tamsin told me about you having sex with Lance, *in front of everyone on that dock.*"

I cringed when Alice's voice rose and averted my eyes. "I was going to tell you right when I got back from the conference, but . . ." I shook my head. Again, I had no excuse.

After skating in silence for a while, Alice started singing along with Karen Carpenter about "love found" and it being "the nearest thing to heaven." Alice always had a beautiful voice, earning first chair alto at State and nabbing the best solos in choir. I was thinking about her and Sutton singing "Need You Now" at the swing choir finals when she surprised me by grasping a stray curl and tucking it behind my ear.

An electric current ran from my head to my lower abdomen. I tightened my grip around her neck, pushing us into each other. She started to massage my upper back, and I sighed along to the tingling in my nether regions as her hand dropped lower down my spine, right before I suddenly screeched in white-hot pain, toppling us both.

It's a Disco Party on wheels! Glitter, skates, and hotpants spell Romance! Join us at the skating rink to celebrate Tamsin and Noah's nuptials. Who knows—maybe you'll find your true love dancing under the disco ball!

DISCO

CHAPTER THIRTEEN
They Came from Everywhere and Nowhere

"Something stabbed me," I yelped, grabbing my arm in pain. People were screaming all around me, but I couldn't see anything through the strobe lights that blinded me whenever I tried to open my eyes. I got separated from Alice and someone bashed into me before they went flying into the wooden safety wall. I tried to reach the wall by inching forward on my skates, but I was knocked to the floor and landed hard on my side. Then I was being pulled across the wood while I protected my head from skates and fleeing bodies. I peeked through my fingers when I stopped moving and saw Alice above me, frantically checking my abdomen and head for injuries.

"Are you okay?" she demanded.

"I'm okay, but I think I got stabbed?"

No one had turned off The Carpenters, so "Top of the World" was still blasting over the speakers while smoke from the dry ice machine filled the tented rink area. "You were stung. Are you allergic?" Alice was already looking at my arm, her hair sticking out in short pigtails that contrasted dramatically with her serious expression. "Can you breathe?" She grabbed my face and poked my lips. "Open your mouth." All the commotion around us seemed to stop as Alice focused on my face.

"Aaahhh." I stuck out my tongue and she declared it not swollen, so no anaphylactic shock for me. Then I saw the source of the humming noise coming out of the still turning, flashing, disco ball. A large, angry swarm of insects was flying from it and attacking the roller skaters young and old, all in their seventies garb. "*Holy Shit.*" I looked at Alice. "There was a fucking beehive in the disco ball."

Alice squinted her eyes. "Those aren't bees; they're yellow jackets—way more aggressive."

"Maggie!" Sutton helped me up while Alice ran to help a crying child desperately holding onto the wall. "Are you hurt?"

Sutton had two huge red welts on his face. "I'm okay, but are you allergic?" I looked closely at his lips to see if they were puffing up.

"No, just sensitive. I'll take some Benadryl and I'll be fine." He looked me over like Alice had. "I tried to get to you sooner, but some asshole, I think it was Trig, ran me over to get out of here."

Just then Mia and James found us on the bench, and we checked each other over, counting stings and anticipating what would turn into bruises. A lot of people were limping around us, cradling arms and heads. An ambulance could be heard in the distance moving toward us. Someone was yelling for help, but I could not see where. We all looked around until James pointed and we ran over to Lena-Elise on the ground with William.

"I don't think he's breathing!" she shrieked, cradling William's head in her lap. Their matching sequined outfits sparkled under the city lantern lights, confusing the gravity of the situation.

"Shit, he must be allergic. Look at his face." I yelled over the music and the screeching. "*Anyone got an EpiPen?*" I screamed into the crowd. William's puffy lips were turning blue, his face so swollen I could barely see his eyes. My god, these asshats and their ridiculous pranks had gone too far. William was a innocent bystander in all of this and now he could die.

Adrian ran over to us and threw an EpiPen at Nic who knelt beside William, flicked the cap off and stabbed him in his thigh. "Hold on William, help is on the way." He put his head down to listen for breathing as we all backed up to let the EMTs through. Nic gave a thumbs up and made room for William to be loaded onto a stretcher and into the ambulance.

"Oh shit, that was close," Heidi said as we watched two ambulances leave the town square. "Where'd you find the EpiPen, Adrian?" She asked, then looked at them closer. "Fuck, you're bleeding." She grabbed some napkins from her purse and held them to Adrian's leg.

Adrian's hair was falling out of their braid, and their shorts had a big rip at the sight of a jagged red scratch on their leg. "It's not deep. I checked. Nothing major." Adrian leaned back on the bench. "Weirdly enough, I found the unused EpiPen by a stool where we put on our roller skates. I was running around trying to find its owner when I heard you."

"Well, that was more than lucky," I said. "I wonder who lost it." I looked around. "Anyone else have to go to the ER?" I asked. A group of locals who kept bees attempted to secure the disco ball, while the remaining wedding party congregated at the picnic tables, drinking heavily by the looks of it.

"No one else went to the hospital," said Mia, resting her head on James' shoulder. She had been in the bathroom when all this went down, thank goodness, so she wasn't hurt. "We're gonna pick up the kids and head home. Can we give you a lift, Heidi?"

Heidi nodded, and the three of them walked off to their car, James giving us a worried wave before they turned the corner.

As Sutton, Adrian, and I walked towards our group, Virginia signaled to us while holding an icepack to her face. "I don't know where the poison ivy rash ends and the stings begin," she lamented, showing us her red, rashy skin. She put the ice pack back on and took a large swig of wine right out of the bottle. "Don't worry, I took some antihistamines for the swelling."

"Hey," I grabbed the almost empty bottle from her tight grip. "Let's everyone go home and watch some Veronica Mars."

"Can we watch Buffy like we used to in high school?" Herschel asked. "We finished the Mars movies last night."

Herschel's eyes were red and I wondered if the bee keepers' smoke had gotten to him. "Yeah, sure," I said, side-eying Herschel. He'd said that there was going to be "something happening tonight," but he had stings all over and his knee was wrapped up. Would he have done this if he had known that he was going to suffer too? I was too tired to think about it and my hip was starting to hurt. "Come on, my group," I signaled, holding my keys in the air. "Follow me."

I head counted everyone as they stumbled into the van. "Hey," I said after I climbed into the passenger seat and twisted around to count again. "We're missing Trig." Lena-Elise had gone with William in the ambulance but everyone else should have been here.

Everyone looked around and shrugged. Well, he could find his own way home, I thought. I leaned back into the seat and slept while Sutton drove us home, but not before I overheard a drunk Virginia loudly whispering to Adrian, "Things could easily get worse."

"Do you remember when we used to watch Buffy at our sleepovers and you used to make us re-enact the fight scenes, Maggie?" Abby asked, handing over a big bowl of popcorn. "What was that episode that had you and Tamsin pretend to go at each other?"

We were huddled together on the couch, Adrian and Abby on either side of me, all of us covered in fleece blankets with the air conditioning blasting. Sutton was curled up on the easy chair, while Virginia and Herschel were lying down on the area rug in front of the TV and fireplace. Virginia rested her head on

Herschel's belly like he was a golden retriever, and Herschel's head rested on a big soft blue pillow shaped like a whale, one of Bri's favorites. We all had ice packs on our stings and bruises and had changed into our softest pajamas.

I thought for a moment before answering Abby, slowly chewing my popcorn. I had my own memories of watching my favorite show with my friends during sleepovers. They made fun of me because I memorized every line of "Buffy the Vampire Slayer," and I recited them verbatim along with the characters. This was apparently annoying as hell to the rest of the slumber party. But reciting lines was a fantastic way for me to calm myself and regulate my emotions, which had been all over the place during puberty. My "weirdness," which now I knew was just me being my autistic self, had been in check until my hormones started raging, and then I was fair game for Tamsin and her minions. They did humor me by acting out scenes while I "directed," and we actually had some fun doing it. Tamsin was a particularly good Faith to my Buffy from the Graduation Day episodes, Parts One and Two. Instead of bringing up any complicated memories, I answered Abby with a simple, "Yes, I do remember," and a smile.

"I think you need more Neosporin on your cuts." Adrian was studying my sliced-up face from my incident with the pine tree and rummaging through the first aid supplies and ointments that we had accumulated over the week. "Here." Adrian handed me an antibacterial tube and an antiseptic wipe.

"I'll take some Calamine." Virginia held out her hand.

Abby sat up and hunted around in the bin as Adrian gave Virginia the lotion. "I thought we had some Cortisone cream somewhere?"

"I got it." Sutton tossed the tube to Abby, who caught it and rubbed the medicine liberally on her face and arms.

"Jeez Abby, how many stings did you get?" Adrian asked, concern on their face.

"Oh, five at last count." She shrugged.

I looked around at this beaten down group who were covered in bruises, swollen lumps, bandages, and smeared in white chalky lotions. As I applied first aid to my own face, I realized that now was the time for honesty before we all got killed. "So, when are we going to talk about the elephant in the room?"

"I don't know what . . ." Virginia began.

Adrian put a hand up to Virginia's haughty face. "Stuff it, Virginia, she knows."

"What *do* you know, Maggie?" Abby asked, then pointed to Sutton perched in his chair, eyes wide and mouth slightly open. "And I suppose he knows what you know?" She leaned away from me on the couch to get a good look at my face.

"Well, I know that y'all are getting very hurt this week and that *somehow*, for some asinine reason, y'all are responsible for it." I looked around at their puffed up, scratched, black and blue faces. Their *guilty* faces. "What's really going on?" I asked.

Adrian, Herschel, Abby, and Virginia exchanged heated looks, communicating silently with raised eyebrows, and pointing fingers. "Fine." Adrian said. "We're being blackmailed." Adrian leaned back onto the couch and covered their eyes with their hands.

"You can't tell her anything more!" Abby yelled, her eyes darting back and forth from me to everyone else. "We were warned if *anyone* finds out."

"Abby, for fuck's sake!" I needed space, so I stood up and headed out of the family room to my kitchen stool, putting distance between me and the others. "You people aren't exactly *Mission Impossible* operatives; it hasn't been hard to figure out who has been behind these 'accidents.'" I made air quotes as I sat on my dad's old stool behind the island. "Herschel, earlier you said something was going to happen tonight. How *exactly* did you get a hive in the disco ball?"

Herschel looked miserable and mumbled something about working at a beehive farm every summer in high school. "So, this morning after I got the blackmail email instructing me, I snuck out, calmed the hive with smoke and put it into the disco ball. Then I transported it in my truck to the square, where I switched out the town's disco ball for mine." Herschel dropped his head in his hands. "My son is allergic to peanuts, so I had an extra epi-pen in my bag, and I left it out at the roller rink just in case anyone was allergic to bees, even though they aren't known to be super aggressive. I just wanted to scare people." He blew out a deep shaky breath and continued: "Only I didn't realize that a swarm of aggressive yellowjackets had taken over the hive." He looked around the group pleadingly for understanding. "I never thought anyone would get hurt."

"Number one," Sutton said with a shiver, "I didn't know that could happen with bees and that's terrifying. Number two, you DO know what a horrible person you are, right, Hersch?" he asked.

Herschel nodded. "I didn't have a choice! The email said that I would lose my job, and then my family would lose their new home. I couldn't do that to my wife and kids."

Sutton looked around the room and pointed to Adrian, "We think *you* are behind the 5K route change."

Virginia scratched her mangled face and glared at Adrian as Adrian nodded yes, face still hidden in their hands. "My job was in jeopardy. One call and I would have gotten fired."

"And the food poisoning too?" I asked, remembering how jumpy Adrian had been in the hallway, clutching onto their bag before the dinner, and how they did not seem to get sick.

Adrian sat up and wiped their wet face. "I wasn't the main culprit, but I helped, when someone asked."

"Jenny, right?" Sutton said and Adrian nodded again, eyes downcast. "How did you do it?"

"Yes," Adrian admitted. "Jenny knows the herbalist in town; you know the one with the tiny store by the stone arch? Anyway, I picked up something called *ipecacuanha* from her, and Jenny and I sprinkled dried bits of the plant in the potato salad, and no one noticed because it looked just like seasoning." Adrian was getting the full glare from everyone who had hurled their dinner and scratched literal holes in their bodies from the poison ivy. Adrian scrunched down in the couch pillows. "I'm sorry, but I had no choice. You all know that."

Sutton then turned to Virginia. "Don't be so mad at Adrian, when you were the one who drugged everyone, weren't you?"

It was Virginia's turn to look guilty. "Lena-Elise got the pills this morning after we received that threatening email, and I still don't know from where. I just helped distribute." She rubbed some more anti-itch lotion on her arms and face, then finished off a bottle of wine. "And we all know what would have happened if we didn't do exactly what he said."

That piqued my interest. "*Who* said? Who's been telling you to do these things?"

The wedding attendants looked at each other before speaking.

"Carl Gleet," Abby finally admitted, looking around nervously, as if she would be struck down for uttering his name.

"Carl? Our classmate who drove off the bridge in front of us fourteen years ago . . . and *died*?" Sutton asked. "*That* Carl?"

"They never found the body, you know," Virginia said, pulling the Christmas patterned fleece tightly around her.

I cleared my throat, trying to get my mind around all this.

"So, you think that Carl, the *same* Carl that we all saw go careening into the lake on graduation night, is now communing with you from his watery grave? By *email*?" I started to laugh.

Cosmo sensed my rising hysteria and put his front paws on my lap and licked my hands.

"Again, no body was found . . ." Abby's voice petered off and she inhaled her vape multiple times while squishing my poor squirming cat Noodle in a hug.

"Um, okay." Sutton looked at me, eyebrows raised, like he was unsure how to continue. I gave him a go-ahead gesture since I was simply unable to think of what to say. "Even if Carl Gleet somehow managed to survive the car wreck and being submerged in a deep, cold, murky lake," Sutton paused to make sure that he had everyone's attention. "You think that for fourteen years he has laid low, not contacting his family or friends, not contacting *anybody*, until he decided to blackmail you all now, during Tamsin's and Noah's wedding week?" When the reaction from every single person in the group was shrugged shoulders, he went on. "And what is he blackmailing you with?"

Adrian put their hand up to speak. "Let's just say that a long time ago a group of us made a bad decision, and then one person in our group made an even worse decision that we believe contributed to Carl's . . . whatever happened to Carl, which I still can't figure out."

"How do you know that Carl is the one blackmailing you?" I asked. "Could it be someone in your group who knew what happened that just wants to mess with you for whatever reason?" I had so many questions, like how anyone could rationally think that we were living the plot of "I Know What You Did Last Summer," for one. But I thought I should just start with the obvious ones.

Herschel and Abby exchanged nervous glances.

"Out with it," Sutton said, leaning forward.

"So, a few months ago, we were all drinking at a bar after the engagement party, and Virginia," Herschel side-eyed Virginia as he said this, "said she felt so guilty about Carl and wanted to do something for the family, maybe on the anniversary. Trig got totally mad and started threatening us that if we did not keep our mouths shut, we would be sorry."

Abby jumped in. "He was slamming his fist on the table, saying that if we had a guilty conscience, to go see a priest or a shrink and get over it, because he would be the one who got into the most trouble if word got out what had happened."

Adrian had been fixing themselves a sandwich beside me, handing me pieces of cheese as they went. "So, we all promised that we would keep our mouths shut, and nothing more happened until a few weeks ago, when we all got emails from Carl Gleet, saying that we had to do these awful things here, or he would tell everyone what we did. We all had to wait to get our instructions until the day before." Adrian took a bite of their sandwich, watching Buffy on mute. "Possibly the emails could be from Trig, even though they were signed Carl, I suppose. But why would Trig want us to hurt each other?"

I nibbled on a hunk of muenster cheese, thinking everything through. "And you won't tell us this terrible thing you did?" Abby, Adrian, Herschel, and Virginia all shook their heads emphatically no. "I see. Bottom line, you gotta knock this shit off, because someone could have died this week. Nothing you did all those years ago could be as bad as multiple innocent people dying today, right?"

"But how do we manage this?" Abby asked. "I'm supposed to fuck up our haunted hotel tour at The Majestic tomorrow night. I've already paid off the workers."

And just like that, we were in cahoots.

"Well," I said, "Now that we know what the left hand is doing . . ."

"We can fake it so *whoever* is blackmailing us will think the plan is still on." Virginia finished my thought perfectly.

The rest of the group nodded. This plan could work and carry us to the wedding and my payday if we got everyone on board. And, not that this was the most *important* reason, but if we could keep this little group going until the wedding was over, I might still get my bonus even after everything that had happened.

"We need to let the others know, including Lena-Elise, and make sure she's not instructed to do anything we don't know about. Has anyone been in touch with her and William?" Sutton asked.

Abby jumped up from the couch, yawning. "I just got a text back from her. William is sleeping in his hospital bed and Lena-Elise got the little couch made up in the room to stay with him. She has her meds, including her sleeping pills, so she just took one to sleep, and they should be back mid-morning tomorrow." Abby then picked up Noodle to claim him for the night.

"Just make sure that she doesn't have dynamite in her purse or anything for tomorrow morning's scavenger hunt," I said as everyone started to file upstairs to bed. "Hey, where the hell is Trig?"

"My guess is that he's staying over with the waitress from the Black Forest Inn that he was flirting with the other night," Herschel yelled down before he got all the way to his room.

"He can text you if he needs to get in the house, cuz I'm locking the door," I said, finishing off the last pieces of popcorn at the bottom of the bowl.

When Sutton and I were alone in the kitchen I beckoned him close. "We *have* to talk to Mark tomorrow," I said. "William almost died, and others could have too." I vigorously rubbed my forehead to make my blossoming headache go away. "But do you think there's a way for Mark to be involved where I still get the bonus and keep my place?" I felt horrible even asking that out loud, but after what happened with Alice tonight, maybe there was a smidgen of hope?

Sutton put his arm around me as we walked to the back door, shutting the lights off as we went. "I don't know. But for now, let's grab a few hours of sleep."

I had put Cosmo on a leash because earlier I didn't want him to rush off chasing possums and deer in the area. He was pulling hard and growling, trying to get to whatever was in the dense forest behind my house. "Come on, Cosmo. There's nothing out there." I yanked on his leash, and we followed the light of the lantern shining above my log cabin door.

Blessings abound as old friends reconnect!
Join us for a delicious brunch, catered
by our favorite café owner, Heidi.
Sit back, sip juice and mimosas and
share your memories and your dreams
for futures filled with love, family,
connection, and warmth.

CHAPTER FOURTEEN
Guess Who's Coming to Brunch?

Two servers didn't bother to show up, so Mia and I threw on aprons and helped Heidi with breakfast *al fresco* while Sutton was doling out mimosas and screwdrivers behind a makeshift bar on my porch. For the hundredth, millionth time, I wondered how on earth I was going to pay back my friends for all their free labor. Fingers crossed that the Carlyons would feel generous after their daughter's wedding and show that in their bonus to me, which I then could share with Mia, James, and Sutton.

Noah looked resplendent in a white button-down shirt open at the neck and salmon-colored shorts. They pulled me aside after I served a basket of fresh croissants and morning buns. "I know this week has been bananas," Noah said, "but I just wanted to thank you for all of your help."

Was Noah really in the dark about everything? They sure looked like the right combination of concern and innocence, which seemed kind of guilty all of a sudden. "Oh, sure," I stammered, looking as uncomfortable as I sounded. When I didn't know someone's true motivations, I could not act naturally at all.

Noah lightly squeezed my arm and said, "I know how much you're doing for everyone, and it's not going unnoticed." Noah smiled their brilliant smile and walked back to their table, humming the Carpenters' tune from last night.

My phone buzzed. Miss Vera texting me, *again*. She may be elderly, but she sure knew her way around a phone.

Miss Vera: **Tell your guests not to speed by my house in the middle of the night, it upsets Richard greatly!**

Richard was Miss Vera's African gray parrot whose cage hung in front of her giant picture window that faced the road.

Me: **Hi Miss Vera. My guests were all home with me at a decent hour. Not sure who drove by, but it wasn't them. hope Richard is OKAYY**

Miss Vera: **I am sure it was one of your people. We are WATCHING. From Vera**

Before I could read more from Miss Vera, my cousin Mark appeared by my side. A jolt of fear ran up and down my body; Mark could make or break my home ownership and business if he lost faith in me.

"Got your message," he said, voice lowered. I had texted him to come to the house.

"Got time to talk after I finish serving brunch?" I asked, shielding my eyes from the sun as I looked up at his tired face. "Did you get any sleep?"

Mark, who had the same freckled complexion as me, took off his worn baseball cap and pushed back his curly auburn hair before putting it back on. "Not really. By the time I got back from the roller rink fiasco, I found a text informing me of some *things* that have been going on this week." Mark raised his eyebrows in an accusing way. "Which I think you know all about."

Shit what did he know? Who told him? I wondered. A *very risky move since we were warned someone would die if we called the cops.*

I searched my cousin's angry face and knew I had to come clean despite the warning. "I was going to tell you everything this morning, I promise," I said as I crossed my fingers behind me (wow, I was doing this a lot lately). I'd planned to tell him only the parts that would allow me to keep this week going as smoothly as possible. But now someone had come forward, muddying the waters.

"Go sit in the shade and get cooled off, and I'll meet you as soon as I can, okay?" I asked.   Mark nodded and wandered over to a table that gave him a perfect view of the party.

"Tamsin's table needs a fresh pitcher of ice water," Heidi said as she zoomed by, looking very professional in her caterer's ankle length white slacks and a blue button down. "And Abby said they were running low on fruit." Heidi rolled her eyes and smiled. She knew as well as I did that the fruit bowl was more than likely still full.

"On it," I said, turning around to head back inside. Mia and I were not dressed up, but both of us looked respectable in khaki shorts and black tops, our hair up in buns. "Gimme some," I commanded as I grabbed the mimosa Sutton was drinking and took a sip. *Shit! My maybe-baby!* I immediately spit the mimosa back into Sutton's glass, faking a choking sound. He grimaced and dumped the drink into a potted geranium plant. *What a time not to be able to drink alcohol,* I thought as I surveyed the seemingly happy group situated outside at tables draped in white linen and topped with gorgeous floral arrangements. Still, denial and compartmentalization were my strong suits so I could just take the damn pregnancy test later.

"I still don't get it," Sutton said as he unwrapped a fruit tray while I filled up a pitcher of water.

"What?"

"Them." He gestured to the group outside. "Laughing, smiling, eating, like they all don't have a care in the world."

"I was just having the same thought. They seem to be very good at faking," I said. "Speaking of fakes, did Trig ever come back last night?" I squinted to try and see if Trig was sitting at one of the tables. "Oh, there's William and Lena-Elise next to Noah's parents. When did they get here?"

Sutton was quiet while looking out the window, distracted. "I don't see Trig. It is not like he's my favorite person in the world." Sutton popped a cantaloupe cube in his mouth. "I mean, don't get me wrong, he was certainly good for a one-night stand, but

I'm worried about him even though I'm sure he was the one who pushed me down at the roller rink."

I was watching a very pale William sip his coffee while Lena-Elise hobbled over to another table on her crutches. I could see people's red welt stings from way back here, and a few people now had casts on their arms or legs. I needed to corner Abby to make sure that no one would get hurt tonight.

"Hey, did you hear me?" Sutton asked, looking at me.

"Yeah, sorry. I was thinking about Abby. We need to check in with her."

"And Mark. Have you called him yet?"

I dropped some more ice cubes in the water pitcher. "Oh yeah. I just saw him outside and he told me that someone had *already* informed him of all the goings-on."

Sutton stopped chewing for a moment, then swallowed his fruit. "Really. Color me surprised. Everyone seemed *very* tight-lipped last night."

"Right? Why come forward now when we had planned to get through the week? I mean, they didn't know we were going to tattle to Mark, but still."

"Who knows. I'm still worried about Trig," Sutton said.

"If Trig is still missing, we'll tell him about that too, okay?"

Sutton seemed satisfied with that answer and went back to his bartender duties while I brought out water and more fruit.

"Thanks Maggie," Abby said, as she walked toward me. "But we're done eating, so you can bring all that back to the kitchen."

I arranged my face into what I hoped was an acceptable expression and not one that exuded a strong pissed off vibe.

"Hey," Abby lowered her voice when she came close. "Do you have something that works on all over pain?" She rubbed her temple and said, "Not just my head, though that hurts too, but like, my whole body hurts, and I know you deal with this sort of thing a lot."

I was indeed a sort of pain connoisseur after dealing with years of autoimmune disease before I had a diagnosis. Doctors chalked my symptoms up to stress, anxiety, needing to lose weight, needing to have a child—you name it—before I was finally diagnosed and put on the right meds. The not knowing before the diagnosis was the hardest part because everyone just treated me like I couldn't handle things.

"I've got some Tylenol and ibuprofen in the house if you think one of those would help," I offered, pointing in the direction of the sliding door.

Abby looked a bit distressed as she answered, rubbing her wrists. "Yeah, I've tried them, but maybe they'll work today. Thank you," she said, giving me a fleeting smile. "My doctor says I just need to get more sleep because I'm too young to have arthritis."

"No problem, Abby." I gave her a sympathetic pat. "Now, are y'all getting ready for the scavenger hunt?"

Tamsin and Noah and their parents had been out early making sure that everything was in place for the hunt. Most things on the list were items that one would find on my land, like feathers, milky quartz, pinecones, and blueberries, but a few special things were hidden.

"Everything is set!" Abby said, regaining her pageant face, her hair in perfect curls cascading down her back, her smile seeming to be tugged up by unseen forces.

"And is everything set for tonight?" I said in a lower voice, making her smile turn into a scowl in a millisecond.

"Being taken care of as we speak. When the actors come at us with real surgical equipment . . ."

"What now?"

"During the reenactment of the lobotomies." Abby flung up her hands in frustration. "You know, the part of the tour when the guests lie down on the gurneys in the creepy old surgical theatre and the fake doctors pretend to do surgeries?"

"Wait. I'm sorry but someone is *bound* to get hurt with this plan." My voice rose and caught the attention of a few people walking by.

"Oh no!" Abby shriek-whispered, pulling me around the side of the house. "I was just going to scare us with the real instruments while we were tied down and then use a lot of fake blood to make people think we got operated on or whatever." Abby rushed on when she saw my face. "But I'm arranging it where only we will be picked as volunteers to be strapped down, so we won't really be scared." She laughed weakly, clearly understanding how atrocious it all sounded. "It'll work, dammit. It will be fun. Now I gotta go find some feathers."

I woke up this morning in a sweat thinking about all the ways this morning could be sabotaged, but it looked like we were going to make it through without incident. *Thank god,* I thought as Abby stormed off clutching onto her scavenger hunt list.

I was about to head back to the house when I noticed someone moving about down by my cabin. Curious, I handed off the fruit bowl at the bartending station and ignored Sutton's protests as I walked down the slope towards the log cabin, following the movement on the other side of the sea wall. Cosmo's head rose from a bush he was inspecting and trotted after me and ran ahead once he saw Alice.

"Alice, what are you doing?"

Alice, clad in gray cargo pants and a forest green t-shirt, was crouched down by the edge of the lake. "Look at this," she said. She pointed to a two-foot-wide section of packed dirt that looked like someone had made a mud slide from the edge of the trees into the lake.

"You know what made this, right?" Alice asked. "This looks old, and the animal is long gone as far as I can tell."

From diligently watching animal shows with my grandma, I knew exactly what kind of big reptile Alice was referring to. My stomach grew queasy as I looked closer and saw that something much bigger than a human must have made those slide tracks. I nodded as I glanced around, hoping Alice was right that whatever made this, probably an alligator, was, in fact, long gone. The happy sounds of people yelling as they conducted the scavenger hunt filled my ears, and I was going to ask Alice about it when I spied a flash of white floating in the lake under some brush. Bending down, I pulled away a branch.

"Alice," I said in my calmest voice while gripping tight onto Cosmo's collar so he wouldn't jump in the water. "Get up here. Now."

Alice knew me well enough to be alarmed. She rushed to me, her eyes widening when she caught sight of the black and white piece of cloth. "What's that?" She asked as she scanned the underbrush sticking out of the water. Before I could answer, she grabbed a stick and pushed at the floating branches, making a squelching sound. "Oh, shit," she said. "Is that—?"

I couldn't answer, too busy gagging. There, floating before us amongst the flotsam, was Trig's leg, still bedecked in the remnants of his black and white hot pants from yesterday, bloated and jagged edged at the thigh like it had been bitten or gnawed on repeatedly.

"I take it this wasn't on the scavenger hunt list." Alice, stoic though pale, stood on the sea wall, poking at Trig's leg with her stick.

"Stop that," I said, slapping her arm. *So much for an incident free day.* Immediately I felt guilty thinking of myself when our classmate (part of our classmate?) was drifting along right by my little cabin. *Right by where I sleep, and where Cosmo was barking and running around last night.* But maybe this was an isolated incident and had nothing to do with me? "Do you think he just got drunk and fell in? And then whatever got him is long gone?" I asked. My voice cracked and I leaned on a large oak tree for support. I felt like I was in a dream, floating along, mildly curious at my surroundings, when a little voice inside me was trying to shout "DANGER."

Alice was already on her phone, probably texting her coworkers at Game and Fish. She glanced at the leg and said, "I don't know what happened here, but those teeth marks on that leg are definitely from a gator. But what I can't figure out is how an alligator got here to this busy cove?" She turned to go into the woods, but then she heard me giggle. Alice looked at me hard as I wiped my eyes and laughed some more. She patted her leg signaling Cosmo over to us and then sat him beside me, I knew, so I could pet him and calm down.

"Look, Mags, I know you and Trig weren't close, but . . ." She took a step back, surveying the scene around us.

"Oh, no, it's not about Trig. I mean," I pointed to our former classmate's body part in the water. "It *is*, but did you know that this isn't even the *first* dead body we've found here, at *my* house, this *week*?" My body was shaking more than my voice, which was vacillating wildly between laughing and crying. The term "sliding off the cracker" suddenly made sense because that's what I was doing.

"Go on." Alice pulled Cosmo and me behind a large maple tree while I proceeded to go off like one of those firecrackers that once lit, spiraled around shooting fireballs everywhere.

"Yeah, so the morning of the sunset cocktail party, I enlisted our friends to wrap up my first dead guest in a rainbow cat printed shower curtain and drive him to a secluded place in the forest, *and then* I made my cousin Mark lie to his superiors and report that the old man died peacefully on the side of the road."

"Go on," Alice said again. "And why didn't you just call Mark when you found him?" Alice was surprisingly calm, her expression more intrigued than horrified as she sat down on a hollowed-out tree trunk. She absently petted Cosmo as they both looked at me.

"Well," I took a breath, trying to decide how much I wanted Alice to loathe me, especially after last night. "I . . . the inspector was there, and I panicked, to be honest. If he found a dead body in my home, then I would have been shut down that day, and you *know* how much debt I'm in. I thought if we could just delay anyone finding out that Mr. Gustaffson . . ."

"Wait." Alice put up her hand. "Not the old janitor from high school?"

"The very one." I stopped pacing and did jazz hands. "And we don't know if he overdosed or was, ah, helped."

"Murdered, you mean."

I looked around to see if anyone was in listening distance. "A possibility. Moving on, I need the wedding bonus, and I thought that we would all make it to the wedding in one piece since these knuckleheads came clean about . . . stuff." I sat down beside Alice on the log and started laughing again. "Might as well start packing now because two bodies are far above my pay grade."

"*Two* bodies?" Sutton said behind us.

"Jesus, Sutton!" Alice jumped up and slapped him on the chest. "You fucking scared me." Cosmo yipped in solidarity with Alice.

Sutton held onto his chest with one hand and a Ziplock bag in the other. "What the hell, Alice?"

"Is that what I think it is?" I asked, peering at the contents of Sutton's Ziploc.

"I went up to Trig's room to look for any sign of him and found this." He held up the bag containing two syringes. "Right on top of his duffle bag." Sutton sat down on the log, placing the bag down beside him. "This is bad, right? We need to find Trig and ask him about what happened to Mr. Gustaffson."

"Ah, well . . ." Alice and I both glanced unintentionally at the water and tried to look away, but Sutton saw us.

"What?" Sutton shook me off and lunged to get a good look in the lake. Unfortunately, Sutton's zealous momentum propelled him too far and he fell screaming into the water, landing right on top of Trig's leg.

"Sutton noooo . . ." Alice and I both yelled, but we were too late. Sutton's screech and fall into the lake got the attention of all the scavenger hunters, and of Mark, whose grimace of rage was more terrifying than the floating body part as he charged at us through the loblollies.

Grab a hammock and absorb all the peace and serenity that nature has to offer as you rejuvenate and refresh lakeside with a quiet book and a frosty lemonade. Tranquility awaits!

CHAPTER FIFTEEN
It Takes a Village

"IT'S TOUCHING ME," Sutton screamed, thrashing desperately away from Trig's gory thigh.

"Stop moving!" Mark jumped over the sea wall, accidentally pushing Sutton's face down into the water as he got close to the chomped-up leg entwined with leaves, old fishing line, and dead branches. "Stay still, Sutton!" Sutton was gasping for air and thrashing near the leg as Mark held up Sutton's sleeve and worked on getting a fish hook free.

"*Ow.*" Sutton tried to pull his arm away and Mark whacked him in the head.

"Quit squirming."

"Everyone has *got* to stop hitting me," Sutton hissed, side-eye-ing the floating leg.

"Oh, that was Dad's favorite lure," I said, pointing to a red and white striped metal spoon that Mark pried loose from Sutton's shirt. "Remember him using that one to teach us how to cast? Those were the days."

Sutton threw me a worried look as Alice smiled, holding a struggling Cosmo back from the water.

"I loved casting, but you just loved watching the bobber for hours, Maggie," Alice said.

I knew Alice was just trying to keep me calm, but I didn't care. "I could have sat and watched a bobber on that old party barge with you and dad for eternity," I sighed, still in my dream-like shocked state.

"And I could have cast just as long," Alice responded.

"What the hell." Sutton stood up from the water looking from Alice to me and back to Alice again, Trig's leg bobbing beside him. "A little help, please." He reached up and Alice and I pulled him up onto the grass.

"What is that?" Mia was suddenly beside me, leaning over to see what Mark was struggling with in the murky lake water. Others had gathered around us, too, still clutching their treasure hunt bags full of pinecones, rocks, moss, and brightly colored plastic Easter eggs.

Mark, after he put gloves on, was doing a bang-up job hiding Trig's leg from the gawkers until Herschel burst through the woods, saw what Mark had and screamed "LEG!" as he flailed toward Mark.

Mark put up his gloved hand and yelled, "*Get back*, this is a crime scene," which only spurred the panicking Herschel on as he tripped into the lake and fell onto Mark, entangling them both with the fishing line and Trig's gnawed appendage. Mark dropped the mess of evidence and put Herschel into a headlock as they thrashed in the water. "Herschel, you have to stop! I beat you every time in wrestling, remember? And this is a crime scene, damnit." He gripped Herschel harder. "Someone needs to call the station and Regina," he shouted to me. "And could somebody get Herschel out of the way?" He asked, dragging Herschel by his head to the shore.

"TRIIIIGG'S LEG! Aiiggh!" Herschel's yelling was garbled as Mark thrust his head under water again.

Noah dodged around us and dragged a now weeping Herschel away from Mark.

"Oh my god," Noah stared at the checkered black and white fabric from Trig's hot pants floating in the foamy water. As Noah held onto Herschel, they bent over to get a better look. "That's from Trig's outfit last night."

"Don't pick it up," Mark warned, holding onto the slimy, pasty-white and bloated leg covered in black hair and weeds. He scanned for any other evidence that might be tangled in the brush. "Get back. . . oh god no, not more of them. Maggie, keep them back!"

I watched the events like they were a movie unfolding.

Abby knocked me sideways as she ran to the sea wall, with Tamsin, Virginia, and Lena- Elise close behind. "NO, it can't be!" Abby screamed. "Not *during our wedding week!*" The other women crowded protectively around her.

Alice and I exchanged an incredulous look while I punched in Regina's number. The shrieking of concerned party goers had reached an unbearable level, so I called for Cosmo as I followed Sutton to my cabin to get him some dry clothes and to hear what Regina thought.

"Hey Regina," I said when she answered. I pointed to a laundry basket full of clean clothes and towels for Sutton and then filled up Cosmo's water bowl. Had to keep the dog alive at least. Then I sat down at my little kitchen table. "We got us a problem here. You need to call the station and head out to the point."

"Body?" I could hear her packing up her supplies as she talked.

"Ah, yeah?" I honestly did not know if you counted a body *part* as a body. I mopped my forehead and neck with a washrag and got up to run it under icy water. "Just a leg so far."

"I see. Tell Mark I will be out there as soon as I can and have him keep everyone away from the area." *Well, that ship had sailed.* I heard zippers zipping and what sounded like Tupperware being snapped shut in the background.

"Will do," I answered and hung up, holding the wet rag over my eyes as a migraine knocked on the inside of my eyeballs. Great. "Get my med bag out of the bathroom, please," I asked Sutton as he came out dressed in a faded pink pair of Patty's Bait and Tackle sweatpants and a SpongeBob t-shirt. He turned around and retrieved my bag while I got a large glass of water ready for my migraine cocktail.

My phone lit up and I assumed it was more harassment from either the water or electrical company, Miss Vera, or Lance's penis, but when I looked closer, I wasn't sure whether to laugh or cry. It was from my old boss, sending me an official job offer for the supervisor position I had always coveted. If he only knew what I had been up to since I left Minnesota.

"Anything interesting?" Sutton asked.

I shook my head and clicked my phone off, instantly feeling bad for lying to Sutton about Lance and my old job, and the possible pregnancy. I offered him an Ativan and he took it while I furiously chewed mine up, hoping that my guilt would go away.

"Are we ready to talk about the recently deceased Trig?" Sutton asked.

"Are we sure that, in fact, he is recently deceased?" I asked. "Maybe he got away from whatever tried to eat him." My head was swimming.

Sutton tilted his head, obviously wondering what to say. "I'd go with yes, he is dead, judging by what was *left of him* in the water."

I nodded. I had never considered Trig a friend, and according to his actual friends Trig was an asshole. But I didn't want him dead, not to mention how bad this looked on my business that kept producing corpses. "So, the two strongest possibilities are that he was drunk and fell into the lake, where an opportunistic wandering rogue alligator far, far, *far* from home just happened to be waiting . . ."

"Or someone helped that meeting along," Sutton mused. "But who would do that?"

"And *why*?" I asked, then my thoughts switched to our family room discussion last night. "Although Trig certainly hasn't been anyone's favorite of late. Didn't Herschel tell us that Trig threatened them a few months back if anyone talked about their alleged secret?"

"Yeah," Sutton answered, rummaging in my med bag. "Don't I have a few of my stomach anti-cramping meds in here?" Sutton paused, then wordlessly held up a pregnancy test.

I stared at my opened medicine bag, not able to make eye contact. "*Not. Now*," was all I could get out.

Sutton stared a moment longer before tucking the pregnancy test back into my bag, then popped two extra-strength Tylenol and his stomach meds into his mouth and washed them down with my water. "So . . . getting back to the question about Trig. Wouldn't it have made more sense that *Trig* killed somebody, like whoever blabbed to Mark or threatened him?"

"Ugh, this is complicated. And don't forget what you found in Trig's room basically could show that he offed the old janitor."

"Nothing about this makes any sense." Sutton sat back in his chair, massaging his temples.

This was definitely a shit show, and I needed to go out there and face the imminent possibility that everyone had already packed up their rooms. Even if I got paid for the time these guests had been staying in my home—and that was a big "if," because once Tamsin's parents found out that I had been hiding bodies and lying to the police, there *still* would not be enough money to pay all my bills—my home would be in foreclosure by Monday morning. Time to think about the present, though. "Maybe not go with the SpongeBob shirt?" I offered.

Sutton looked down at what he was wearing. "Well, you tell me what *is* appropriate for an afternoon tea following the discovery of a chewed-up gam of a man you recently had sex with?" Sutton's eyes widened. "*Oh my god*, will they think *I'm* a suspect?" Sutton jumped up and ran to my closet. "I have to find something that doesn't scream *guilty*." He looked in the mirror. "What does Spongebob scream?"

I rolled my eyes. "You were with *me* last night, remember?" We fell asleep watching *Monk* not long after we left the main house, and Cosmo woke us up several times with his barking."

Sutton was pulling out dark clothes and throwing them on my bed, shaking his head at every article. "Would this work?" He held up a black silk t-shirt.

"Yes, and I'm pretty sure a pair of your khakis is in there somewhere." As Sutton rummaged around in my closet, I thought again about last night. Everyone was in the house except for Lena-Elise and William, who were in the hospital, and Trig, who as far as I knew, never came back to the house. I had locked the doors and turned on my security system. I checked my security app to see if anyone had gone in or out of the house at any time in the night. "The front door was opened at around three this morning," I said to Sutton as he changed. "And three times again all in the same hour."

"We need to tell Mark that. You should screenshot it and text it to him."

"Okay." I did that and drank some more water, thinking over this morning's activities, trying to pin down who had been where, when. Abby had already dressed and gone downstairs when I entered the kitchen. Virginia and Herschel were not far behind. Adrian had come down from their room right before I had headed outside to help Heidi set up for brunch. Lena-Elise and William were wearing clean clothes at their table outside, so they must have gone into their rooms before brunch and changed. I did not yet know the early morning's whereabouts of Jenny, Tamsin, Noah, or their families.

"You look like a forest witch." Sutton brushed my frizzled curls back into a twist and secured it with a comb. It was getting more humid by the minute, and this morning's weather report warned of a severe storm brewing in a day or so, which could mean anything from a light rain to a full-on thunder and lightning storm that could knock out power and wash out roads. A few years ago, the dirt road connecting us to the city was closed for a week because of torrential rains and flooding. I could feel the pressure in every part of my body. The brushing felt good, but my migraine meds were not working yet, so the pulling gave me more of a headache. "Here." Sutton tried to put lipstick on me, but I batted him away.

"I'll do it." I dotted on some color and got up to find something suitable to wear, settling on a white linen shirt and gray linen pants: a respectable outfit for a respectable host who didn't run a bed and breakfast for murdered and dismembered guests. "Hey, you got that plastic bag from Trig's room to give to Mark?"

"Yep." Sutton pulled out the evidence and looked at the syringe and little bottles in it. "What the hell does our high school janitor have to do with any of this?"

"I'm still stuck on the timing of everything," I said, pulling on my clean clothes. "It's not a coincidence that someone texted Mark last night, and now someone in the wedding party ends up dead."

"We *were* warned about would happen if someone told the police." Sutton looked out the window and spotted Mark. "Now's my chance to hand over this bag."

"Good idea. One question is, who told Mark?" We put on our shoes and opened the door. Cosmo was exhausted from today's events, so I left him in the cabin.

Before walking out, Sutton asked, "And how did the killer find out?"

Reunited and it feels so good!
We've only just begun celebrating
Tamsin and Noah's magical week,
and there's so much more to come
here at Henry's Point B & B.

CHAPTER SIXTEEN
What's a Body Part Between Friends?

"Of *course*, we are still going on the pub crawl, and of course, the wedding is still on." Tamsin stared at me like I had tentacles growing out of my head. "Why wouldn't it be?"

This was a fresh take on murder at a wedding. I perched on my favorite stool in my kitchen and stole a quick look at Sutton, who was sitting beside me trying to discreetly blow a huge plume of marijuana smoke back toward the mudroom. We were not interested in another lecture from Tamsin about the perils of the cannabis plant; we'd heard it from her all through high school. Sutton looked just as stunned by recent events as I was, but that could have been the weed. "Um . . ." I gestured to the direction of the lake shore where Regina, Mark and a crew of people had found more of Trig's things, mostly hidden under a submerged log.

"*That* has nothing to do with our big day," Tamsin huffed. Her eyes were wide and her normally smooth, perfect hair was sticking up above her face, which was red and shining with perspiration. "As soon as Mark and the police are done with their interviews, we can get ready for the pub crawl and tour of the old Majestic, just like we planned!" Tamsin actually clapped and did a little jump in the air.

"Tamsin, your best dude has been eaten," Sutton said, eyeing Tamsin like she might just shed her human skin and be an alien underneath.

"But . . ." Tamsin tried to talk over Sutton.

"But nothing. There is no *but* here, you frizzled tart!" Sutton shrieked. "And what does Noah think about having a wedding without their best friend standing next to them?"

That comment brought Tamsin's energy down a bit. "They . . . Noah, is understandably upset." She looked around as she talked. "But they know that accidents happen and . . ."

"An ACCIDENT?" Mia walked into the kitchen from the mudroom, gawking at Tamsin's cavalier attitude. Mia's eye make-up was smudged, and her shiny black braids were haphazardly wound in a loose bun. "Are you serious?" Mia tilted her head to catch me inhaling Sutton's extra weed vape under the kitchen island ledge.

Abby entered too, also worse for the wear in the humidity, sporting pit stains under her pink blouse and a halo of fuzz that escaped her recent up-do. She stood partially in front of Tamsin in a defensive stance, beads of sweat rolling down her face. "What else could it have been besides an accident, Mia?" Abby asked.

Mia stared at her incredulously.

"Accident or not," I said, holding up a finger and mouthing "food please" to Mia. "Don't get me wrong, I'm still Go Team Wedding, Tamsin, but, um should we look at maybe toning down the festivities when someone in your wedding party has just been . . ." Searching for the right words, I glanced out the window and saw Regina clad in a dark blue CORONER jumpsuit slowly maneuvering a cart laden with a black, leg-sized zippered bag through the loblolly pines.

"Aren't you the least bit upset that Trig is dead?" Mia asked as she grabbed a bowl of dilapidated melon balls leftover from brunch and placed it on the island.

"Of course we are," Virginia said. "How could you even ask that?" Instead of her hair up in its usual fun, spiky layers, it was flattened against her head, and her makeup streaked down her face, revealing a dull red rash and a few scattered welts.

"Well . . ." Sutton began as he pulled the plastic wrap off the fruit bowl.

Abby cut in. "Most of us weren't even that close to Trig anymore because he was a dick, which makes sense now that we know he was the one behind all the blackmail stuff. But we *are* planning a tribute to him at the reception."

"Wait," I said, mouth full of cantaloupe. I swallowed hard. "*How* do we know *Trig* was behind the blackmailing?" I remembered that there was a suspicion about Trig using blackmail to keep everyone from revealing their Big Teenage Secret, but was there proof?

Abby and Virginia exchanged glances and then looked to Tamsin for guidance. She nodded at Abby to continue.

"I was worried about Trig when I got up this morning," Abby said, "so I went into his room to see if he had returned, and I found this." She reached into her pocket and pulled out a phone. "The threats and the blackmail—it's all in here."

"Trig didn't have a passcode?" I asked, leaning forward to watch Abby scroll through all the texts and emails that were sent to all of us. She went to his emails and held up the phone to show me one from "Carl Gleet" to her.

"He did have a passcode, but I got it right away." Abby clicked off the phone and put it back into her pocket. "It was 1-2-3-4."

"Okay, even for Trig that seems way too easy," Sutton said, frowning.

"Honestly, he had such a big ego that he probably didn't think anyone would be able to take the phone from him." Abby wiped her neck with a cool rag and sighed. The heat was starting to get to all of us.

A collection of "ahhs" and head nods went around the room. But how did Trig's phone end up back in his room? *Why didn't he have it on him when he ended up in the lake?* I pointed to Abby and Virginia. "Were either of you up around three this morning?"

"Why?" Virginia asked.

"Someone or *someones* came into the house around three this morning." I held an ice cube to my forehead as I spoke, praying that the last of this migraine disappeared fast.

"That must have been Trig," Abby said. "He must have dropped off his phone in his room before going back out to the lake."

Sutton picked up Noodle and stroked his fur as he paced back and forth. "Didn't we lock the front door, though? And didn't the door get opened and shut several times?"

"Did we?" The weed was clouding my head a little, and I could not remember for sure. "I think we did, but how did Trig or others get in then?"

"And if it was Trig, why did he go back outside, without his phone?" Mia had covered her whole face with a cool wet dishtowel and was leaning back in her kitchen stool.

That stumped us all, and we sat in silence for a few minutes until Mia took off her dish towel and turned her chair around to look at Virginia, Abby, and Tamsin. "Knowing that Trig blackmailed you, are you going to come clean to Mark about all your shenanigans?" She stared down Abby, who pushed Virginia in front of her.

Virginia stared hard back at Mia then spat out, "You should never have gotten first flute chair in high school."

"Seriously?" Mia asked.

Abby and Tamsin, though apparently confused by Virginia's outburst, nodded vigorously in agreement.

Sutton shot off his stool and stood protectively in front of Mia: "What the hell do our past band seat assignments have to do with the fact that *all* of you have done your best to sabotage this week and hurt people in the process?"

I realized a little late we were taking sides, so I also scooted off my stool and shambled over to stand with Mia and Sutton, followed by a haze of the weed dab I'd just hit, again. As we squared off like dancers in West Side Story, it occurred to me that Tamsin did not seem the least bit surprised when Sutton mentioned the sabotage or the blackmail. Could she have been involved? Tamsin had always been a person to get what she wanted, but what would she gain by ruining her own wedding? An image flashed through my brain of her glaring at me in town the other day. *Hmmmm.*

"You messed up Tamsin's audition by making out with her boyfriend Herschel the weekend before at Abby's party," Virginia pointed her finger at Mia.

Sutton's eyes widened and he leaned in closer.

Virginia continued: "Tamsin was too heartbroken to play *Pour Some Sugar on Me* on key and totally bombed."

Tamsin held up her hand to Virginia. "Hey, it wasn't that bad . . ."

"Yes, it was," Virginia said, shaking her head sadly. "It was."

"Virginia, I think you might want to look into the concept of letting things go," Sutton ventured. Virginia shot him a look.

"Hold on," Mia interrupted. "You're still mad about Herschel?" she asked. "You might have thought you were exclusive during high school," Mia said, "But that guy got around, and not just with me."

I nodded. Tamsin dated Herschel almost all through high school, until she started dating Noah in her senior year. I had wondered how Herschel was feeling about this wedding after he dated Tamsin for so long. I shook myself; Herschel was married now, and it was time for me to take charge. "Okay, none of this," I gestured around, "is helping anyone. And soon Mark and the other officers are going to crash this party and ask us a *lot* of questions." I made painful eye contact with everyone. "Are we going to tell the police the truth?"

"Of course we are," Tamsin answered, "But not, like, *every-thing* needs to be said, right?" She looked at Virginia and Abby, her eyes pleading.

Had I really completely missed Tamsin's involvement in these recent sabotage events? I watched her fidget with her clothes, obsessively checking her phone. Again, what would she have to gain by sabotaging her own wedding? *Wait*, was Tamsin part of the group that did something bad in high school?

My thoughts were interrupted by Mark and Officers Nguyen and Peterson knocking on the glass sliding kitchen door. Lynn Nguyen graduated a year or two after me, and her family owned the hardware store in town. I liked her but I was not fond of Harlan Peterson, who transferred here from another town a few years ago. Mark told me that he harbored a grudge for never being promoted to detective and was hoping for a better chance of advancement in Majestic Springs, where his uncle was chief of police.

I motioned for them to come in while Sutton discreetly waved away the lingering vape smell in the kitchen.

Where Officer Nguyen was all lean muscle and on the short side, Officer Peterson was large framed and tall. His ruddy face was dripping with perspiration, and his uniform was blotched with sweat stains. Officer Nyugen's light brown face was also showing signs of the weather, but her hair remained in a neat tight bun. I was hoping that she would interview us together, but she indicated to Tamsin to join her in the library, while Mark asked Abby and Virginia to meet in the living room. That left Mia, Sutton, and me with Officer Peterson. *Shit.*

Officer Peterson's eyes swerved to us when everyone else left the kitchen. "Think you were going to get away with covering up all these crimes, Maggie?" He hitched his navy blue pants up and stood taller, making the kitchen feel smaller and more hot and cramped.

Before I could say anything, Sutton, my attorney, thank goodness, put his hand up in a "stop" motion. "Harlan, I mean, Officer Peterson," Sutton corrected himself when Harlan's eyes narrowed. Before continuing, Sutton stumbled and caught himself on a kitchen stool.

Oh good, I thought, my lawyer was very, very stoned for this talk, which was quickly turning into an interrogation.

"Officer Harlan Peterson," Sutton began again, once stabilized, "Why would you think that Maggie is involved at all?" Sutton tried to make a serious face, but one side of his mouth kept curling up, as if to stifle a giggle.

Peterson took a long look at Sutton before deciding to ignore him and focus on me: "For starters, both bodies—yes, Maggie, I know all about Mr. Gustaffson—were found on *your* property. And from what I've gathered, strange occurrences have been happening around town, and they all tie back to your little wedding party."

I blew out a breath that I didn't even know I was holding. "Okay, technically . . ."

"You're the common denominator, and when there are hoof-beats, look for horses, not zebras," Peterson said, as he trimmed one of his fingernails with a hunting knife.

"Wait, isn't that what doctors are taught?" Sutton scratched his head. "Which I've never understood anyway."

"It means . . . it doesn't matter what it means," I said. "What matters is that I'm completely innocent." I turned to confront Peterson. "Do you really think that I am sabotaging my own guests? And that I gnawed off Trig's leg?" I threw my hands up in the air. "*Why* would I do any of this?"

Officer Peterson leaned his elbow on the kitchen island. "That's what I'm trying to find out," he said, still maintaining painful eye contact with me. "I know about your financials, Maggie, or lack thereof. That makes you vulnerable to blackmail. I also know that you and your friends here weren't looking forward to these people coming to stay in your home, so maybe you're trying to make their lives miserable, payback for all the times they were mean to you. My nephew went to your school. I know things."

Sensing danger, Mia grabbed Sutton's and my arms. "We have to go to the bathroom," she announced.

"All of you?" Officer Peterson asked.

"Yes," Mia said, pointing to her belly, like that explained it.

As we started walking to the bathroom like Dorothy and friends down the Yellow Brick Road, Peterson called out, "Together?"

"Yes!" We replied in unison and dashed into the bathroom, locking the door behind us.

"What should we do?" I whispered, knocking the vape from Sutton's hand. "Stop hitting that! You're a lawyer!"

"We need to get our stories straight," Mia said, vigorously straightening the bath towels.

I was starting to feel the woozy effect of migraine meds, Ativan, and now a butt-load of weed coming together in a perfect fugue state. Perhaps this wasn't the best course of action to take before being interrogated about a dead body . . . er, *bodies*, but what was done was done.

"Well, obviously Peterson has it out for me," I said. "Maybe you two also. What we don't know is what the others are saying. Do you think they are going to mention being blackmailed by the ghost of Carl Gleet who was really Trig?"

Mia shook her head. "My guess is that they're going to say as little as possible. Although, if they mention Carl, it might move some of his suspicion off of you and us. What do you think, Sutton?"

Sutton was rocking back and forth on the toilet cover humming The Reading Rainbow theme song. Mia nudged him and he grabbed the sides of the walls to steady himself. "What?"

"You're the lawyer. What should we say?" I was getting paranoid, thinking about all the ways Officer Peterson could come after me. "Hey!" I hit Sutton on the shoulder, and he fell over to one side, his head now leaning on the wall, higher than a kite. We now officially had no lawyer.

Loud knocking on the bathroom door made us all jump.

"Coming," Mia said, grimacing while pulling Sutton up. "Be vague in your answers," she whispered, before opening the door.

Get ready for a night you won't forget in beautiful downtown Majestic Springs starting with The Majestic Pub Crawl! Vans departing at seven o'clock sharp. Don't be late!

CHAPTER SEVENTEEN
There Goes That

"So, what exactly did Officer Nguyen ask you, Tamsin?" Heidi leaned towards her at the Black Forest Inn Biergarten, our last stop on our pub crawl. We were all—minus Trig, of course—sitting under a large tent, crammed together at two tables. Even with fans blasting cool air, it was still sweltering, and we all had the frizzy hair and smudged make-up to prove it.

Tamsin delicately blotted her forehead with a square napkin advertising a new lager on tap. "Officer Nguyen just asked like, where I was last night and early this morning." Tamsin yelled over the German oompah band and furtively glanced at Noah, who was staring down at their drink. "Obviously, I was with Noah and my family at the Jablonskis' house—we went there right after the unfortunate bee incident."

"Is that what you called it? *Unfortunate*? Like an accident?" James shouted over the music, holding his ice-cold beer mug to his bald head.

"Well, it was!" Tamsin retorted.

Everyone's eyebrows startled up at that curt answer, but nobody pushed further. I looked around at the motley crew before me: Abby's and Adrian's faces were covered in stings; William's face was still swollen, and both he and Lena-Elise looked like they had not slept well. Noah's wrist was in a cast from the yellowjacket/bee-capades. A few people, including Virginia, still bore traces of a poison ivy rash, and bruises were now blooming on Herschel's neck from Mark's headlock in the water.

Before I could think about that any further, Sutton loudly asked Abby, "So what did Mark say to you and Virginia?" She was fanning her face and, at the sound of her name, turned and glared at me.

"There's nothing to tell," Abby said. "Mark asked us about our whereabouts since we got back from town last night, and . . . stuff like that." She looked down at the menu and turned her fan back on.

"You want us to believe Mark the detective didn't inquire how all of us have gotten brutalized these past few days at what were supposed to be fun pre-wedding get-togethers?" Mia's lips pursed, her eyes roving over every guilty party. The oompah band finished their song and Mia lowered her voice. "I hope you told both officers that Maggie, Sutton and I had nothing to do with anything." She stared pointedly at Abby.

When Virginia saw that Abby was done talking, she ventured into the conversation. "Mark mentioned that he received some intel that some people involved with the wedding were, um, messing things up." She took a swig of her beer, then another, longer one, tilting her head back until the last of her drink slid down her throat.

"And how did you answer that, Virginia?" William's stare from his still swollen eyes appeared to bore straight into Virginia's soul.

"Ah . . ." Virginia blushed pink. "I . . ."

Adrian came to Virginia's rescue from down the table. "Look, I think I speak for us all when I say that we are all very deeply sorry." Adrian made a prayer motion with their hands and bowed their head before continuing. "We didn't feel that we had a choice . . ."

"Screw your bowing, Adrian; of course you had a choice." William stood up so fast his leg bashed the table and rattled a few glasses, spilling beer and froth over the surface. A Lederhosen clad accordion player scooted up to our group, played exactly one note, then hurried away when he saw William's seething expression. "Even when your back is against the wall, you still have a choice." William glared down at Lena-Elise before walking away from our group.

If the guilt on Lena-Elise's face was any evidence, she'd clearly come clean. She quietly cleaned up the spilled beer with extra napkins. Everyone watched William leave, and a few people mumbled how bad they felt that William got caught in the middle.

Speaking of feeling bad, my insides suddenly felt like they were being gripped by claws, signaling the start of one of my *exceptional* periods. Time stopped, and I was alone, back in the little blue bathroom that Lance and I had shared in Minneapolis, holding another negative pregnancy test. "*Nothing lost; nothing to miss,*" *Lance had said.* My gut spasmed and I gritted my teeth, clenching my thighs together. Time to compartmentalize.

"Excuse me," I mumbled, rising clumsily to go to the bathroom. I promised myself that this time I'd allow myself to grieve, but I'd have to do it later. Out of the corner of my eye I spotted Mia getting up from the table. "Got any tampons?" I whispered huskily, as we walked down a dim hallway.

"You know what's weird?" I asked Mia. I appreciated her for always carrying tampons, even while pregnant.

"What?" Mia was splashing water on her face as I came out and washed my hands. She moved closer to me.

I took a deep breath and looked in the mirror at us both, Mia with her swollen belly and me with my scratched-up face and swollen eyes. I took another slow breath. Then another. "I thought that I was pregnant, but . . . I'm not." I was going to continue, but a sniffle hiccup stopped me.

"I thought something like that might be happening." Mia smiled gently. "I was waiting for you to tell me when you had a wild hookup with some stranger."

"Well, I unfortunately have a few dick pics from the hookup himself, if you ever want to see." I didn't have the heart (or the courage ?) to tell her it was Lance.

"Duh," Mia said. "Always up for a good laugh."

"I'll send them to you," I said before I leaned my head against the wall, trying to grasp the words that were bouncing around in my head. "You know, Lance and I tried for a few years with fertility treatments, but with endometriosis, and the Sjögren's Disease diagnosis, well . . ." I squashed a tear that was making its way down my face. "We stopped because Lance said he didn't want a baby that could be *like me*, autistic and sick and broken." He had since told me over and over that he didn't mean it, but once those words were spoken, they couldn't be taken back.

"Oh sweetie, first of all you're not broken." Mia rubbed my back as she spoke. I wondered fleetingly how many heart to heart conversations like this we'd had over the years in public restrooms when one or the other of us was having a crisis. "How do you feel about having a baby, now that you are no longer with that shithead?"

I hated lying to Mia, but I couldn't tell her about Lance right now. "I think I have to just let it go for a while, because my emotions are too much. But yeah, I think, someday, having a baby on my terms might be important to me."

"Well, okay then!" Mia smiled and hugged me, just like I could handle it—not too tight, but not gumby bodies either. She knew I needed a distraction. "Let's rejoin the group—and you can have a drink now."

"Did anyone tell the police the truth?" Heidi asked as we sat back down. Even in a tank top and shorts, Heidi was sweating in the sweltering heat. Strands of her blond hair stuck to the sides of her face and neck.

"I told Mark that our pranks got out of hand, and he seemed to buy it." Herschel shrugged and tossed a few shelled peanuts in his mouth. He may have been acting nonchalantly, but the puffiness and redness around his eyes suggested that he had been crying over Trig.

Sutton signaled the Bavarian folk-dressed server for another round. "What did Mark say about Trig pretending to be Carl and threatening you all?"

Sutton and I had changed outfits, and like everyone else, we were wearing the least amount of clothing possible to still legally traipse out on the town in this heat wave. I hadn't planned to join the bar crawl or The Majestic Ghost Tour tonight, but Tamsin heavily implied that her dad loved to see me helping with the guests and that could influence his generosity in bonus giving. *Would it though, after everything, or was I just being played by Tamsin again like in high school?* I was shocked that my guests were still staying with me, much less that I was still in the running for a good bonus. Fingers crossed that with Trig's untimely death, the sabotaging would stop, and it would be smooth sailing until after the wedding, when every one of these dinks would leave my home forever. Hell, maybe after this wedding *I'd* leave my home forever and take that job in Minneapolis. The peace and quiet of a remote job and working quietly at home with Cosmo and Noodle sounded like heaven right about now.

Abby turned her personal fan to maximum speed and got extremely interested in watching a few little kids jump around in a sprinkler set up in the middle of the town's square. Hard to believe that we had been here just 24 hours ago, getting ready to skate the night away.

"Hey Abby." I raised my voice so she could hear me over her fan's buzz. "What did Mark say when he saw Trig's phone?" When Abby did not answer, I asked again, louder.

"What?" Abby looked the picture of innocence, her eyes wide and mouth in a little circle. "Oh, I didn't think Mark needed Trig's phone."

Every head turned toward Abby.

At seeing my shocked face, she rushed on. "I kept the phone because Jenny told me that since so many people saw him drink so much that night, it's clear his inebriation caused him to fall into the lake, so what was the point in giving Mark the phone? The phone didn't make him walk into the lake or anything."

Alice glared at Jenny, who was sitting next to her. "That info wasn't supposed to be public yet."

Trouble in paradise, I hoped? Still, I felt bad for Jenny, who withered under Alice's steely gaze.

"How'd you know about that stuff, Alice?" Herschel washed down his peanuts with a frothy mug of freshly poured beer. We were keeping our server quite busy filling our rapidly emptying glasses and bowls of nuts, which we ate up like demonic squirrels in the warm glow cast by the bare lightbulbs strung above our heads in the biergarten tent.

Alice sighed, giving Jenny one last glare. "I am now officially involved in the investigation because of the alleged alligator. Game and Fish are always brought in when there is a suspected animal attack, even if it seems very unlikely." She slid a few inches away from Jenny and put her backpack in between them.

"So, then it really was, for sure, a gator who got him?" Herschel looked like he was going to cry again as he clutched onto his beer mug.

"Well," Alice hesitated, obviously wondering how to say what happened to Trig without setting off Herschel. "From the um, marks on his leg, and from the preliminary toxicology results we can determine that he, at some point, met up with an alligator . . ."

Noah, who had been noticeably quiet so far, crashed their mug down and got everyone's attention. "So, we're supposed to believe that a very drunk Trig just *wandered* into the lake, in the middle of the night, and no one saw or heard him? And he was *silent* while he was being *eaten* by a rogue alligator wandering far from its natural habitat?" Noah looked around, their big brown eyes pleading for an answer as to why their best friend was dead. Trig and Noah had been close ever since daycare and had stayed close even though their personalities were almost exact opposites. "And I don't buy that he was blackmailing or threatening any of you," Noah said. "Why would Trig do that? He *just* told me how he was in such a good place and taking care of his mental and physical health."

Another costumed server came to take our order, took in the awkward mood of the table, said she would bring a couple more pitchers of beer and appetizers and zipped away. Noah looked like they had not slept in days or shaved. Their black hair was covered by an old baseball cap, and their t-shirt was wrinkled and stained.

A few people shrugged their shoulders; others murmured, "Who knows?"

I guessed that no one wanted to tell Noah about what Trig had been up to, because then they would have to admit to whatever terrible thing they did fourteen years ago. This was not my circus, and these were not my monkeys, so I kept my mouth shut. I looked around at the guilty parties, all averting their eyes, not wanting to lock eyes with Noah. I kicked Abby's leg under the table and raised my eyebrows at her, hoping to get her to say something, *anything* to help Noah understand the situation better. But all Abby did was move out of kicking range and stare down at her phone. *Coward.*

Noah stood up from the table and threw some money down in a huff. When Tamsin started to follow them, Noah put their hand up to her and walked away.

"Oh shit," Sutton whispered loudly to me. Abby glared at us above her personal fan, and Virginia made a "tsk" noise while patting Tamsin's back.

Adrian's mug must have been one of the glasses that William knocked over because Adrian gave up looking for it and started drinking straight from a pitcher. "I think Noah should know the whole story," Adrian said, after finishing the last drop.

"I think we all deserve to know the whole story after this week," Heidi said as she finished wiping up the spilled alcohol and threw the used napkins away. The server came back with more pitchers, two large charcuterie platters and baskets of bread and crackers. Heidi and James helped distribute the food around the tables, while the rest of us sat in uncomfortable silence, munching on meats, rustic bread, and a large assortment of cheeses, waiting for someone to speak.

When I could not stand the silence anymore. I wiped my face that was full of crumbs and said, "Doesn't anyone think it's weird that Trig disappeared for hours after the skating rink fiasco, then dropped off his phone in his room and somehow drowned before or after an alligator attack?" I took an exceedingly long swig of beer. Then another. "And I could have sworn that Sutton and I locked the front door, so how did anyone get in?" I thought about mentioning the link between the dead janitor and Trig, but then I would have to admit that my best friends and I had committed several possible felonies, so I let that one lie.

"What does it matter now, anyway?" Tamsin looked up from her phone. "I mean, Trig is dead. He obviously felt very bad about hurting us all, making us do terrible things to each other, and that's why he got really drunk and accidentally drowned."

"Yes, and then he was eaten," Abby added, supportively.

Virginia nodded.

"That's a very convenient way to look at it," Heidi said, looking suspiciously among the three of them. "But I agree with Maggie. I don't know if I buy Trig coming into the house at three in the morning, very drunk and not waking anyone up, and then walking in the pitch dark into the lake. What if he was not alone? Didn't Maggie say that the door was opened several times?"

"Everyone was in their rooms or in the hospital, according to the police," Jenny said, earning another glare and eyeroll from Alice. "Oops. Shit, you guys, I accidentally saw this stuff on Alice's computer, and I've had way too much to drink." She mouthed "*sorry*" to Alice, who was now studiously occupied with buttering her hunk of peasant bread.

As Alice tucked her hair behind her ear, she caught my eye and smiled shyly. My insides did a flip and a deep blush crept up my neck, remembering Alice's hands on my hips. Then my mind traveled to that horrible night when everything went wrong: when I broke Alice's heart, and when I made the decision to leave home and go as far away north as I could get from my mistakes. That was also the night that Carl Gleet had died, fourteen years ago tomorrow.

A low rumble above us cut through the silence, and we all looked up to see heavy, dark thunderclouds rolling in. Cool rain misted our hot, perspiring faces and a collection of sighs escaped our lips. Finally, a break in the oppressive heat.

Tamsin ignored the impending storm as she read a text on her phone. She looked triumphant and announced, "Noah and William are together, and they say they'll meet us later at The Majestic for the tour, so, all is forgiven. I say we take a cue from them and honor Trig by making the most out of the rest of the week." Tamsin was clearly ready to forget the last four days and to go headlong into a tour of one of the most haunted hotels in Majestic Springs. As I looked at the confused and alarmed faces around the table, I wasn't sure everyone shared the same frame of mind.

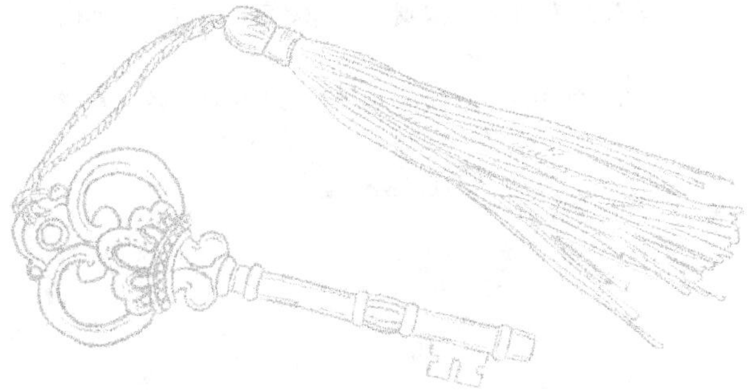

Grab your bestie and hold
on tight! We're headed to
The Haunted Majestic Hotel,
where nightmares come to life,
adorably!

CHAPTER EIGHTEEN
I Ain't Afraid

Lamplight was replaced by moonlight filtering through low hanging clouds and pine branches as we drove out of our village. Patches of fog hovered around the tops of the oak and poplar trees, and as the fog swirled, I saw how easy it was to imagine ghosts in the forest. I also realized how much beer I had consumed in a brief time as the world swayed around me. No pregnancy, so who cared?

"Get off, Maggie, you reek of beer," Abby said, pushing me away from the window. I was sharing the middle seat of the van with Abby while Heidi, one of the only two sober people in our group—Lena-Elise drove the other van—maneuvered us up the winding dirt road that would lead to The Majestic. I had mixed feelings about this tour. On the one hand, the new owners had spared no expense in revamping the old hotel which included a new spa and a restaurant featured in one of those foodie shows. On the other hand, the whole premise of this "haunted" hotel was built on the agony of thousands of patients, including people with my autistic symptoms, that were forcibly housed here when The Majestic was an asylum in the early-to mid-twentieth century. I shuddered thinking that I would have been most likely committed at that time.

"Was The Majestic *built* to be an asylum?" Abby asked, trying to remember the history.

"No," Heidi answered, leaning forward to see better through the heavy rain pounding on the windshield. "The Majestic was actually first called The Majestic Springs Hotel and Healing Waters, built around 1880 or so."

"Oh yeah, that one guy who started bottling up the hot springs water and selling it as a magical cure-all made so much money that he built a place for the rich to get away from the summer heat," Virginia added from the front seat. She must have filled her to-go mug with beer from the restaurant because that certainly was not coffee wafting from it. Smart.

Sutton added to the history: "Another abhorrent reason not to celebrate this place is that we all learned about the town's history in school, and the teachers conveniently left out the parts where white settlers stole the land and natural springs from indigenous people and then turned a hefty profit."

"Typical," Virginia snorted.

"When did the hotel turn into the asylum with all that experimental surgery stuff?" I poked Virginia and she handed me her cup. Yep. Beer.

"Hold on, looking it up," Sutton replied from the way back seat and made a "give me" motion for the now communal drink. He was squished between Herschel and Adrian, who was snoozing on Sutton's shoulder, and Sutton had to wiggle forward to get the cup from me. "Okay, found something on Wikipedia. In 1905, a man originally from Indiana calling himself Dr. Belfry—interesting note here: he wasn't actually a medical doctor but made his fortune by selling a patent for a musical instrument—bought the dilapidated Majestic Springs and Healing Waters Hotel and made it into what he called a sanitarium for those who had lost hope."

Heidi slowed down for a tight curve before asking, "If he wasn't a doctor, then who did all the experimental surgeries?"

"Oh . . . ew, he made a shit ton of money from surgeons that travelled to the later named Majestic Springs Sanitarium to teach brand new surgeries in the Grand Surgical Theatre, which is still preserved for tours," Sutton read from his phone, taking another drink before Herschel wrestled the cup from him.

"I bet the patients didn't have much say in anything," I said, thinking of all the types of patients I'd read about, including women suffering from so-called hysteria; children; men with PTSD, before that was an official diagnosis from serving in wars; and anyone whose family had given up on them or were desperate for a cure. "In all cases that I read about, the rights of each patient were signed away, so Belfry and his visiting doctors had free reign."

That reminded me of something. "Hey Abby, did you straighten stuff out with the workers there so they won't accidentally hurt us?"

Abby turned from the window where a branch had just scraped against it. The road was getting narrower as we climbed further up the mountain. "Yeah, everything's cool."

"What exactly does that mean, Abby?" Heidi glared at her through the rearview mirror. Heidi was probably no more interested than the rest of us in getting stung, drowned, rashed or anything else that the wedding party had made us endure this past week.

Abby stopped rubbing her wrist and held it up to me. Instead of answering Heidi, she asked, "Does this look swollen to you?"

I leaned over and examined Abby's reddish, puffy wrist. "Yeah, a bit. How long has it been like this?"

"A while, same with a few other joints."

Even in the dimly lit van, I could see Abby's worried frown. "I have a great rheumatologist in town. I'll text you her info." No matter what nefarious things Abby had been up to this week, I recognized that unique fear and was happy to help. "I could go with you to the appointment, if you like." She nodded and returned to look out the window.

As we got further up the mountain, The Majestic emerged from the clouds, lit up by moonlight. Through the rain and fog, I could make out steeply pitched roofs, pointed arches over the rectangular leaded glass windows and doors, wooden trim that looked like carefully stitched lace, and hunched gargoyles of all sizes guarding the hotel from their high perches. As much as

I loathed the history of this place, I couldn't help but be a bit curious too. I was even excited for the possibility of a ghost spotting. Still, a nervous pang poked my insides.

The car took its final turn around the side of the mountain, and then we turned off the main road onto the long, tree-lined driveway of the hotel. If I had to take a stab at describing this enormous building in front of us, I would throw some 19th century English manors, a few early 20th century American asylums, and the castle from Beauty and the Beast into a bowl and then mix them up to make one big, haunted dollhouse. Heidi pulled into an open space at the end of an extensive line of cars parked in front of the main entrance, lit up by a dazzling display of lanterns that looked like they came straight out of a Victorian gothic novel.

"Wow, this place is popular," Herschel said. "Look at all the cars!"

"It's not raining too hard yet, so if we book it, we won't get drenched." Virginia unbuckled her seatbelt and bolted out of the van.

We followed her, weaving through the cars in the parking lot in a snakelike pattern then ran up the stairs and into The Majestic.

I whacked Sutton as he shook his wet hair like a cartoon dog, spraying me. He laughed and crashed into my side, which caused me to bump into a fancy dressed older woman I recognized from our town hall meetings. I mumbled an apology as she ran her eyes judgmentally up and down our cut-off shorts, tank tops, and multitude of casts, bandages, and welts. We reeked of beer and pretzels and more than a few of us were stumblingly inebriated. Although, they could just well have been staring at the fact that we looked like we had been in a horrible accident.

Sutton raised his eyebrows at me and stifled a giggle as we meandered through the main hall, running our fingers along the dark paneled walls. We passed an enormous fireplace with a dark green marble mantle set with dusky pink velvet furniture. Tamsin was standing at the massive front desk, made from the same dark wood as the paneled walls, gesticulating wildly, her voice rising above the hum of the crowd waiting for the tour to start.

Not wanting to be associated with whatever Tamsin was demanding from the wedding party, Sutton and I headed for Mia, James, and Heidi crowded around a fancy bulletin board.

"Honest to god, a *barbeque* night here?" Mia shook her head. "I just don't know how I feel about that."

"I mean, I heard that John Holter from that famous St. Louis BBQ restaurant is running the kitchen now, so let's not be too hasty," Heidi said.

"If he's in charge of the BBQ, I definitely could look the other way from where the good doctor's collection of jars with body parts was dug up a few years ago," Mia said.

"Yikes," James chimed in. "Oh look." He pointed to another activity. "We can dress up like zombies and have a paintball tournament through the cemetery."

"I'm most certainly going to hell for this considering the history here, but shit, I'd be down for that." Sutton looked out one of the huge glass windows just as lightning illuminated windblown tree branches scraping against the glass. All of us jumped as a crash of thunder shook the windowpanes.

Herschel jogged up to us, spilling a bit of his drink before he took a big swig of it. "You should hear Tamsin have a go at management. She's gotten that down to an art form."

"What is she bitching about now?" Heidi asked as we all turned to look at not one but three employees in smart suit jackets and bow ties from another era. Around us, women dressed as '20s flappers held out trays. Sutton nudged me and my eyes traveled to where he was pointing: two people dressed in ripped white garments with what looked like blood spatters all over them were lurking among the potted trees. Several guests were taking pictures of them as they peered through the foliage.

"Tamsin wants our party to be alone on a tour and she wants us to go *first*, of course." Herschel tipped his head back and drained his glass, then grabbed another drink from a wandering flapper. "Apparently there's a big surprise, and she wants us away from the crowds."

Watching big Herschel stumble and catch himself on a velvet couch, I surmised that he was dealing with Trig's death by sousing himself. He was also staring at Tamsin.

"How long did you and Tamsin date again?" I asked, trying to sound casual. I grabbed a champagne glass and downed it in one gulp before putting it back on the tray, earning me a glare from the server.

"All through high school," Herschel answered, slurring his words a bit. "And beyond, maybe." He gave me a meaningful drunken look and then turned his gaze to Noah walking in the door with William, both soaked from the storm.

"You mean . . ." I was going to ask what exactly "beyond" meant but was interrupted by Tamsin clapping her hands together and calling out to her wedding party to join her.

Mia took my hand and whispered, "Here we go." I grabbed a wine glass for me and a Shirley Temple for Mia as we walked through the lobby. We met up with the rest of the motley group who were in various states of wetness and health. Good old Lena-Elise was trooping along on her crutches, with a still swollen William at her side. Virginia and Abby's stings and poison ivy rashes were still bright red as they haphazardly lined up behind Adrian and Alice, who was Jenny free. *Too bad.* Behind us, Noah was showing James and Sutton a camera or some other sort of device that fit in his hand, while Heidi joined Mia and me.

"Let's hope that Abby took care of whatever she was supposed to do." Heidi leaned between Mia and me and whispered. "I'm just not up for any more shenanigans."

"Talking about shenanigans," I pulled Heidi and Mia closer as we walked down a dark red wall with candle-like light fixtures flickering around us. I was slurring my words a bit, but no one seemed to notice or care. "I swear Herschel just told me that he and Tamsin were still goin' at it."

"What?" Mia clapped her hand over her mouth and then said in a quieter voice, "You're shitting me."

"Tamsin has been acting weird this past week," Heidi said, nodding in agreement to the possibility of the affair. "But Herschel?" We all looked ahead to watch Herschel stumble into a wall and spill his drink on the thick, blue diamond patterned carpet. Adrian took Herschel's glass out of his hand and set it on an ornate dresser, then put their arm around Herschel's shoulders as they walked.

"Makes me wonder if Herschel was actually in favor of Trig sabotaging the wedding or maybe just a part of it," I mused. "He'd certainly have something big to gain from Noah and Tamsin breaking up."

Before Heidi and Mia could respond, the tour guide, a young man named Nathan wearing a doctor's coat and scrub cap, signaled for us to be quiet.

"Take a peek in here and then I'll tell you about Althea." He swooped his arm toward an open door, and we all took turns looking into an exam room from Dr. Belfry's time. The light fixture reminded me of something from a Doctor Who episode: four long, spindly silver legs dangled from the ceiling with bowl-like metal contraptions hanging from each leg, all with a bulb inside. An old wooden exam table filled the cramped room, with a steel cart topped with gleaming silver instruments lined up neatly on a cloth, its lower shelf holding a large basin with bloody rags spilling out of it.

As I leaned in to get a better look, my back rubbed up against the peeling foam green paint on a chalk white, crumbly wall. I felt someone brush my shoulder and was pleased to see it was Alice. I smiled at her, hoping she couldn't see me blush as I moved out of the way so the rest of the group could see the exam room. She rolled her eyes at the spectacle and pointed to a break in the crowd.

"What do you think of the hotel makeover?" Alice asked when we drifted away from the rest of the group.

"I like the new business it will bring to the town," I said, trying desperately to sound smart and sober. *Do not look at her boobs.* "And I'm impressed with how the owners crafted the modern decor in the café and gym, but also hold onto the feel of another time." I clenched my knees together and cringed inwardly. *I am so full of shit.* I glanced into another treatment room with "Hydrotherapy" written in big black letters on the old oak door. "That being said, I'm not sure how I feel about making entertainment of all this suffering."

Alice nodded and whispered, "Ghost hunting is huge now," just as Nathan the Tour Guide started telling us about Althea.

"... be on the lookout for a young teenage girl who died *right in this very room* while giving birth." Nathan's eyes widened as he spoke. "Many guests have seen and heard her wandering these very halls, calling out for her baby."

Oof. That hit me right in the ovaries. Now was not the ideal time to think about my pregnancy-but-not-really-pregnant scare, but I could not help it. I was past thirty. I didn't know how my health issues might impact baby incubating, and my fertility issues were ongoing, so if I truly wanted a kid, I needed to get my act in gear.

"Hey Alice." I nudged her. "Do you, or have you ever thought about, you know, children in the future? In *your* future, I mean?" *Oh my God why am I asking her this?*

To my surprise, Alice smiled and nodded. "Oh yeah. Besides the fact that I'm a first-generation Greek here in the states and I have been told since birth that it's my duty to produce lots more Greeks, I actually like the idea of having kids one day. Why?"

"Just wondering," I said, barely able to keep my grin from spreading into Joker territory. I was going to ask something else when I noticed that our group was moving along.

Noah held out that small black sensor object he had been carrying around and James and Mia circled around him.

"What is that?" I asked Alice as we all scanned the corridor, looking for anything that might resemble a spirit.

"Noah's a ghost hunter; didn't you know?" Alice's brown eyes twinkled in the soft light coming from the candle fixtures. "I think that's why Tamsin was making such a big fuss about making sure the tour goes well." She went on to describe what an EMF was, how it could pick up sounds that human ears were not able to hear, including ghost voices, by an electromagnetic radiation signal. I nodded sagely, pretending that I understood exactly what the electro-thingy was and that I knew all about devices that record Casper the Friendly Ghost and his friends.

"Those Casper the Ghost films were such weird movies; the way that ghost was just a dead little white child with a gruesome backstory." Alice's whispering breath tickled the hairs on my neck. She had a point.

I involuntarily shivered as the hair on my arms stood up. Was that Alice's breath or something else? Alice's breath was never this cold before, though. I looked around for an open window or an air conditioning vent to explain the cold rush of air I felt and for which I couldn't find a source. Alice noticed my unease and I showed her my goosebumps.

"Looks like Althea is trying to get your attention," she said, looking behind me, then putting her hand on my arm for a moment. I reveled at the warmth of her skin on mine.

"There has to be an open window around," I said, trying to hide my suddenly hot, blushing face. "I mean . . ." I stumbled for words. "Maybe the storms brought hail?" I peeked into the next room where a large window took up most of the back wall. One of the panes was halfway open, its oily black crank sticking straight out. "See?" I pointed to the open window, the forest barely visible through the rain-streaked pane. "Always a rational explanation . . ."

The words caught in my throat as Alice suddenly thrust her arm in front of me. The pale stricken face of a young man appeared suddenly on the other side of the old wavy glass pane. The man wearing a red hat and brown zippered jacket was a ringer for Carl Gleet the night he drove his pick-up into the lake. Alice's hand gripped my upper arm hard, and I opened my mouth to yell, but only a squeak came out as Alice dragged me toward the door.

Meet up for a ghostly good
nightcap at The Majestic Veranda
to refresh and swap stories about
all the spooky specters you
encountered on this magical
night. Let the fun continue!
Cheers!

CHAPTER NINETEEN
Scooby Do or Die

Alice grasped the back of my tank top and pulled me out of the room and away from the ghost of Carl Gleet in the window. My precious wine spilled a bit as I tumbled into the hallway. We looked at each other and then peered around the open door, my eyes slits, hers wide open.

"Is Carl still there?" I asked, now with fully closed eyes. I was a baby. Full stop.

"Nobody is there," Alice said. "Open your eyes and check for yourself. And there is no way that was Carl." She walked slowly over to the window, then went on her tiptoes and searched outside. She looked back at me and shook her head. "Nope. No one there. We probably saw an owl or something."

"An owl that closely resembled our deceased classmate? And was wearing his hat?" I was a master at denial and compartmentalization, but that was a stretch. I crept up to the window and closed my eyes again, afraid to see a dead man looming outside of a haunted asylum. With one eye barely open, I scanned the parking lot and the forested mountains in the background.

"Wait," I turned to Alice who was already halfway out the door. "Isn't that a pick-up by those trees?"

"Hey, you guys are missing the tour . . ." Sutton jogged over to the window, balancing his wine glass carefully as he went. "What are we looking at?"

"Don't know how it could be." Alice clucked her tongue and pondered for a moment before continuing. "But it sure does look like his."

"What looks like whose?" Sutton, frustrated and pouting, nudged himself right in front of the window and said, "All I see is the creepy forest and a rusted out old truck." He drained the rest of his wine and looked again.

"Remind you of anyone's?" Alice asked, signaling to the very impatient tour guide that we were coming. "Come on." She pulled Sutton and me away from the window.

"But what about what we saw?" I asked. "And don't tell me that truck is just a coincidence."

"*Whom* did you see, and *what* does that car thing have to . . . wait. WAIT." Sutton got shushed by Nathan as we all started walking in a group again down an exceptionally long hallway. "Was that *the* truck? Carl's truck?" Sutton whisper-shrieked as we followed the crowd down a flight of industrial concrete stairs.

"What are you three gossiping about?" Adrian turned around and asked before I could answer Sutton.

"Carl Gleet's outside," Sutton squeaked before I punched him on the arm.

"What the fuck, Sutton?" Abby tried to hit him too, but Sutton dodged. "That's not funny, with Trig dead now and everything." Abby looked forlornly at her empty glass and grabbed my still half-filled one. I didn't dare protest as she finished it off.

"I'm not trying to be funny." Sutton pointed at Alice and me. "They're the ones who saw him."

Those in earshot, namely Virginia, Adrian, Lena-Elise, Heidi, and William all turned to us as we bottlenecked at the bottom of the stairs.

"Ow! That was my bad ankle, Adrian."

"I'm sorry but William ran into me first." Adrian made a face when they realized they had spilled some wine down Lena-Elise's back. Adrian handed the glass to me and tried to discreetly blot Lena-Elise with their shirt, but Lena-Elise shrugged Adrian off.

"Hey everyone." Lena-Elise looked at her phone and then back up at us. "It's after midnight."

"And now it's officially the anniversary of Carl's death . . . or whatever," William said, looking sad. William had dark circles under his eyes, probably from his night in the hospital. I was surprised that he'd come out with us at all.

"Hey guys, the best part of the tour is coming up, so please stop chattering and find a place in the auditorium." Nathan, clearly done with us, opened an old wooden set of doors to a room that was a lot bigger than the other exam rooms. As we filed in, I saw that it was two stories, with an open gallery at least five rows of bleacher seats high, and a black railing that sat atop the cement block wall where another tour group sat. Lining one wall were several long sinks, metal carts with wheels, stainless steel shelves over the sinks with various sized containers on them. Surgical instruments were spread out on tables next to three operating tables. A large chalkboard stood in the corner of the room with a diagram of a brain drawn on it.

"What are you playing at?" Lena-Elise poked my knee with her crutch. The last of my newly acquired wine spilled onto the cracked tiled floor and I regretfully set the empty glass on a shelf.

"It was a mistake," I whispered, my hands up in surrender. "I didn't see Carl Gleet in the window. I made a mistake, okay?" I said again as we filed through the auditorium, passing by black and white framed pictures of patients, their bodies sliced open on operating tables under spotlights that snaked down from the ceiling. In some of the pictures, doctors, a few of them smoking, peered over the railing from the galley above.

This time Tamsin admonished me to be quiet, staring me down until I cowered behind Heidi.

"*Alright*," I mouthed.

A scantily clad woman with an impressively real looking head wound wrapped in gauze handed us all glasses of wine, bless her. She sauntered off, her ripped, stained hospital gown flowing around her.

Another tour guide, also dressed as an old timey doctor complete with a white, button-down lab coat, was dramatically explaining about a young soldier who'd been brought to Dr. Belfry to cure his seizures, most likely caused by biological warfare from WWI. "For some reason, Dr. Belfry, not a surgeon, was convinced that amputating the man's leg would cure him of his ailment and proceeded to do just that."

Just then another doctor—an actor, of course—raised a huge rusty saw and rammed it down on a dummy lying on the surgical table. "Blood" sprayed the air, causing many to jump and clap. Jonathan, the other tour guide, laughed. "Be sure to hold onto your legs, because *this soldier* has been known to grab people's appendages as they walk through The Majestic."

"Hey!" I yelped as Sutton pushed me in front of him as a bloodied "soldier" lurched in front of us, growling and making attempts to snatch at our legs. I teetered and bumped into Alice, who laughed and made a show of protecting me by putting her arm across my chest. I didn't mind at all.

"We now ask for volunteers for the next part of the tour." Nathan's eyes gleamed as four steel surgical tables were pushed in by alarmingly beefy "orderlies."

"Um, guys?" Abby was backing away from the crowd and heading toward the back door. "Those are not the actors I paid off."

I looked at Abby, then looked more closely at the men in ill-fitting scrubs and masks, and holding what appeared to be real scalpels, surgical saws, and ice picks. Granted, because of the booze and the marijuana I'd had earlier, I was also seeing double, but still, this looked bad. They had their sights on our little group, and not the other people in the stands or around the surgical tables.

As the creepy orderlies slowly headed toward us, the other wedding party members got the hint that something nefarious was happening and, with solid grips on their new drinks, turned and made a beeline for the door.

"Where are you all going?" Nathan, clearly pissed, tried to push through to stop us from leaving. "Tamsin said that you all volunteered for the fun part."

Speaking of Tamsin, where was she?

As Heidi and Mia held open the massive oak doors, our little group hurried through into the hall, bumping into walls and into each other as we scurried. Weirdly, the lumbering orderlies were still keeping up with us as we accelerated through the corridor.

"They still have their sharp things!" Virginia shrieked, her head whipping back.

"Look out!" Abby called, leaping over a piece of broken concrete.

"Why are they following us?" Sutton called out from behind. "Wait! I can't keep up!"

"I don't remember this being a part of the tour." Noah dutifully held out his recorder with his injured arm as we picked up our pace and rounded yet another corner until we hit a dead end.

"Hey! Where did the orderlies go?" I looked frantically around the hallway. *Where was Sutton?* "THEY TOOK SUTTON!" I screamed.

"Here!" Alice opened a stairwell door and waved her arms frantically to get the attention of the wedding party, who were milling in various states of confusion and fear while clutching their wine glasses.

Heidi joined Alice. "Let's go down to the next level. The only place for them to go is to the basement. Move!" Heidi yelled, grabbing people's arms, and pulling them through the door.

Mia and I used one of Lena-Elise's crutches and a decorative sword grabbed from the wall to jam the hallway doors shut. "That should trap them in the basement," I called, as we fled down the concrete stairs and headed toward the open door with a faint glowing light pouring out from it.

"Watch out!" Abby yelped and karate-chopped a ghost actor in the throat who fell roughly to the ground.

"Oh my god, Abby, he was just doing his job." William tried to help the guy up, but he clutched his neck and scampered off.

"Well, how was I supposed to know?" Abby said as she frantically looked around for more attackers and Sutton.

"You are *literally* the person who was supposed to know, Abby. Jesus!" Mia threw up her hands and motioned us all ahead.

At first glance, the basement looked like any other early 20th century hospital's lower floor, but no sign of Sutton. Adrian flipped a switch on the wall and the overhead fluorescent lights flickered on, lending an eerie strobe-lit quality to the already disturbingly institutional feel of the grayish walls with their peeling paint and ancient brown speckled terrazzo floor. I started checking in a side room when I heard thumping and a squeaky wheel sound.

"There!" Virginia pointed to the four "orderlies" of substantial build pushing a struggling body shaped sheet on one of those surgical carts from the auditorium. The orderlies ducked into a room on the opposite side of the hall from us and before we could get to them, the heavy industrial door slammed shut and locked, then thudding sounds like they were pulling the cart down the stairs.

"Abby," I hissed, futilely pushing on the door marked "TO BASEMENT." *I thought we were at the basement?* "You told us you took care of everything."

"I did!" Abby wailed. "I don't know who those freaks were. And did you say you saw Carl Gleet here? Did Carl Gleet take Sutton?"

Everyone stared at me as we turned around and raced to the other side of the hallway. Jesus, I completely forgot about the Ghost of Carl Gleet. "Oh god," was all I could get out before gasping for breath again. We bottlenecked into a tiny stairwell that went down into darkness. "I'll tell you later. Keep up!" I sucked in a big gulp of air, my lungs burning from the running. My legs were shaky and hurting too, but I couldn't slow down with Sutton still in danger.

As we hurried down yet another staircase, this one clearly not meant for guests, we stepped over rat droppings, got our hands and hair caught in spider webs and were overpowered by mildew and rotting smells.

"In the horror movies," Herschel began, "isn't it super bad to go underground?"

"Shut up, Herschel," Alice said, smacking him in his beefy arm. "Not helpful."

Just then everyone's heads swiveled toward the pounding of steps at the far end of the basement. We started running through yet another dimly lit, smelly corridor. Lena-Elise was piggybacking on Alice and carrying her one remaining crutch, and Tamsin and Herschel were whispering to each other as they darted along with the rest of the crew. Even running after creepers, Noah and James were still getting all they could out of this ghost tour by holding up the recorder and pointing out to anyone who would listen that it was lighting up red, whatever that meant.

Just as we heard the other staircase door being pushed open, Virginia motioned us into a room. "I saw them push the cart in here, I think."

We crammed into a concrete floored morgue with large steel drawers lining one wall. A muffled wail emitted from that side of the room. *Sutton was in a morgue drawer!*

Herschel, Tamsin, and Noah were closest and started flinging open the long morgue drawers made for bodies of the recently dead.

"Found him!" Yelled Noah, pulling a white sheet from a duct taped Sutton and then helping him sit up. Sutton's eyes were huge as Noah gently tore the tape off his mouth and his wrists.

"Ow!" Sutton rubbed his mouth as I pushed Abby over to give him a hug and Virginia handed him her glass of wine.

"Are you okay?" I quickly looked him over, lifting up his arms and checking out his legs for damage. "Did they say anything? Why did they take you?"

Sutton batted me away and dramatically flung back his hair. "No, I'm not okay." He gave me a side eye and sipped his wine. "They told me to give everyone a warning: 'Quit talking to the police or more of you will die.' Now, please take me home immediately. I've been *handled,* and not in a good way."

"Wait a second," I said, leaning on an open morgue drawer for support. "If Trig is the person we thought was doing the sabotage stuff, and he's dead, WHY IS THIS STILL HAPPENING?" For the first time, I wasn't immediately thinking about keeping my home and business, but of our very survival. Two people were dead, both connected to me, somehow. Sutton could have easily been hurt, or worse.

"You said that you saw Carl?" Lena-Elise asked, holding onto William. "Could he be the one behind all this, you know, if he's alive?"

"Weirdly enough, I can't think of another candidate for wanting to hurt us," Adrian said.

I looked around at all the people in the moldy morgue—Noah looked too busy with his lit-up recording device to notice Herschel and Tamsin, who had reappeared, talking in low voices to each other in a corner and touching each other's arms a little too intimately. I whispered to Mia who had just walked up to Sutton and me. "I'm thinking Herschel and Tamsin never quit seeing each other. Just look at them, and right in front of poor Noah."

Since there were no chairs in the morgue, I reluctantly sat down beside Sutton on the morgue drawer and tried not to think of all the possible decaying body fluids that were most definitely somehow still on the stainless steel slabs and seeping into my shorts, which would need to be burned. I sighed and glanced at Alice, who was brushing cobwebs from her shirt. "Okay. It looks like those guys are gone, so I might as well tell you all that Alice and I *might* have seen someone that had the same clothes on as Carl . . ."

"*And* the same truck outside of The Majestic," Sutton interrupted, rubbing his red face where the tape had been.

Heidi raised her hand. "Like, was he in the room, or . . ."

"No, more like his head was kind of, sort of floating outside the window," Alice answered, frowning.

"In the dark, in the rain, from across the room, you're sure you saw a dead man?" asked James, scanning for a way out of the basement. "Shouldn't we be more worried about an actual person that's threatening us?

"Hey everyone," William said, walking up a half flight of stairs and yanking on an old door marked "Emergency Exit" in between two old crank windows. He pulled hard and the door creaked open, letting in the smells of rain and freedom. "Whew! Let's get out of here."

"No arguments there," Sutton replied, as I helped him to his feet.

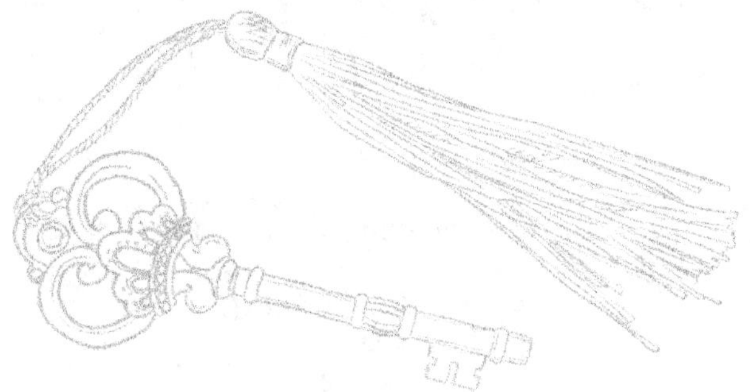

Climb into your favorite jam jams and munch cookies and warm milk before retiring to your cozy beds. In the morning, you'll wake up to fresh muffins, hot coffee, and Tamsin's floral arranging tutorial where everyone can center for the serene spa day ahead.

CHAPTER TWENTY:
Dark Night of the Soul

"So, was it Carl trying to kill us or not?" Abby demanded. She stood on one side of my kitchen island, hands firmly planted on the butcher block, and I stood in the same position on the other side. Sweat clung to our hair and faces, and both of our tank tops were blotched with perspiration. The storm had subsided for now, but the humidity pressed in as thick as ever.

I'd hoped Alice would come back to the house with us, but she and Heidi got out of the van on the way here. Can't say I blamed them after an evening filled with violence and a possible visit from our dead classmate.

I had to think carefully about how I answered Abby. "Whatever was in the window looked like . . . a person, if it even was a person, dressed like Carl was dressed . . . that night?" I trailed off, feeling the stares of most of the wedding party boring into me. "Obviously, someone knew it was the anniversary and was playing a horrible prank on us."

"But why? And who were those guys at The Majestic?" Abby pushed on. Cosmo jumped up and put his paws on her legs, earning him pats on the head and a treat from the bowl on the island.

"Tamsin texted me about that." Herschel scrolled on his phone and stopped when he found what he was looking for. He threw away some paper towels that he used to wipe his sweaty neck and face and said, "Nathan the tour guide was pissed that we ran out and ruined the best part of the tour and told Tamsin that if we didn't want to participate why did someone from the wedding party call ahead to set it up?" Herschel scrolled down some more. "When I asked Tamsin who called ahead, she said that Nathan didn't get a name, but interesting point here— Nathan said that he had never seen the workers who were dressed as orderlies before that night."

"So," Adrian said after a few moments of us all absorbing this latest information, "a Carl-like person slash apparition shows up at the same place we are on the fourteenth anniversary of his supposed death, and we get chased and Sutton gets kidnapped by suspicious actors slash orderlies wielding actual weapons." Adrian paused to stuff another Oreo in their mouth. Someone found my stash of cookies and made a spread of them on the island. "So maybe Trig wasn't responsible for the blackmailing emails after all."

Mia waved a chocolate chip cookie in the air before she spoke. "The phone was found in Trig's room, along with the bag showing that he probably murdered Mr. Gustaffson."

I tried to get Mia's attention by making a cut-throat gesture, but it was too late.

"What?" asked Adrian, Abby, Herschel, and Virginia almost simultaneously. William and Lena-Elise stared wide eyed at Mia, then they all turned to me.

"What does our old janitor have to do with this?" Virginia's suspicious tone matched the general feeling in the room. "And did you say *murdered?*"

Well shit. "Okay, so, before you all came, we had a small . . . incident here . . . in the house, that involved a man that . . ." I could not finish the sentence and looked to Sutton and Mia for help while shoving two cookies in my mouth.

Sutton cleared his throat and wiped his brow with the back of his hand. "We were asked by the police not to speak of the incident, so . . . our hands have been tied." He gave them his best lawyer voice, and I hoped that that would settle everyone down, but nope.

"Oh, that is some bullshit," Virginia said, shaking her head.

"Again, Mia said 'murdered.' Are you telling us that our old janitor was murdered *at this house* that we are now staying at, and you all think Trig did it, and you didn't tell us?" Abby's voice rose with every word.

"It's not like any of you have been very forthcoming," Mia accused the group. She picked a chocolate chip from her cookie and slammed it into her mouth.

Virginia had just eaten the crème from her Oreo and still had a bit on her lips when she spoke. "Yes, we did some shameful things and kept some stuff from you, but *not* a dead body . . ."

"*Some* things?" Mia spat. "You roofied my husband. He was naked in a swamp!" Adrian raised their hand in the air to speak but Mia cut them off. "And you still haven't told us what really happened on graduation night, so who's really keeping secrets here?"

I went to wash the chocolate off my hands and when I turned the handle a loud sputter erupted, but no water came out. I shook the handle of the broken faucet and not even a drop emerged. *Oh no. Not now. We could not have a water malfunction now.*

Lena-Elise peered over the butcher block island. "What's wrong with your sink? It was working fine this afternoon." She looked exhausted as she pulled her hair back and secured it in a ponytail.

"Ahhhh, it's fine." I was trying to think what the last email from the water company had said. I swore they said I had water through the weekend. *Shit!*

"It's not just the kitchen," Sutton walked in from the mudroom. "Water is out everywhere."

"Sometimes this happens when there's a storm," I lied. "My guess is that the water will be working in the morning." Another lie. "So, everyone, take an emergency jug of water from the kitchen up to your bathrooms and you should be fine." I gave a weak smile as my eye twitched. I had taken so much more prednisone this week to get through, my body was starting to react poorly to it with an upset stomach, jitteriness, and a tight chest. Add my period to the mix and now I was just tired and wanted some down time.

I had a flash of a memory of hiding in the grade school lockers for an entire day, keeping myself busy with a piece of string and a few buttons while the entire school administration, the police, and my dad looked for me. I was perfectly content in the dark with my buttons and string, all alone where there were no loud noises, no one to grab me or yell at me. Soon after that incident, I was formally diagnosed with autism, to the surprise of no one.

Mia knew I was lying through my clenched teeth and mouthed, *"Can I help?"*

I shook my head, and she gave me an exasperated look and said, "I'll be back in the morning. I really want to talk to you about plans for the acreage behind your house, okay? And remember, my dad is picking up Cosmo and Noodle in the morning for their grooming appointments."

Mia kissed my cheek and hugged Sutton. As she walked out of the house, she glared at the rest of the group.

Sutton was passing out water jugs to my guests as they begrudgingly took them upstairs. I thought the conversation was over, but Sutton came over to the island to hash it out some more.

"Shut it." I seethed as quietly as I could when Sutton brought up, yet again, the ghost of Carl Gleet.

"But . . ."

"But nothing." My eyes darted to the stairs then back to Sutton. "Look, for some reason, our friends and paying guests do not seem to be too bothered by the fact that the person responsible for the blackmailing may not, in fact, be dead, and that there apparently is a killer on the loose. I want to keep it that way, so keep the booze and the weed flowing." I was back to survival mode. This side of me scared even me, but it couldn't be avoided.

Sutton made himself useful by bagging up the remaining cookies while I wiped down the counters, but he could not stay quiet. "Why?"

"Well—" I thought hard about what I was going to say next because it did not paint me in the most positive of lights. "Because all I have to do is get through these next few days by convincing everyone not to go to the cops, and then I get paid, which means that I can pay my bills and keep my home."

"But aren't people in real danger?" Sutton whispered, glancing up at the ceiling where we could hear voices and footsteps. "I just don't buy that story Tamsin told us about those guys back there 'just doing their jobs' . . . and someone *was* outside the hotel to scare us, driving the exact truck Carl had in high school, which means that *someone* is still out there, which you know very well." He took the cookie bags and stored them in the pantry, then grabbed a water jug for my cabin, which would of course have no water either.

"Give it to me," I said more roughly than I meant to. "And I'll lock the house and set the alarm before I go to the cabin, so everyone is safe here."

"You mean before *we* go to the cabin." Sutton studied me, not sure what to say next. He had graciously volunteered to stay with me this week to help, even taking off work, which I tried to talk him out of many times. And now I was repaying him by starting a fight.

I was too tired to mask my exhaustion and frustration. "Me. Before I go to *my* cabin."

"You're being ridiculous, and . . ."

"Then go home. You have your own home, remember?"

Sutton's hurt face was almost more than I could take, but I pressed on. I put my hand up to stop more conversation. "You obviously think that I'm only thinking of myself and putting my guests in mortal danger because of a ghost and I'm too tired to get your morally superior take on this because I'm that desperate for money."

"You know I've always been on your side, but I honestly believe that we should have pulled Mark in earlier." His direct eye contact made me feel like I was trapped in a fishbowl. "Maybe if we would have said something right when we found the janitor, Trig would still be alive."

"But then I would have had to cancel the wedding party and would have lost out on all the money," I retorted.

"I know. But I have a terrible feeling that we are all going to lose out on a lot more than money. Be here alone if you want." Sutton walked out the door, closing it softly, leaving me with a horrible feeling in my stomach and a tight throat. After he left, Cosmo and I locked up the house and made our way alone to the cabin.

The next day, as Heidi whipped up a fabulous breakfast in my kitchen, I stood silently reflecting on how normal everyone was behaving, as though we hadn't just been chased by surgical knife-wielding weirdos hired by an unknown ghost, or semi-sure we'd seen an apparition, or gotten threatened, or in an emotional spiral after Trig was taken out by an alligator. There was a vibe in the air: a manic, fearful energy that no one was talking about.

We all stuffed ourselves with three different kinds of quiche, fresh squeezed orange juice and homemade pastries straight from the oven while engaging in vapid small talk. Too bad Cosmo and Noodle were at their beauty appointments today and missing out on all these scrumptious crumbs that kept falling to the floor.

As we dipped our flaky, buttery croissants into real hot chocolate, Tamsin brought in a dolly piled high with large plastic bins. "Clear the table and make sure to wipe it down well," Tamsin said, signaling to Virginia and Herschel to help her unload.

"Why are we doing the flowers in here again?" Adrian asked, gathering the last of the breakfast dishes up. They looked at Abby, who was still finishing. "Give it. We have to clear the table." Adrian put their hand out only to have it slapped away. "Abby, stop it!"

Abby clung stubbornly to her bowl, using a morning bun to sop up the remaining dregs of hot chocolate. "I'll bring it to the sink when I'm damn good and ready, not that it will do any good there."

I shot Abby a glare. That comment was the umpteenth crack about the non-existent water. We were getting by without it, but not without a lot of grumbling and complaints. After reluctantly admitting the water still wasn't working, they were making plans to take turns showering at the Jablonski's after craft time.

"But the storm stopped last night," Virginia had pointed out earlier, between gulps of coffee made with our dwindling bottled water supply. "You told us that the water would come back if it stopped raining."

I sighed, my lie coming back to haunt me. "I don't know what to say, Virginia." I had refilled her coffee and pushed over the creamer and sugar bowl to keep her distracted so I could escape her questioning.

Someone had just laid out a plastic tablecloth to protect my ancient oak kitchen table, and Virginia and Adrian were pulling out all sorts of decorations from the containers and placing them down on the middle of the table. "Careful with the etched glass bowls, they cost me a fortune, and we don't have extras." Tamsin grabbed a bubble wrapped bundle and gently set it down, then motioned for another one.

"Where do you want these?" Lena-Elise held up a package of glue guns and a clear bag full of glue inserts. Lena-Elise, like the rest of us, was going about this activity like a robot following directions.

"Just place them every few feet so people can share," Tamsin answered. "And Virginia, make sure there is a battery-operated candle by every bowl, and enough dried flowers and twig things for each piece. We want these flower arrangements to be perfect," she barked.

As Virginia distributed the candles and flowers, everyone found a place to sit around the table that once held my family. I always sat where Adrian was now, by the window so I could look out onto the lake, and close enough to the warm fireplace for those bone chilling ice storms we got. My cushion was still there, made from fabric scraps that I used to carry around singing Dolly Parton's *Coat of Many Colors* very, very off key.

"Remember when we had to pull an all-nighter getting all the decorations ready for prom?" Lena-Elise said, knocking me out of my reverie.

I sat down beside her and reached for a glue gun and awaited instructions as the group reminisced about their glory days of high school.

"Oh yeah," Abby responded, then set a bowl and candle in front of me. "Glue these sticks and flowers together around the candle, after arranging them in the bowl." As she started working on her own centerpiece, she asked, "Why *did* we have to redo the prom stuff?"

"Everything got wet when someone set the smoke alarms off and the sprinklers soaked the gym." Adrian did not look up from concentrating on loading their glue gun for a second round.

Virginia giggled. "Well, I think that was because we should not have been smoking so much green while working."

And so, the chatter went on as we worked feverishly on Tamsin's vision for a perfect reception. By the third time I had wiped my perspiring forehead, I looked around and realized that the others were working up a sweat too.

"Hey, could you turn the air conditioning up?" Tamsin asked, using her shirt sleeve to mop her own gleaming brow. "It's been feeling pretty warm in here for a while."

Warm and sticky. I wondered where a window might have been left open when I realized that the kitchen lights above the island were now off and so was the . . . *oh no. No no no. The electricity.* I slinked to the light switch, hoping that no one was watching while I flicked it on and off, then tried another switch. Nothing. No lights. The electricity had been shut off. I grabbed my phone and quickly scrolled through all the warning texts from the electric company, but none of them indicated a power shut off today. I heavily sat down next to my kitchen table. *Fuck.* FUCK.

While I was trying to figure out how to tell my guests that

they not only had no water, but they must also stay in an un-air conditioned, one-hundred and thirty-year-old house in the middle of a heat wave, Noah came in the sliding door flush with excitement.

"I finally got this thing to work!" Noah held up their ghost tracker thing and pushed the PLAY button. We all put our glue guns down and listened to our own voices screech and yell as we frantically searched for Sutton at The Majestic Haunted Tour gone awry.

Noah fast forwarded and pushed play again. "This was in the morgue where James told me he heard something funky." We patiently listened to us all prattle on in the morgue, straining to hear anything that resembled a voice from beyond. Noah turned the volume up all the way. "This was right before we walked out, I think . . ." Noah said.

Everyone leaned in just in time to hear my voice say, ". . . Tamsin and Herschel never quit seeing each other. Just look at them, and right in front of poor Noah."

Everyone froze. Virginia dropped her candle onto the wooden floor, its batteries scattering across the kitchen. Noah stood still, staring at their ghost device, which was now clutched in their hand. Tamsin, mouth open, looked from me to Noah, then to Herschel, then back to Noah.

"Hey," Herschel stood up from the craft table and put a handful of little twigs down. "I don't know what Maggie was saying, but . . ."

Tamsin jumped up and ran over to Noah, who backed away from her immediately. "That's all wrong; you can't believe that." She reached out to Noah, who shook her hand off.

Noah's face turned hard. "Actually," they said in a deadly calm voice, "that's the first thing that makes sense this week, especially after what happened the other night." Noah glared at Tamsin, eyebrows up. "I would not waste your time on those centerpieces since they won't be needed anymore." With that, Noah stormed out of the stuffy kitchen.

Tamsin whirled around to face me. "You did this! Why would you say that?" Tamsin stuck her finger in my face. "And you wonder why we all stopped hanging around you."

I looked at Herschel, who was red in the face and concentrating hard on gluing a fake rose blossom to a candle. "I heard it from a solid source," I said, hearing how weak that was. My face likely matched Herschel's in blotched redness, shame creeping up my neck.

"Because of your inability to be even slightly human, my wedding is off. Now, turn up the damn air conditioner." Tamsin stormed outside, then came back in to grab the van key. "Does anyone want to get out of here?"

"I need to shower and for some reason, my phone isn't charging," Virginia said.

"The power is out, isn't it?" asked William, unplugging his phone, and putting it in his pocket.

I shrugged. I was too tired to speak. One by one, my guests trudged up the stairs to get their shower supplies and a change of clothes to escape the hell I was trying to charge them for while Tamsin slammed her half-done centerpieces into bins. Then they hauled out their bags and left me all alone in the house, with a huge mess of dirty dishes in the sink that I couldn't wash, and a table full of dried flower bits and glue gun sticks.

I was calculating how many days I thought Tamsin's parents might still consent to pay for, when I received a text from Mr. Carlyon:

TWO deaths on your property? Trust me I will make this very public. You are in breach of your contract—no payment forthcoming!

I was screwed. There would be no paying my mortgage or my bills, and now with the truth out I could never rent to anyone ever again.

I was so distracted from thinking about what in the world I was going to do, that I wasn't paying attention to a screenshot I was sending to Mia of Lance's penile portrait with his contact **"Lance the Man"** at the top. I was trying to lighten Mia's mood since her baby had decided to lodge painfully on her bladder. I also didn't want to keep lying to Mia about the penis's owner, and I really needed her help to decide what to do with the whole situation and whether to take the job in Minneapolis now that all this was going to hell. A simple screenshot with his name at the top would do the trick. I texted:

Here's who I hooked up with a few months ago, and thinking about getting back together- need to talk it through with you

Almost at once my phone blew up with texts:

WTF

Why did you send this to me???

Wtaf.......

isn't lance your ex

NOT BAD!

uh

And the most mortifying of all, from Mr. Carlyon:

YOU ARE A DISGRACE.

My breath froze in my throat. Had I sent Lance's dick pic to a group text made for everyone in the wedding? No. Noooooo. Despite the hot day, my body shivered cold as I looked at my phone again and confirmed the hideous truth. I had sent Lance's dick pic to *everyone*. It was a fact. In the past. Unchangeable. Not fixable.

Oh GOD, that meant . . . Alice! I frantically checked who had already sent me texts, when her response flashed across my screen:

Good to know. Thanks for the public humiliation. Again.

With trembling fingers, I tried to text her back, but she had already blocked me. I threw my phone down on the kitchen table, tears burning my eyes. My head ached but my heart hurt more, and my stomach felt like an animal was gnawing through it. I tried to think of something, *anything* positive that could come out of this horrible situation that I'd put myself in, but nothing came to mind. So what if that job back in Minneapolis was great pay? I would be at home all alone during the day, sitting at my computer. No water trouble, or peeling paint, or irksome guests, but also no Sutton or Mia, or my beautiful, messy house that holds all the memories of my family. But I would have Lance again.

Who was I kidding? I blew my snotty nose and swiped the hot tears from my face as I thought about all his shitty texts and calls. He never asked about how I was, never volunteered to help me down here. "Shut it down and come back up north, where you belong," he told me when I asked him what I should do after my dad died. Lance was always about Lance. He was predictable and my safety blanket for so long that I had stopped imagining a life without him. And now I had nowhere to go because of my bad choices. Sutton was mad at me, Mia was going to be busy with another baby and certainly didn't want her already crowded house more crowded, and I was just a burden to everyone.

Time to face the music and call the real estate agent, whose card was somewhere in the library. My throat had an awful tight feeling as the room swam through fresh tears. I couldn't sit anymore and curled up in a ball under the kitchen table on the braided rug like I used to when I was younger, trying to hide from a world that was always too much for me.

As I rocked back and forth, I saw that some asshole had stuck gum underneath my table. When I tried to pull it off with a tissue, I felt that the substance was hard and circular. I yanked hard and it finally came free. As I held it in my hand, I recognized what it was from all the TV crime drama I watched. Someone had planted a bug in my kitchen.

Spa time for our cherished wedding party! Please enjoy our gift to you: a day filled with pedicures, massages, manicures, and facials, compliments of the Carlyon family. Lunch and drinks provided at the Majestic Springs Premier Spa and Hotel.

CHAPTER TWENTY-ONE
You Make Your Ancestors Cry

I turned over the listening device in my hand, peering at it closely to make sure it was the same one I had found on the internet. My momentary excitement drained away as I came thudding back to earth. It did not matter who or why someone planted this bug under my kitchen table; it wouldn't bring me the money to pay for my home.

Then I remembered that Mr. Gustaffson had been under the table one morning when I walked in. He'd said he was picking up his napkin that had fallen, and that made perfect sense to me at the time, but now it was suspect. I wandered into the library as I thought this through, shutting a loose panel door on the wall that opened to one of the hidden passageways in the old house. I thought about all the times Mia and I snuck in there to drink and found my dad's forbidden cigarettes, which he'd promised he had given up. The passageways went up all three levels of the house, so my moonshiner and bootlegger relatives on every level had a safe place to hide during Prohibition.

I stood in the library and held up a framed picture of Karen and Angus, my great-great grandparents, both in dungarees and standing in front of the little log cabin they had built themselves before starting on their beloved Victorian. The same log cabin that I was lucky enough to stay in now. Funny enough, my great-great grandma had been on her way to become a homesteading wife in North Dakota, but met Angus on the way there, and the rest was history. A history I now had to sell.

For four generations my relatives had managed to keep this home and lake property in the family through the Great Depression, wars, and personal tragedies. When my grandfather died when my dad was only eleven years old, my grandma turned this place into a boarding house. And all it took me was one short week to lose it. The best option was packing up Noodle and Cosmo and going back to Minnesota, because I couldn't imagine living in Majestic Springs knowing that someone else was walking through my forest, fishing off my dock, and living in my home.

"We gotta leave, Noodle." I picked up a framed picture of my dad cuddling Noodle on his lap, sitting in his favorite leather chair by the window. Yes, I'd go back to leading a quiet, predictable life, which I had been secretly daydreaming about since I started getting the house ready for the bed and breakfast. But now that my suddenly chaotic, loud, busy, and people-filled life was about to change back, grief swelled up in me like a tide.

But I had to grow up now and face the trouble that I'd gotten myself into. I found the number of the realtor who had told me that she had some buyers in mind and sat down on the worn and elegant leather green couch to call her. My cell phone dinged yet again, and I wasn't surprised to see it was Miss Vera up the way. Yet another person who was mad at me because I was ruining her quiet neighborhood. Just super. Well, she would be ecstatic to know that there would be no more loud and rowdy guests disrupting her evenings. I started texting her back that soon she would have wonderful new neighbors with hopefully a lot of muscle-car driving teenagers, when a picture came through with a text that read:

My ring camera picked this up. I told you it was one of your guests. From Vera.

I blinked hard. Then blinked again. The picture was of a light colored, four door sedan and at the wheel sat William, time and date stamped around the same time that someone had entered my home in the middle of the night. The night William was supposed to be at the hospital, when Lena-Elise said she had slept surprisingly well on the pull-out bed in his room with the help of a sleeping pill. This was also around the time Trig was supposed to have died and yet somehow a phone and a bag of drugs that implicated him as the murderer of Mr. Gustaffson and the email blackmailer appeared in Trig's room.

I dropped the piece of paper and ran up the stairs to William and Lena-Elise's room. I felt a tinge of guilt when I started tossing William's stuff around in his suitcase, but all those feelings disappeared when I encountered a bag of more listening bugs hidden in a shoe. A noise made me jump. William could come back here at any minute to pick up his stuff, but the sound was just my old and spindly maple tree scraping against the window. The wind was picking up outside and it was getting darker.

When I looked back down at William's suitcase, I noticed the edge of a plastic bag protruding out of the lining, and what was in it shocked me even more than the bag of bugs: a series of pictures of a teenaged William with Carl Gleet. William had said he barely knew Carl, but not according to these photos. I took the pictures and ran back down the stairs, pausing to catch my breath and wondering if I had taken my meds that morning.

Slow down. Back to basics. I breathed in and out, lowering my pulse and swallowing whatever was rising in my throat. Thoughts of my seemingly innocent conversations with William drifted around in my mind. That he was in town that weekend before the guests arrived when the janitor was murdered. And where did he say he worked? At a therapy place in Little Rock, where he shared patient information with the other therapists. A bell rung in my head, and Noah's words at the biergarten came back to me: "We're proud of Trig because he has been taking really good care of his physical *and* mental health." That could easily have meant that he was seeing a counselor. Trig lived in Little Rock. Could Trig's therapist have shared confidential information from Trig's past with William? What if Trig told his therapist about what happened to Carl that night?

I swore William had said that he didn't know Carl because he hung out with students in our grade, but the photographs in his suitcase of them told a different story. Curiosity got the best of me, and I hurried back into the library, sweat trickling down my back and chest from hours without air conditioning. Rain pelted against the divided glass bay windows, and I wondered how the road connecting us to the rest of the town was going to hold up under a second storm assault.

I turned on my dad's old radio and thanked him for always making sure that the batteries were fresh. I moved the dial around until I found the weather station. The forecaster was warning about flash flooding in our area, and a severe wind and tornado watch. While I was listening to the genuinely concerning weather report, I scanned the cherrywood bookshelves until I found what I was looking for: my high school yearbook.

"Are you in here, William and Carl?" I asked out loud, flipping through until I found a picture of the two in question, dressed up for spirit day in our school colors, both giving a thumbs up. I snapped a picture of it with my phone and continued to skim through the book, stopping dead at another picture of William, this time standing with none other than our old janitor, Mr. Gustaffson. They knew each other.

I snapped that picture too and sent it along with the ring camera picture of William driving the car and the pic of William and Carl in a group text to Mia, Alice, and Sutton with an "eyes wide open" emoji and the words,

WILLIAM DID EVERYTHING

Mia called me first, followed a millisecond later by Sutton. "Hold on, I'm adding Sutton. "You there?"

"What's . . ." Sutton started to ask but I cut him off.

"Mia, you still there?"

"Yep. What the fuck is happening?"

"I second that," Sutton yelled over the engine of his car and the roar of the rain.

"Are you on your way to Maggie's too?" Mia asked, her voice also competing with a car and the storm. My heart bounced in my chest with elation and fear when I heard that both Mia and Sutton were on their way.

"I don't know how our road is. Be careful," I warned as I started to pull candles from the cupboards. Suddenly, charcoal black clouds rolled in low. The house got very dark. Anxiety buzzed my chest. "Where do we keep more candles?" I asked, glad my friends were still on the phone.

"Try the shelves inside the kitchen's secret passageway entry," Mia said, then swore at another driver. "People are nuts out here. Watch out, Sutton."

"Yeah, I'm noticing," Sutton replied. "Don't try to take Logan Road, there are cones blocking the entrance. Shit, I think it's washed out entirely, and that might mean flooding at the Jablonski's." Rain pelting the windshield drowned out his voice. "We'll call you back," he yelled.

I hung up and tried not to think about Sutton and Mia out on the roads as I opened the passageway door and searched the shelves for candles. A bag of extra blankets and pillows had been opened and the contents were spilled out on the floor. I needed to talk to everyone about safety issues like this. I stepped over the mess and finally found an apple pie scented candle. I made a mental note to clean up the passageway, which I didn't remember leaving in such a state of disarray.

The sound of a door slamming jolted me with relief. "You got here!" I said as I turned around to greet Mia and Sutton.

"We did."

I jumped to the sound of William's voice and slowly crept out of the passageway. "Ahhh, hi. Why are you here?" I asked.

William was standing in the kitchen, dripping wet, with Lena-Elise, Virginia, Herschel, Abby, and Adrian. "Since we can't stay here, we need our stuff and thought we'd get it before the storm got too bad."

I froze and stared at William, grateful I wasn't alone with him. Then I scanned the rest of the battered little group. "I'm so sorry," I said. "I had no idea that this would all happen this way."

"You certainly did a number on Tamsin and Noah, Maggie. And that . . . text was something. Not that I'm surprised that you did all that," Abby said icily as she headed up the stairs, shining the flashlight on her phone.

"Hey, I just repeated what Herschel told me." I turned to Herschel, and he shrugged but kept silent. He was clearly not going to help me. The hairs on my neck prickled when I saw that William was staring at me. Should I say something to the rest of the group? He had to be the one behind sending those emails that blackmailed everyone into hurting each other. And he very well could have killed Trig and the janitor to cover his tracks. And all that added up to him still wanting to hurt those who were responsible for his friend's death, exactly fourteen years ago on a stormy night just like this one.

Lightning flashed through the kitchen and we all jumped. Another flash illuminated William's hard, unreadable face and gleamed off the keys he was holding. I clamped my mouth down hard to silence my chattering teeth.

"You driving everyone, William?" I asked, raising my voice over the long rumbling of thunder. "Aren't the roads around the lake really bad right now? Like, easy for a van load of people to go off a bridge? Like your good friend Carl Gleet did?" I maneuvered myself closer and closer to grabbing the keys, but they were still out of my reach.

"What the hell is wrong with you, Maggie. Really?" Lena-Elise said, holding her bag in one hand and her crutch with the other. She stood at the bottom of the stairs next to Virginia, their rattled expressions mirrors of each other.

William looked down at the van keys and then back to my eyes. He remained quiet, motionless as the others came down the stairs with their suitcases and backpacks, all murmuring to each other.

"Hey Maggie?" Adrian hesitantly stepped toward me, their face lit by dancing candlelight. "Um, it's been a really stressful day for all of us, so I'm not sure what this is between you and William. But I think it is best if we all leave so you can collect yourself."

"Why don't you ask William about his best friend from high school?" I turned around. Even though there were no lights on, I could still make out everyone's confused faces in the dim light. "You know who his best friend was, because you're all responsible for his death."

Gasps overlapped each other; hands flew to mouths and loud exclamations of denials filled the kitchen. I breathed in the sharp scents of cinnamon and apple spices from the candles spaced about the room. William's eyes narrowed.

"Go ahead William," I goaded him, edging closer to the keys in his hand. If the wedding party did not believe me, and they went with William and he hurt—or even killed—them, I would never forgive myself. Sutton was right: it was my fault things had gone this far in the first place. "Tell them that you've been so angry about Carl's death for all these years, that when the opportunity fell in your lap, you devised a plan to get revenge."

"What's she talking about, William?" Lena-Elise pleaded, leaning on her crutch.

"Maggie has obviously had some sort of breakdown, which isn't surprising with the recent death of her father, her unwise relationships, and the failure of her business." William's voice was maddeningly soothing, just like you'd expect from a condescending therapist. He nodded sagely in my direction and rage spiked through my body at the mention of my father. William motioned for everyone to follow him as he spoke. "We need to be patient with Maggie now, and I think the best we can do for her is to give her space, so let's go back to the Jablonski house and . . ."

William started for the door, and everyone turned, as though to follow him.

"Tell them why you were here at the house yesterday morning at three a.m. instead of at the hospital where you said you were," I said, just as a sopping wet Sutton and Mia skittered into the kitchen through the mudroom door and stood between William and the rest of the group.

"She's right," Sutton said. "And she has proof."

Everyone turned toward William, then back to me. "If you don't believe us," I continued, here's a photo supplied by my extremely nosy neighbor Miss Vera." I retrieved my phone out of my pocket and pulled up the picture of William driving past Miss Vera's ring camera. I held it up triumphantly for all to see.

Abby leaned in and grabbed my phone. "That's a picture of a sick bird."

I took back my phone and swiped to the right picture. "That was Richard, Miss Vera's bird . . . forget it. Doesn't matter. This is it here." I handed the phone back to Abby.

"What the hell, William?" She turned it for him to see. "The time says 2:58 a.m. Why weren't you in the hospital like you and Lena-Elise said you were?" She paused and her hand flew to her mouth. "Oh My God! That's when Trig died. Did you kill Trig?"

"And funny how all the evidence from Mr. Gustaffson's death was found in Trig's room right after you were in the house, plus the blackmailer's phone," Mia added.

William's eyes were huge and darting, a feral energy that I had never seen before crossed his features. His hands balled into fists, his jaw clenched tight, and he was visibly shaking. "Look, I admit that I started the blackmailing. I wanted you all to have the shittiest week possible and I started planning this the minute I found out about what happened that day. But I swear I had *nothing* to do with Trig's death, and I just heard about the janitor's death today. I. Didn't. Kill. Anybody." He pronounced each word carefully, bitingly. "Unlike you people, who have *no* remorse at all." He spat. "Monsters."

"Hey, we didn't kill anyone either," Herschel slurred, handing my phone back. He addressed William, "And if you're talking about Carl Gleet, he drove his truck off the bridge all by himself." Herschel threw his hands up in the air, as though washing himself free of any accusations from years ago. He went back to his own bottle of whiskey that he had been drinking from, and gulped down another third.

Under the glow of the Yankee candles, I could see Virginia crying and Lena-Elise wiping her eyes. Even Abby's eyes shown bright from her tears. They felt guilty for Carl. "What happened to Carl Gleet?" I asked. "It's time to get it out."

You might think you've been having fun, but you ain't seen nothin' yet! Get ready to don your best cruise wear for dinner on the famous Majestic Springs Riverboat, followed by a sunset cruise with fancy drinks. Salut!

CHAPTER TWENTY-TWO
I Know What You Did That Night

"Nobody was supposed to get hurt." Adrian sat down on a kitchen stool. They slowly twirled a cinnamon spice candle around as they continued speaking. "We just wanted to sneak into the vice principal's office and grab the evidence that proved we cheated on a final."

"We would have lost our scholarships and everything." Virginia jumped in, exhaling smoke as she spoke. She'd somehow got ahold of a fat joint she'd found. Abby grabbed it from her and pulled a drag so long I thought she might pass out. I held out my hand for a turn.

William was dimly lit by the candles, his expression wary and forlorn. He fingered the van keys in his hands as he listened. I watched him through the marijuana haze wafting through the sticky, hot kitchen. Eye contact was acutely painful for me, but I maintained it with William while I took a large hit from the community blunt, afraid that if I took my eyes off him for even a second, he would hurt someone as badly as he was obviously hurting.

"We found out that another student had turned in an envelope with photocopies of the test answers and a list of our names on the morning of graduation, so we thought that if we could just get that envelope, no one would get in trouble." Abby talked as she carried over several bags of cookies and opened them all up on the island. "We just didn't think anyone would be in the office at that time, because the administration was supposed to be preoccupied with the start of graduation."

"But Vice Principal Kinsley surprised us," Herschel jumped in, slurring his words loudly, trying to be heard over the crashing thunder. Herschel, barely able to stand at this point, motioned for the joint and took a long hit before passing it to Sutton. "We pleaded with Kinsley, but he said he had already called the police, so we knew we were fucked, biiiig time." Herschel wandered off into the living room, where he plopped down on the couch and promptly started snoring.

The group looked at each other in uncomfortable silence (save some furious cookie munching and the crackling candles). Finally, Virginia said, "Yeah, Kinsley told us the police were coming to arrest us, and then Trig asked to talk to him alone. We were stunned, but Trig was insistent, so we left the two of them in the office and got in line for graduation."

"And then about twenty minutes later, Trig came and said everything was taken care of," Abby said. She was also sweating profusely, her coral t-shirt sticking to her chest.

"Isn't anyone going to admit what Trig did?" William asked in a low voice, barely audible. "He caused Carl's death."

"Is that why you killed Trig?" Mia had taken her phone out, no doubt to call the police, which is what I should have done once I figured out that William was a murderer. She looked down at her phone, then up to me with a troubled expression. She mouthed "no service." *Fuck.*

"Again, I didn't kill anyone," William said. "There are things in life more important than revenge, like friendship. Carl taught me that, and you all helped me remember it." He looked at Lena-Elise. "Carl wouldn't want me to hurt anyone, so I'm choosing to let my anger go." William let out a deep breath and tears glistened in his eyes.

"Maybe, but if you didn't kill Trig and the janitor, then who the hell did?" Sutton asked, weed smoke escaping from his nose and mouth as he spoke. "And my money's still on you, by the way." He pointed to William and went on. "You've had the means, motive and the opportunity this past week and in my book, that makes you the prime suspect."

"I'm not on trial here," William said, then pointed to the wedding party. "They should be. I said I'm trying to let it go, but you're not making it easy."

"It was *Trig*, not any of us. *Jesus.*" Abby rolled her eyes. "*He* was the one who bribed the vice principal to forget about the cheating and to redirect the police to a different crime that was committed that day, *not us.*"

"Redirect the police to a different crime? A DIFFERENT CRIME? That's how you remember it?" William was indignant. "Trig and the vice principal manufactured the so-called different crime they pinned on Carl. And you say you weren't involved? You made the choice to stay quiet after Carl died." William spat out every word, shaking his head in disgust. "Trig paid the janitor Elias Gustaffson to open Carl's locker and plant the fundraiser's cash bag. The vice principal knew. Carl was a child."

I sat down heavily on the last open kitchen stool. I knew what was coming next in the story. Mia stood behind me, her arms resting on my shoulders. I held onto her hands as William continued.

"After the police dragged Carl to the station in front of everybody, he lost it. He was so humiliated and scared that as soon as his parents picked him up from the station, he went home and drank so he could forget what happened. But he did not forget, and he got in his car. And we all know what happened next. Carl left me a voicemail on my phone about how frightened he was and what he was going to do, but I didn't understand the implications of what he was saying at the time. I was just a kid too." All the fight left William with these last words. He crumpled into a chair by the sliding door.

No one spoke. We shared the rest of the joint and ate cookies in silence. Finally, Lena-Elise got up from the counter and walked over to William. "Did you start dating me just to be here this week?" I could see that it took all her strength to ask the man she loved if he was just using her.

"At first, yes," William answered. "When I found out what Trig had done . . ."

"Oh no," Lena-Elise sobbed.

"Sorry for interrupting." Virginia raised her hand. "But how *did* you find out?

"Not in the most ethical way," William answered. "But since Trig is dead, and I hated him, I don't care about confidentiality anymore. He was seeing my partner for therapy, and he admitted everything to him. My partner didn't know that I went to school with Trig, so when he told me certain details about his patient, I put it all together. I finally knew what had happened to Carl. How Trig had driven him to his death."

"So, then you found me on Instagram and *innocently* asked me out?" Lena-Elise's voice had taken on an edge.

William sighed, not quite able to meet Lena-Elise's laser gaze. "I swear, that in the beginning I was only trying to get into your group to find out who else was involved, but then I fell in love with you." Lena-Elise started to cry and moved away from William. She sat down beside Abby and Virginia, who both hugged her and glared.

"And I swear on Carl's life that I didn't kill Trig or the janitor, and I didn't blackmail you all week either," William said.

"What?" Sutton's head flew from where he was resting it

on the kitchen island. His floppy hair was plastered against his face. "You just said that you had been planning this for months, and now you're telling us that you didn't do the blackmailing?"

"I started to, in the beginning, yes." William grimaced, shifting in his seat at even admitting that. "But then the phone that I was using to email you all was stolen out of my suitcase along with a picture of Carl and me. I did not see the phone again until I heard a loud commotion and found it outside by the lake."

"Was the commotion caused by . . . the gator?" Virginia asked quietly.

Knowledge dawned on the stoned faces around the room.

"Oh my god," Sutton gasped. "An alligator did eat Trig." Abby nodded at him, eyes wide.

William continued: "All I saw when I got down to the shore was Trig's leg stump, and I knew it was too late to save him. I saw my phone, and I thought I had the perfect opportunity to end all the revenge stuff. I decided to hide the phone in Trig's room, and that way, no one would think I had anything to do with his death."

"How'd you get into the house?" I asked, thinking again that I was sure that I had locked the door.

William shrugged. "It was cracked open, so I assumed Trig had left it open before he went outside and . . . well."

"It wasn't Trig." Virginia piped in, looking a tad sheepish. "I let Tamsin inside."

"Wait. Tamsin was *also* here around the time of Trig's death?" Adrian looked around, confused.

"Tamsin came over here to make sure the sabotaging had stopped. She didn't come here to kill the best dude." Virginia glared at Adrian. "I can't believe you'd think Tamsin would have something to do with a reptile-involved death."

But honestly, I thought to myself, it made sense. Tamsin was determined to have a perfect wedding day, and if she got wind that Trig was the one behind the blackmails, maybe she just went for it.

Adrian stood up from their stool and started pacing the kitchen. "Did Tamsin leave right after talking to you, Virginia?"

Virginia looked momentarily thoughtful, then nodded her head vigorously. "Yes. Tamsin had borrowed a bike from the Jablonskis, and she told me that she was going to take the old logging road back."

So, Tamsin was here that night, sneaking around on a bicycle. I guessed that most of us were thinking the same thing: Did Tamsin kill Trig before she hopped on her ancient ten-speed and peddled on out of here? William looked more innocent with every passing minute, and so did the alligator.

"Why did you have the listening devices and recordings in

your room, William?" I asked. I wanted to believe him, but some things were not in place yet.

"I found the bag in Trig's room. I didn't want to be implicated in the blackmailing, so I took the bag just in case. I know how bad that sounds."

"So, *you* didn't make us attack each other with drugs and bees?" Abby asked, slurring her words a bit. She had found a bottle of tequila.

"Yellowjackets," we all corrected her in unison.

William continued, on a confessional roll now, "I admit, I did plan the poison ivy and the food poisoning, but that's as far as I got when Trig stole my phone. I would never, ever tell anyone to fool with a hive. And honestly, at that point, my heart wasn't in it anymore." He turned to me and said, "Maggie, remember our talk right here in the kitchen before the naked boat ride?"

The naked boat ride had eclipsed that particular conversation in my memory, but now I nodded over the tequila bottle that I had tipped into my mouth. It made sense, what William was saying, but there was something gnawing at the back of my mind.

"I told us both that we needed to heal ourselves, and I listened to myself," William said. "I had to let my anger go to move ahead with my life. He turned to Lena-Elise, still in the arms of Abby and Virginia. "My new life."

The tenderness in William's eyes was real, no matter what lies he might have told.

"So . . ." Sutton gave up pulling his wet shirt away from his body in the humidity and just took it off. Several of us watched approvingly as the candlelight's shadows played over his hardened abs. Sutton continued, "Trig probably killed the janitor so he would not squeal on him after he helped plant the evidence and set bugs all over Maggie's house. But we still don't know why he did that. And Trig took over the blackmailing for reasons we also don't know. Plus THEN he got murdered or eaten by an alligator, or both, which still does not make any sense at all, William. You can see that, right, buddy?"

"I know it looks bad," William said. "I know that it would make a lot of sense if I did all these things, but I *didn't*."

"I believe you." Lena-Elise wiped her face and attempted a smile. "No matter how angry you've been at us, and you have had every right to be, I know you're not capable of murder." She got up and walked over to William and took his hands.

"I believe William too, as nutty as it all sounds," Mia said.

"Yeah, it does make a lot more sense that Trig was the bad guy in all of this," Abby said. "So, let's get our shit together and go back to the house so we can get ready to go home whenever the cops will let us go. Because there certainly isn't going to be any wedding." She started to rise from the stool but sat back down as Mia turned up my dad's old radio.

"Logan Road is out. Do not attempt to drive on it. Stay tuned to this station for more storm updates."

Mia turned the radio back down and held up her phone. "No cell service either, so get comfy."

"Ugh," Abby huffed and went using her cell phone flashlight to dig in the fridge for dinner. "We can tell Mark that Trig was responsible for the wedding pranks to get him off our backs then. Shit, we can blame everything on that weasel."

"You can certainly try, Abby, but I have other plans." We turned together to find . . . Trig, emerging from a secret passageway, smiling widely as he pointed a gun at us.

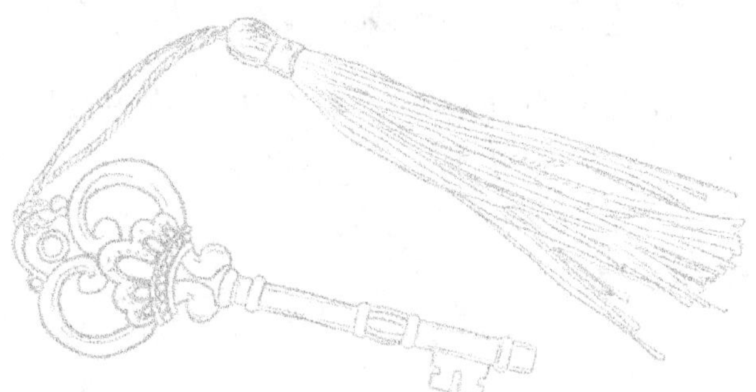

Everything's coming together
for a perfect ending to a perfect week.
Let's gather and make a toast:
To love! To enduring friendships!
To certain bliss!

CHAPTER TWENTY-THREE
Who Saw That Coming?

Sutton screamed. Abby whirled around, dropping a bag of salami on the floor.

"ARE YOU FUCKING KIDDING ME?" Virginia bellowed.

"What the *hell*?" I yelled, staring at a very alive Trig, with two very intact legs who had just appeared in the room out of thin air. "Wait, have you been living in my fucking *walls*?" I asked, staring at the open entry to my secret passageways.

"Oh, you figured it out. Congratulations," Trig sneered. He flicked the handgun in our direction. "There's a bag of zip ties on the shelf behind me, Sutton. Get them and start tying everyone to chairs."

He couldn't be serious.

Sutton, still standing directly behind me, asked in an almost non-shaky voice, "Why me?"

"Cuz you're good with your hands, bitch."

Sutton managed to look both proud and offended at the same time before Trig turned his gun on Virginia, William and Lena-Elise, who were trying to slip out the sliding door.

"Oh, no you don't, William. Get back in here and go sit on one of the kitchen chairs. Can't have the main character leave. You too, Virginia and Lena-Elise."

"I have no idea what's going on," Lena-Elise whimpered as she and William limped hand in hand to sit on my old spindle backed chairs. Virginia stood defensively behind them.

Abby glared at Trig, who was dressed in all black à la Tom Cruise in "Mission Impossible."

"Just let us go," William said. "And what do you mean, I'm the main character?"

"*Someone* was blackmailing us when we arrived and that meant *someone* knew the secret of what really happened to Carl Gleet and was ready to expose it. But I needed to figure out who it was and how to stop them," Trig said. "That was the puzzle, and I like puzzles. So, I came here and . . . oh my GOD Sutton, just put it around their hands and tighten it, Jesus Christ." Trig mimicked pulling the zip tie tight.

Sutton raised his hand.

"Dude." Trig gave Sutton a look. "Do you have a question? You don't have to raise your hand."

"Can Maggie help me with the zip ties?" Sutton asked.

I shook my head vehemently, incredulous he was asking this. Sutton, already sick-looking from the heat, pleaded with his pathetic puppy eyes in the glow of the Yankee candlelight.

"Fine," Trig said, gun now directly pointing at me. "But Sutton's pretty face won't save you if you fuck it up." Thunder claps and whistling wind competed with the noise of branches banging against the house. Trig's chin lit up pale under the black bill of his hat when lightning flashed in the windows. His eyes were hidden as a slow smile spread across his face. "I always did enjoy watching you walk, Maggie. Let's see it."

"You're disgusting," Abby snarled.

I didn't know if it was the oppressive heat, the storm raging outside, my swollen joints, or the growing realization that this mad bastard had the balls to threaten people I cared about in MY family's ancestral home. We were moonshiners and smugglers for Christ's sake. I thought about Trig watching us from the peepholes in the passageways that my own relatives had made to protect us and my blood boiled. Fuck this asshole. "Shut up, Trig," I growled at him as I marched over to Sutton and grabbed the zip tie bag from his hands. "What are we even doing zip tying each other?"

Trig laughed and nodded at William. "Douche-canoe over here gave me the best idea. Once I figured out that William was only faking getting sick from the food poisoning, I knew that he had to be the one blackmailing us. But I didn't know why he was the one doing it. So, I had to find out, naturally."

"You took my phone that night, didn't you?" asked William, his face flashed white in the lightning.

"Yep. I found it and saw the pictures of you and Carl Gleet, but I still could not understand which of these assholes told you the truth. Imagine my surprise when I looked up where you worked, and I realized that *I* was the asshole." Trig did his best Joker impression, waving and sneering. "I found out my shit therapist had their shitty office at the same shitty place you have yours. The little snitch must have talked to you. Even with no names, the story is recognizable. I should have known you can't trust therapists."

"What is your plan?" I demanded, glancing angrily at Trig while I loosely zip-tied Mia.

Trig shot me a look that said I should not push him too far. "As I was saying, I figured out that spineless William was still crying over his bestie Carl Gleet, and that he was trying to, very clumsily I might add, blackmail us. From there, I knew that he would be the perfect scapegoat for all the loose ends I needed to tie up." Trig looked around the room with a look of almost genuine benevolence. "I know you can all understand. If word got out that I caused a teenager's death, bribed school officials, and cheated on tests, I would get kicked out of the Bar Association and lose my license." He crisply adjusted his plain black baseball cap. "Now, *that* dog just won't hunt."

"You still haven't said whose leg that was in the lake." Mia spoke up. Leave it to pregnant and stone-cold sober Mia to fact check the maniac.

"Good catch, Mia. You always were smart," Trig said. "I did have helpers this week, but for reasons that I don't owe you an explanation about, they needed to be dispatched. Especially after one started getting a conscience and blabbed." Trig paced around, waving the gun. "Obviously, I had to take care of him. Did you know that this guy actually texted Mark and tried to *warn* him? Can't get good help anywhere."

"What guy? Who?" I asked, trying to think who was missing. "Who was that helper?"

"Who knows alligators?" Trig teased, twirling his gun around his finger.

"Oh my god! *Gary!*" Sutton cried.

"Who the hell is Gary?" asked Adrian, sucking back on a bottle of my dad's Cutty Sark Whiskey from the sideboard.

"The guy who ran the alligator petting zoo before it was shut down. I *knew* that couldn't be a wild alligator here," Sutton said. He sat down on the remaining kitchen stool and Adrian offered him the booze.

"The alligator guy was our guide at the caves too," Lena-Elise said. "He was standing really close to me when I fell. Did he push me?" asked Lena-Elise, raising her head hopefully from the table.

"No, Lena-Elise," Trig said, not unkindly. "You're just a klutz."

"Okay." Lena-Elise took that in stride and laid her head back down on the table.

"Trig, your plan isn't making sense. How can you be suddenly alive again without raising suspicion?" Mia, ever the detective, pressed Trig again.

"Simple," he said. "It's even easier for me now than before when I had to make it *look* like William left the hospital to kill Gary here at the lake. Imagine my surprise, *again*, when William showed up here, destroying his own alibi of being in the hospital." Trig laughed so hard he had to wipe his eyes as the thunder clapped.

"What about the janitor, Mr. Gustaffson?" I asked. "You didn't get William's phone until after the janitor was killed."

"The janitor—Elias—helped to plant evidence in Carl's locker all those years ago, so of course it's believable that William killed Elias too. William was so enraged he just snapped." Trig flicked a fly off his arm and blandly continued: "But reality is more boring. Elias got cold feet even after the enormous bribe I gave him. He wanted to go to the cops and confess, especially after messing with the dock and putting the listening device in your house. He knew someone could get hurt, so I had to get rid of him." Trig turned to me. "Honestly, Maggie, you really should have better security here. I've been living quite comfortably in the passageways and you never suspected a thing. I even turned off your electricity and water without you guessing I was here."

"You did that? Why?" I asked.

"I saw the overdue bills and knew I could fuck with you," Trig answered. "I can turn it all on again whenever I want." He motioned for me to sit on the last remaining stool and zip-tied my hands behind my back, which made my swollen joints throb.

"Okay, that's all well and good, but your shorts were on the dead guy. How do you explain that you're alive?" Abby asked.

"That's easy," Trig said. "I'm going to tell the cops that William, who is an extremely sick man, made me take off my clothes before he was going to kill me here at the lake, but I escaped and have been in hiding ever since, afraid to come out after I got away from him. He *must* have made Gary put on the hot pants and then killed Gary at his own farm and let the alligators feed on him before he dragged him to the lake. People will think William put the hot pants on Gary to make everyone think I was dead so no one would look for me."

"Hold on. Just hold on." William's hands were zip-tied to his chair, so he thumped his elbow on the side of the table. "Carl is dead. And if you killed Gary, then who did Alice and Maggie see at The Majestic?"

"Oh, that was me. Gary bought Carl's truck at auction years ago, and I thought it would be funny to drive it to the Majestic and dress up as Carl on the anniversary of his death. And I wanted to send a message through the orderlies I hired. Sorry, Sutton." Trig winked. "I didn't know who they were going to pick."

Sutton glared back. "So, you just picked up where William left off and kept forcing the wedding party to sabotage each other? Why?"

Trig sighed and scratched his face with the handle of his gun. "I wanted as many people as possible to be neck deep in bad shit, so when the time came to decide to call the cops or not, everyone would first think about their own role in everything. You guys are really slow, and *really* selfish about saving your own skins." He shook his head at us.

"But you let yourself get drugged, why?" Sutton asked.

"Free drugs, man. Why not?"

As Trig laughed again at his own joke, hope swelled in me when I glanced outside and spotted Alice and Tamsin in a flash of lightning hiding behind the lawn chairs on the porch. I nudged Mia with my foot, and very carefully nodded toward the door.

Mia, who was weirdly flexible with pregnancy hormones, had been working on getting her hands free. As she was busy with that, I tried to get Sutton's attention, but he was finishing off the Cutty Sark with Adrian's assistance.

"Trig, what is your endgame? The police will know what has happened the second they talk to us," Virginia pointed out.

Trig took a moment to look around the room at each of us with another slow creepy smile. He was enjoying dragging this out.

"Good catch, Virginia. The police will *not* know anything because, tragically, I will be the sole survivor who didn't die in an awful murder by fire," Trig said.

We all looked up at that.

"You planning to burn my house down now?" I asked as Abby stood up, still strapped to her chair.

"Sit down, *Abby*," Trig warned, pointing his gun at her. "You too, Maggie."

"I think not, *Trig*." Abby started waddling toward the door, her arms zip-tied around the spindles. "I'm not waiting around to be burned to death, so fucking shoot me if you have a problem with that."

"Okay."

I thought the blasting noise was thunder at first, but then Abby and her chair went down, hard. A resounding crash, or maybe the screaming came first.

"ABBY!" Mia yelled, lunging forward from her stool after breaking free from her zip-ties. "Jesus Christ, Trig, what have you done?" Mia grabbed a dishtowel from the counter and held it to Abby's chest. Of all the times for giant Herschel to be passed out drunk in the living room under a pile of dog blankets!

Sutton and I made moves to help Abby, but Trig blocked us, his back now to the sliding glass doors. Tamsin and Alice took this opportunity to sneak in the door while Trig was busy waving his gun in our faces.

"You guys wanna try next?" Trig's shaking voice betrayed him, exposing his cratering façade. "I was going to offer most of you a way out, but not if you don't stay put."

"What kind of way out, Trig?" William asked, his face gray in the shadows as he watched Abby writhing on the floor. Mia managed to get Abby unhooked from her chair and was trying to help her.

"Well, not you, William. You've gotta die no matter what." Trig shrugged, like it could not be helped. "But the rest of you, who all have their hands dirty in some way or another, we could make a deal."

"And burn William and my home down in the process?" I asked, trying not to let my gaze linger on Alice and Tamsin as they crouched down behind the island.

"You should die because you've always been so annoying," Trig said to me.

Tamsin was gesturing and trying to tell me something, but I couldn't figure out what. She was holding up her fingers, three fingers on one hand and then twenty-one with both hands. Why did I know those numbers? Three and twenty-one. So familiar.

"You're losing your house anyway, Maggie." Trig's eyes darted from Abby then back to me. "I've seen all the bank notices. Now at least you can get insurance money out of it."

Tamsin motioned again. Three and twenty-one . . . *Buffy*! That was my favorite Buffy episode where Buffy and her friends take on the serpent Olvikan. The one I made us all act out over and over when we were kids. I nodded to Tamsin to show I under-stood while Alice duckwalked over and silently cut my zip-ties.

"So," I said loudly and purposefully, once Alice was safely behind the island again. "It's been a long road getting here for you, for . . . Majestic Springs," I paraphrased the mayor's speech at Buffy's TV graduation, the one right before the mayor turned into a monster, hoping that everyone would remember the episode.

"What?" Trig frowned and turned to me.

"Um, yeah. There's been achievement, joy, good times . . ." I could see realization dawning on some people's faces, but also a healthy amount of confusion.

"Maggie, what . . ." Willliam started to ask, but Lena-Elise, recognizing the plan, ever so slightly gestured with her head towards Alice and Tamsin.

I continued while I still had Trig's attention. "And there's been grief, there's been loss. Some people who should be here today . . . aren't." As Tamsin and Alice positioned themselves behind Trig, I said much more forcefully, "**But. We. Are.**" Then we made our move, just like in Graduation Day, Part Two.

"Xander, TAKE 'EM DOWN!" I screamed. Alice jumped on Trig's back, and even though Trig was twice Alice's size, she clung onto his neck like a demented monkey. Tamsin and I went for the gun at the same time. I thought I had Trig's arm secured, but he jutted out his forearm and knocked Tamsin hard in the face. As Tamsin went flying to the ground, Virginia jumped up and tackled Trig from the side. The four of us tumbled to the floor, and for a scary second Trig pointed the gun at us, finger on the trigger.

"Journey's end, dude."

This was when Abby pulled out a round house kick *grand battement*, honed from years of ballet training. By god she grand battemented that gun right out of Trig's hand. She then high-fived me before collapsing on Tamsin, her shoulder soaked in blood.

Alice had secured her arms around Trig's neck and was using all her strength to choke him out while Mia and I sat on his legs and zip-tied them. Finally, he passed out and we secured his hands too.

"I got phone service!" William shouted over the melee. He and Lena-Elise had managed to escape their binds while we fought. "I'll call for an ambulance if someone else can call Mark."

Herschel wandered in from the living room, still clutching his almost empty bottle. "Heyyyy, what happened in here?" He rubbed his eyes drowsily.

"Long story, Hersch." I rubbed my sore wrists and then took a swig of my dad's Cutty Sark, feeling the satisfying burn down my throat.

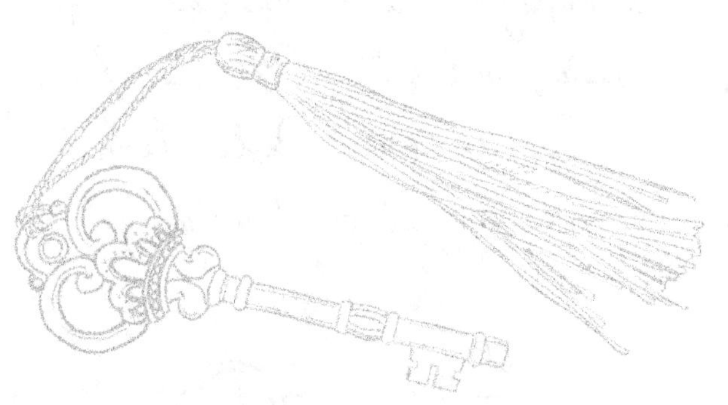

Tamsin and Noah's big day!
Hair and makeup first, then a light
buffet, and don't just fill up on
champagne, Ha Ha! Vans depart for
Elena's on the Lake Restaurant and
Premier Event Destination
precisely at 1pm. Here we go!

CHAPTER TWENTY-FOUR
Love is a Flower You Must Fondle

"Everything is ruined." Tamsin sighed.

I had to agree with her as we walked around the flooded wedding venue, a once beautiful restaurant and garden on the lake. Elena, the owner and manager for over twenty years, waved at us bravely as she wrestled a shop vac. My rain boots made squishing noises in the several inches of water that covered the dance floor where Tamsin and Noah would have had their first dance. "I mean, at least you and Noah made up and still want to get married, right?"

"Yes." Tamsin nodded so vigorously the bandage on her face slipped, and she delicately put it back in place. "We absolutely do."

As soon as Noah heard about the attack, dangerous as it was, they grabbed a motorboat from the Jablonskis' dock and roared over to make sure Tamsin was alright. Soon after, the real reason Tamsin and Herschel had been conspiring at The Majestic became clear: they'd been planning a surprise bachelorx party for Noah. All these years I'd judged Sutton for gossiping and now it was my big mouth that had really caused some pain. I glanced at Tamsin before I spoke, not sure of how to approach this. "So, do you postpone the wedding until . . ."

"No." Tamsin gestured around the vast empty restaurant space. "I don't need all of this. Not anymore. I just want to be married to Noah. That's all." She smiled wide.

"Well, if you really don't need all the pomp and circumstance, I might have a way to accomplish that," I said.

Tamsin stopped walking and flood water swished around her galoshes. "How? I don't even have a dress because all our stuff got ruined in the flood at the Jablonskis' house while we were saving you all."

"How do you feel about a vintage themed wedding?" I asked.

Alice straightened Cosmo's floppy pink bow while I pushed back the baby buggy top for Noodle to peer out. My cat, nestled grandly atop a pink satin pillow, was now calmly nibbling the bow that had been on his head. Alice and I were decked out in my great-grandparents' clothes—me in a 1920's linen dress, complete with bright blue rain boots, and Alice looking simply adorable in my great-grandpa's button-down shirt, tie, and dress pants. His newsboy cap fit her perfectly, with her dark hair sticking out from underneath it.

Because my family were all packrats, there were plenty of costumes to go around. Everyone had worked all day cleaning up my lake point and hanging twinkle lights and flowers throughout the pine, oak, and willow trees. After refreshing showers, the whole group gathered together, resplendent in vintage clothes that had belonged to my grandparents, aunts, cousins, and uncles.

Roberta and her hair and make-up crew came out and treated the wedding attendants to spa treatments while we tied bouquets made from wildflowers. Virginia and Lena-Elise salvaged some decorations from the flooded wedding venue and attached gorgeous fuchsia- and salmon-colored bows to chairs and tree trunks. Bri, Shaun, and Mia collected shiny rocks, pinecones, and milky quartz from around the property and made sparkling and earthy centerpieces by arranging them in clear vases. Everyone was enjoying working together to transform this shipwreck of a week into something transcendent.

Adrian tipped their derby hat to Alice and me as they and Virginia walked slowly down the flower-petaled aisle. Adrian's delicate silk skirt, which I think had belonged to my Great Aunt Erna, flowed about them as they walked. A beaming Noah stood at the end of my point, the sunlight glinting off the lake and reflecting down from the green tree leaves above them. James and Herschel had constructed a gorgeous arched trellis made from tree branches and twine, where Noah and Tamsin could exchange their vows.

Cosmo barked happily at William, dressed in a 1920's era suit and bow tie, and at Lena-Elise, who, like Abby and me, was wearing a dress that flowed in the gentle breeze. William looked adoringly at his girlfriend Lena-Elise, whose crutch was bedecked with a string of marigolds. She smiled back at him as they walked the rest of the way to the arch.

Jenny, Herschel, and Abby were up next. Jenny wore one of my relative's suits and I hated to admit how cute she looked in it. I stole a glance at Alice, who was trying unsuccessfully to put Noodle's bow back on his head in the baby carriage. When Alice looked up, I assumed she would ogle cute Jenny, but Alice wasn't looking at Jenny. She was looking at me.

"Just so you know, Jenny and I broke up," Alice said, her fingers masterfully avoiding Noodle's love bites as she rearranged his satin pillow and re-tied Cosmo's leash to Noodle's baby stroller. "Not that my breakup has anything to do with Mia spilling the beans that you mailed your signed divorce papers to Lance and the lawyers," she said. Her eyes lit up under my grandpa's newsboy cap.

My hopeful heart leaped. Cosmo stood proudly between us, and I reached down to pet him, my fingers finding calm in his familiar soft, short hairs. "No, of course not," I said, trying, and failing, to suppress my grin.

Herschel and Jenny pushed Abby down the aisle in a bedazzled wheelchair. Her arm was in a cast to which we'd glued pale pink flowers to match her dress. Luckily, the bullet had gone right through her shoulder flesh, missing bone and major tendons, but she still required a shit-ton of pain killers, as evidenced by her giggling.

And then it was time for Tamsin. Everyone stood up as a string quartet played Brandi Carlisle's song "You and Me on the Rock." Even I felt a tightening in my throat and had to wipe away a tear as Tamsin's and Noah's eyes met, smiles wide across their faces. I glanced over at Sutton, Mia, and James, who all looked like they had walked out of a tea party from the 1920's. Mia's hat matched Briana's, both wide brimmed with a row of tiny purple flowers around them, and James, Sutton and Shaun wore matching suspenders that they had found in my many attic trunks.

My great grandmother's wedding dress fit Tamsin perfectly. Champagne colored satin lovingly clung to her body as she slowly walked down the aisle accompanied by her beaming father. She held a simple bouquet of yellow and purple wildflowers that we'd picked from the point.

Earlier that day Mr. Carlyon had given me a check for way beyond what we'd previously agreed. "You all worked so hard to make my daughter's day special and to keep her and Noah safe. I hope that you will continue to keep this place going, Maggie. You have the magic touch with your guests." He patted my arm and walked away while I tried not to faint. It was more than the money. I was finally able to take a deep, full breath knowing that I could keep my family home.

Mia and Sutton came to stand by Alice, Cosmo, Noodle, and me. Sutton nodded over to Noah and Tamsin. "Would you look at those two love birds all married and happy now?" He said, twirling the ribbon around Noodle's head as Noodle batted it with his paws. "Maggie, I do declare that you are the perfect host."

"Who would have thought?" I smiled as Tamsin and Noah shared their first married kiss, pleased that I had a part in making their dreams come true. "Maybe I can be a host after all," I said. "But I doubt that we are ever going to get a crew as wild as these people again, right? That's impossible! Plus, it will be strange letting guests stay in my home while I sleep in the cabin, but it is the price to pay to keep my home. I'm down for it."

"You might not have to sleep in the cabin forever," Mia said. "See all your land back there?" She pointed to twenty acres of forested land behind my home.

I looked at the expanse of pine tops rising up over the mountain and nodded.

"I . . . well, *we*," Mia grasped Sutton's hand, "have a plan." They looked at each other and grinned, then they both looked at me.

"Are you telling her about *the plan*?" Heidi had just joined us, taking a break from preparing the wedding dinner in my kitchen.

"Does everyone know about *the plan* but me?" When everyone including Alice nodded, I laughed and made a "do continue" gesture.

"We could build cabins and a small community space to hold retreats and workshops and such." Mia was so excited her words fell over each other. "We've all talked and we want to be in this together. Heidi will provide catering, James's construction company will take on the cost of building and then get a share of the profits, Sutton will deal with the legal stuff, also getting a share, and I will coordinate the retreats and activities."

Everyone looked at me, waiting for my reaction. "Alice," I turned to her. "What do you think?"

Alice was looking at an old, dilapidated stone structure on the land that used to be the barn. "Well, I'm thinking that barn would be the perfect spot for an animal shelter, for animals like Athena the possum." She beamed.

I could have my home back. I suddenly had a vision of my Aunt Mary's bedroom with a crib in it and dogs and cats and yes, a possum running through the house as we all congregated together in the kitchen for a family meal.

Maybe this really could work out after all.

the end . . .

for now . . .

ABOUT THE AUTHORS

Elizabeth Land Quant.

Born and raised in North Dakota, Elizabeth is a disabled, queer, autistic writer, wife, and a mom to three very cool kids. She holds degrees in the Classics and Political Science from St. Olaf College, and splits her time between Minneapolis, Minnesota and Hot Springs, Arkansas. Elizabeth has published in The New York Times, Disability Acts, The Manifest-Station, The Red Noise Collective, Unleash Lit and Tangled Locks. She is the proud co-founder of The Unpopular Publishing Co., co-creator of AutisticAunties.com, and happily rents out adorable little cabins with shelves full of books in Arkansas.

Signe E. Land.

Big sister to Elizabeth, Signe also hails from North Dakota, Minnesota and Arkansas. She is a queer disabled autistic writer plus other secret things. Co-founder of The Unpopular Publishing Co.; co-creator of AutisticAunties.com; co-owner & operator of our book-filled getaway cabin resort at Cooper's Point, Lake Hamilton, Hot Springs National Park, Ouachita Mountains, Arkansas.

FIND US AT:

AutisticAunties.com

for F*CK THIS MURDER

news & content, blog, about us,

and so much more!